Anything Anytime Anywhere

ERIN SPINETO

SEA PEPTIDE PUBLISHING

ANYTHING ANYTIME ANYWHERE

For Information, Contact:
Sea Peptide Publishing
Carlsbad, CA, 92011
www.SeaPeptide.com

ISBN-13: 978-0-9882065-8-8
August 2023

To Michelle.
For always being ready and willing
to accompany me on all of my wild
adventures. You make everyone of
them exponentially better.

Read Me Diabetes

Diabetes can be a confusing disease that has a language and behavior all its own, just like most chronic conditions. It plays a role in this novel, but, because Billie thinks about it so little, it is explained only a little.

If you want a deeper explanation of her diabetes—Your Diabetes May Vary—or you are confused, The Diabetes Appendix in the back of the book will catch you right up or introduce you to the would of type 1 diabetes if you haven't experienced it yourself.

It is arranged by page reference so you can read it all beforehand or flip to an excerpt as needed.

Prologue
Six months ago...

BILLIE

I hate this day.

I wish it would jump off the calendar and burn in hell.

I wish I never again had to have an October 7.

And this year is worse with the paddle out and the memorial surf contest.

And the interrogations.

"How are you *doing*, Billie?" With the most somber faces. And the hand patting, the hushed tones, the expectations that I'm supposed to feel one way or another.

Some will only be satisfied if I'm completely over it and happy to have moved on with my life. Others only if I'm still overcome with grief. Either way, I can't muster up the right emotions for anyone to be appeased. The only thing I feel is hate for this lousy date.

And the deep, deep desire for it to never reappear again.

When some old beach boy gives me the, 'you guys were inseparable as kids' speech, I'm officially done. Clearly we weren't all that inseparable or we all wouldn't be here today preparing to paddle into the ocean, sit in a circle, throw our lei's into the water, and remember him, would we?

I turn my back to the maudlin zombies and wander off the beach.

The Lahaina waterfront is filled with tourists carrying surfboards following their instructor like ants to the local kook break, photo-happy families stopping at every landmark on the walking tour brochure, and watermen fixing up their floating money pits.

With each step away from this morning's spectacle, the weight lightens. If I can simply get through this day and survive it, by next year I will find some way to sleep through the whole damned thing.

Right foot in front of left, left in front of right, not quite certain where I'm headed, I allow the sun to heat my skin, hoping it will burn the paper in my hand, the one I cannot seem to let go, the one that reads, "Five years later, Brent's light still shines. Come paddle out with us and remember."

I squeeze behind the family who has paused in the middle of the sidewalk to take yet another picture, not really caring if I photo-bomb it. I'm quite certain they have at least four hundred more pics just like it already.

The steps of the old courthouse look to be as good of a place to kill this day as any, so I head in that direction.

"You know what cures all that ails you?" a deep voice pulls me from my weariness.

I cast my glance towards the sound and find a kind face waiting for some reply from me. I'm not sure I can summon one.

He lays down the dock lines leading to a decent-sized fishing vessel, one of the many lined up on these docks promising to take the tourists out for a day they will never forget. In only a pair of faded blue trunks, his tan arms are on full display, strong and muscular from time on the boat. "You look like you could use some time on the water."

Sounds exactly like what my dad would say when I had a bad day.

When I was a kid and the world became too big for my little kid mind, my dad would grab two paddleboards and say, "Looks like it's time for some salt," and we'd paddle until my problems washed off into the water. No matter how overwhelming my concerns felt, once I hit the sea, nothing ever appeared as monstrous.

My final year on the Pro Surf Tour, I came home after a series of miserable losses ready to throw in the towel. I arrived at my parent's house for Sunday family dinner and within seconds my dad could tell I was in a bad place.

"Looks like it's time for some salt," he offered.

"Dad. I just spent the last five weeks in the ocean, and it only made things worse."

"Well then, I need some salt," he said sweetly. "And my paddle buddy."

"Fine," I grumbled like some spoiled teenager, even though I had left my teens years ago. I followed him to the edge of our yard where a palapa covered a rack packed with surfboards and paddleboards.

He pulled a fourteen-foot paddleboard and paddle. "Technically, you may have been in the ocean during your contests, Billie, but you've forgotten how to be in the sea."

I spun my paddle in my hands, looking at all the stickers on the blade, companies that dictated a large portion of my life. Maybe I had been distracted by the hustle and work it takes to be on tour.

Carrying my neon green Yolo board, I hustled to catch up to my dad at the edge of our property. Making his way onto the dock, he laid his board in the water and stepped on. I copied his rehearsed movements.

We paddled down the Nalu River that snakes its way from our backyard to the mouth of the river 2.2 miles away where it empties out at Nalu Kai Harbor. The backyards of houses I had drifted by thousands of times before pulled the travel tension from my body.

Dad stopped and waited for me to catch up to him. He pointed to the water a few feet ahead of him. A small rock protruded from the surface of the water.

When I came alongside him, I realized it was no rock. It was a monstrous turtle having a staring contest with my dad. Knowing my dad, he was probably telepathically having a deep philosophical discussion about the meaning of life with the creature.

The turtle turned my way and flashed me a welcoming grin. For a seemingly endless time, we let the current pull us along, drifting down river together, until, at last, Mr. Turtle yawned and sank below the surface until he faded away into the deep green of the channel.

I looked at my dad, who grinned back briefly with satisfaction, knowing he brought his daughter back to the rhythm of the water. We paddled on towards the beach as I began to share with him the terrible mind space I had been in during the last leg of the tour. By the time we reached the beach, all the stress that had been piling up was gone.

Sometimes my problems took more time to solve than the few miles to the beach and back, so we would turn into the wind and keep paddling as long as it would take to get back into the right headspace or for Dad to dispense his wisdom. But that day, knowing Mom had dinner waiting for us, and feeling already lighter, we turned around at the harbor and headed home.

And the whole way, Dad simply listened. It was like this time, he didn't need to say a thing. All the sage advice he had shared on this river over the years came flooding back to me. The lessons about staying in the present. Appreciating the ocean. Controlling what you can and letting go of what you can't.

By the time we reached our back dock, the entire last leg of the tour had been wiped from my mind. I was ready to make the most of my break and to finish off the year strong.

A velvet-edged voice coaxes me back to my mournful Lahaina reality. "You know, we leave in only a couple minutes." The man points over his shoulder. "You want to hop on board, go catch a few?"

"Catch a few?" Why is basic conversation totally beyond me today?

"Fish. I run a fishing charter and we have some spots left."

Fishing sounds like torture, but being out on the ocean is exactly what I need to wash this morning away. His glowing smile and waterman's body certainly don't hurt either. "Sure. Why not?"

The sun hangs high over puffy clouds barely moving in the sky. The other people on board have been fishing practically since we cast off. Some commotion a little while ago probably meant they caught something, but I have only been watching the water pass under the hull of the boat.

The sea has done what it always does. Washes away the pain. Recalibrates the misery-meter. I have already made it through half of this dreadful day, I will make it through the rest. And tomorrow will be better. Overflowing with sunshine, warm water, and joy. Just like the other 364 days in the year.

My life on Maui is brimming with all the things I love. I just lost sight of that today. But the salt has brought me back. The salt and Ryder Jax, the captain of this lovely vessel.

"You ever fish before?" Ryder is holding a pole, standing next to me. I think he actually wants me to fish. Silly boy.

"Not really."

He hands over the rod, reaches into the bait bucket, and pulls out a squirming, silvery fish. "You have to make sure the hook goes through the jaw. Otherwise, it will fall off the second it hits the water and you won't catch a thing," he says while presenting the tiny fish.

I grimace. "Sounds painful."

He laughs as he plucks the hook from the air and holds it out for me.

I'm not usually the type to play dumb to get a guy to help, but I'd do just about anything right now to have him stay right where he is. "How is that again?"

He mimes baiting the hook one more time, but there's no way I'm actually going to do that to this poor fishie. I've had enough of death today. When he looks over his shoulder to check on the other fishermen, I let the hand with the baitfish hang over the side of the boat and release it, hoping Ryder doesn't see.

I pull my hand back and mime hooking it before saying a silent prayer that all the little fishies swim far, far away from the minefield of hooks surrounding us.

He leans on the railing next to me and tips his head to the water, nudging me to cast.

I do it quickly so he can't get a clear view of my empty hook. "Ryder, give me a hand with this," his deckhand calls and my captivating tutor vanishes to tend to his work.

I pretend to reel in my line a bit, but really I'm simply watching the horizon as it rises and falls with each passing swell. The pink orchids around my neck float up in the breeze. I was supposed to place the lei in the water this morning after sitting in a circle with those who loved Brent and listening to them speak about how he should have still been here and all the inspiring things he would have done.

But it's all just words. Should. Would. None of it means a thing.

I lean my pole against the railing, lift the lei from my shoulders, and drag it over the railing, letting it flutter in the ocean breeze, while I gather the resolve to release my grip and let it fall to the water below. It floats up and down with the swells, through whitecaps, losing a few petals as it drifts, until, at last, it is pulled from my view. Just like Brent.

"You getting lucky today?" The sound pulls me back into reality, but the words are a little hard to make sense of.

"Sorry?"

"Fishing. You catch anything?"

Instead of finding Ryder back to instruct me in fish murder, I turn to meet the adorable passenger's charming smile in full force. Picking up my pole again, I give the reel a couple idle spins. "Not yet."

He leans in to whisper like he's letting me in on some deep dark secret, "There's an art to it, you know?"

"Oh yeah?" I can play along with the best of them.

He reclines on the railing confidently. "I can teach you if you want."

Who am I to say no to that?

And he does. Between hilarious stories, amusing pop songs with rewritten lyrics, and hysterical attempts at tongue twisters, JJ attempts to teach me a skill I have no intention of acquiring. But no matter how much he tries to entertain me, and how much I try not to let it, my attention keeps moving right over JJ's shoulder to Ryder, now flanked by the only two other women onboard.

When Ryder catches me watching him, a contented grin overtakes his features, which produces the widest smile I've had on my face all day.

"I think you have a bite," JJ buzzes.

There's no way I caught anything without bait. But I reel in my line just the same. No need to admit I'm cheating at this whole fishing thing.

When my hook comes up empty, JJ reaches for another baitfish. "Looks like he stole your bait." He hooks a new one on. "Don't worry, we'll get you a fish, I promise," and he spends the next hour trying.

When Ryder finally points the boat towards home, I take it as my cue to give up on torturing innocent creatures and make my way to the foredeck to hang my feet over the edge, hoping to touch some of the salt water that has been bringing me the relief I needed so badly today. It may not be quite as relaxing as dipping my whole body in it, but at least I can be touched by the spray from the bow.

One of the girls who has been surrounding Ryder all day shrieks as she points toward me, "We have to do that." Her friend hoots in agreement and follows her my way, feet swinging over the edge as they drain a few more canned Margaritas.

When we make our way into shallower waters, the swells pick up, sending the dizzy ladies tumbling into each other. I really don't want to see them go overboard.

Ryder's voice comes over the PA. "We're gonna start hitting a little swell up here in a minute. It may be time to head back to the cabin."

The moment he finishes his announcement, we dive into a trough and hit the other side with enough force to send cold mist onto two pairs of sunburned legs. That's all the encouragement they need. They help each other up and make their way back.

I spin around as if to ask Ryder if his briefing was an order or a suggestion.

He nods his approval.

The swells toss gusts of salt water over the bow as we dip into troughs. I kick my feet into each one like a little girl joyfully swaying on a playground swing. We shift course a bit to drive head-on into the swells making the spray that much bigger. I spin towards the wheelhouse to find Ryder a massive, self-confident presence. Did he do that just for me?

He seems to answer with a knowing nod.

I flash him a grateful smile and turn back to enjoy my exhilarating ride back.

Once back at the harbor, Ryder and JJ take pictures with the guests and their prized catches. Looks more like JJ is less passenger and more deckhand helping out Ryder.

I end up stalling, not sure if I want to be back on land ever again. Or perhaps it has more to do with not wanting to walk away from Ryder without finding a way to see him again.

By the time I disembark, Ryder is on the dock tidying the lines JJ tossed aside after tying up the boat.

I stop in front of him. "Thanks for this. You'll never know how much it meant to me."

He drops the dock lines and stands to face me. "No worries. Let me know the next time you want to head out. Really, anytime you want to go." He rubs his hand over his short brown hair, and tilts his eyes back to me, on the verge of saying something meaningful.

I wrap my hands into the hem of my neon pink t-shirt and stare at the cartoon Gorilla on the front hanging off the side of a building holding a surfboard.

With his foot, Ryder taps the now coiled lines on the dock, nudging them towards the edge, out of people's way.

I lift my eyes to his face, begging him to ask me out or to give me an opening to ask.

But he doesn't, and I'm so distracted by his ice-green eyes, full of life and pain and hope, that I lose the ability to speak. I accept the fact that this was not the beginning I had hoped it was—it was simply a brief respite from a torturous day—so I turn, heading up the dock.

As I pass JJ washing off the boat, he tosses the hose in the water. "Hey, wait. You forgot to take your picture," he calls out.

This coaxes a laugh from me. "The only thing I caught was a baitfish."

"I'll count that." JJ jogs to the bait bucket and pulls out a fish and yells, "Let's go, Jax. One more pic for Billie here."

JJ wraps his arm around my shoulders as we make our way to the front of the Captain Jax Sportfishing sign and cleverly says, "I think the printer ran out of ink during the last picture we printed. Maybe I could print it out later and bring it your way. Tomorrow night? We could grab some food, too?"

"Sure. I could eat."

"Awesome. It's a date." JJ makes no attempt to hide his excitement as Ryder joins us. "Hey, Jax, you mind setting up the camera again?"

Ryder nods, sets the tripod on a faded, black x on the ground, and rejoins us, standing on my left.

He's looking off towards Lahaina town when he scrubs his hand over his hair again. When he looks down at me, I find it impossible not to return his irresistibly devastating smile. His mouth softens like he is finally going to say what I could see hiding behind his eyes all this time. The prolonged anticipation is almost unbearable, but the words never come.

Without breaking our stare, I lift my hand and tilt my head as if to ask permission before wrapping it around his waist. In answer, he steps closer.

"Oh, wait, your fish." JJ hands over a three-inch 'Oama.

It would take much more than a baitfish to convince me to move my hand from around Ryder's body, so I clutch it with my right and hold it up for the camera.

And, then, I hear Ryder's voice. "GoPro, take a picture."

Chapter 1

RYDER JAX

I pop my head out of the balmy saltwater and shout, "Billie!"

She doesn't hear me and for sure doesn't see it. The clear waters of Nalu Kai in Maui slowly turn a deeper aqua ten meters out. Two hundred meters further, where the ocean turns a deep cobalt and the sandy shore drops off into the depths, a dark shadow moves along the ledge. As it glides closer, the sleek outline of a juvenile tiger shark comes into focus.

Shit.

Billie continues swimming exactly like she lives life, without a care in the world, even though a ferocious predator is in the water with her.

I sprint to tap her ankle and she lifts her head. Pointing to where the threat has moved, I warn, "Shark."

"What?" I can't tell if she is terrified or excited.

"Shark. Wait for it. It'll surface again." I point it out to her as its fin breaks the surface at two o'clock, ten meters away. "There."

"Hey there, Sharkie," she says sweetly. A huge grin lights up her face and excitement fills her sea-green eyes as she turns back to me. "That's incredible."

I love that that's her reaction while I'm trying my best not to piss myself. After years of training, I may be more at home in the water than on land, but that ease does not extend to a beast that could remove a limb in one bite.

I take four measured breaths to slow my heart rate. You can't show fear when a shark is nearby. They feed off that stuff. A shark can pick up the static electricity on a balloon five miles away and I'm struggling to avoid ringing the dinner bell.

Billie, on the other hand, puts her head down and follows the beast underwater for a few meters. When she passes me, I have to seize her around the waist to stop her from chasing a tiger shark.

A Tiger Shark.

She stays wrapped in my arms underwater, watching it until it fades into the dark of the sea. When she raises her head, she's pissed. "Why'd you do that, Ryder?"

"It's a shark, Billie." It's like I'm speaking a foreign language, so I stretch out the word to make sure she understands. "Shaaaarrrrrk."

"I know." Her eyes dim with disappointment from not being allowed to chase it or pet it like it's Spooner, her adopted street puppy.

"We should go back in," I offer.

"You just want to avoid a loss. I see how slow you are this morning, Ryder," she teases, the only person I know to use my first name.

"Oh yeah?" I take off only to have her catch up to me, pull my ankle back, and swim right over me.

When we make it out to the half-mile buoy in record time, we both pause to tread water for a moment as we take in the view of the shore. Even at this distance, I can see Spooner sitting in one of the Adirondack chairs angled to take in the sunset at the edge of my yard. Wherever Billie is, that puppy can be found. I'm surprised he hasn't followed her out here.

The sun glints off the neon green of Billie's bike leaning up against the other chair making it glow in front of the dark olive of my house at the other end of the grassy expanse. With Billie bobbing in front of the picture-perfect scene, I realize there's not much else in life I need.

"You good?" I ask, knowing her blood sugars can drop quickly out here.

She checks her watch. "163," she reports before clicking another button. She flashes me the stopwatch ticking away.

"Fastest one yet. Let's see if we can push it on the way back," I say.

That's all the info she needs. She sprints to shore.

I ride her heels all the way in.

When she hits the sand, she dashes towards the grass at the edge of my yard, the official finish line for a swim race. It's a short run, maybe twenty meters, I could outrun her on the soft sand, but I get more joy from watching her celebrate than I would if I beat her.

She jumps up on the berm, hands raised in celebration. "And in first place," she announces like this is an Olympic sport, "beating her closest competition by minutes, folks, minutes, Billie Styles." She spins to greet her imaginary, cheering fans. "Oh, my God. What is that?" she squeals.

I scan the yard for the threat. What have I missed?

She bounces around, slapping wildly at her back and shoulders. "Get 'em off! Get 'em off me!"

I survey a panicked Billie. During her revelry, she must have backed through a web crammed with newly hatched black and yellow spiderlings. They have spilled from their home to cover her back.

I step in to wipe off the spiders, but she's a dog trying to catch her own tail with all her hopping and spinning. "Hold still, so I can get them."

"Hurry. Oh, God. Get them off me."

It takes a while to get the rogue monsters off her back. The whole time she is shaking and making these adorable noises like any one of the spiders could do her in with one little nibble. I'm laughing the entire time at a girl who will swim after a tiger shark but is terrified of a few tiny spiders who probably still have all their baby teeth.

Ensuring I catch every last little monster, I slow my hands on her back, her flesh cool under my palms. I have to lift the string of her top to swipe out one who has found a comfortable spot cuddled up next to Billie's skin. When the final spider has been vanquished, I let my hand linger on her lower back, not wanting this moment to end. Leaning in closer, I laugh out, "I don't think I've actually seen you scared before. It's kind of cute."

She slowly spins toward me, wrapping my arm around her in the process. She's regained her confidence as if her freak-out didn't even happen. "I don't really do scared," she says with a boldness I don't want to admire, but can't avoid respecting, and, God help me, my body is not immune to that smile.

My mind is trying very, very hard to compensate for my body's shortcomings, though. With my arm still around her, she is only inches from me, her lips ensnaring my focus. She drops her cheeky confidence as those lips fall open and she pulls in a breath.

My eyes rise to find her gazing at me and I swear she's begging me to lean in a bit more. Who am I to deny her? I begin to close the distance between us.

Until I remember.

I immediately lift my hands from her hips and hold them up while retreating a few paces. "Shit. Sorry." I scan her face for any indication I have totally screwed things up, but I can't tell anything from her ever-cheery smile. I retreat one more step. "I... Dammit. I should go."

Still no sign other than her joy-filled grin. I gain a couple more meters from that major screw-up. "I'm gonna go."

How the hell did I let that get away from me so fast? I spin and head toward the safety of my house before realizing leaving like that was totally rude. Great way to add insult to injury, Jax.

I turn back to Billie who is in the same position I left her. "But you... you should stay. Finish editing your photos. Enjoy the beach. I'm gonna go."

She laughs off my weirdness and drops into an Adirondack, spinning sideways and slinging her cute little feet over the armrest.

Jax, you selfish bastard. When are you going to knock that shit off?

Chapter 2

BILLIE

Ryder is hilarious when he gets all flustered like that. And sure, maybe I push things a little to enjoy watching him freak out, but it's all harmless fun. I never cross any lines. I would never do that to my boyfriend, JJ.

I clip my insulin pump back into its port on my bum, take my phone from my bag, and recline in the sun. I swear, Ryder bought these chairs just for me. If I turn sideways, they fit perfectly.

Time slows as I glance over my shoulder and am greeted by the perfect view of Ryder showering off on his back deck. Always a man of routine, he showers off with the same ritual every time. Not that I've watched him enough to memorize it or anything.

He lets the water hit his face before spinning and tilting his head back as he closes his eyes and allows the warm water to pour over him for a solid minute. Then he plucks the soap from the storage bin next to the shower and lathers everything from his hair to his feet, rinsing it all off in one fell swoop afterward.

He picks a navy towel from the outdoor rack that is somehow always packed with fresh towels, wraps it around his waist, and slips off his trunks, hanging them on the now-empty hook on the wall. He replaces the soap in the storage bin and closes the lid. As he makes his way to the back door, he turns and catches me ogling him.

Time snaps back to full speed as I turn back to my work, smiling even bigger now. When he disappears inside, I can finally focus.

I have to head into the office for a meeting this morning, so I'll have to put a rush on this morning's posts. Piper wants to "talk," which usually means I'm gonna get another earful about her wanting more from me.

Maybe I should come prepared with some new ideas. I've been playing around with the idea of rigging up the half-mile buoy with one of my old GoPros, so I can take a pic every time we go for a swim. But I still haven't worked out how to retrieve the pics from the camera when I'm finished—perhaps an app on my phone that will automatically connect and download it as we glide by without having to even remove it from its waterproof case on my thigh—but if I mention it, she'll push me to finish it and I really don't care enough to have a deadline on the idea. Plus, by now, she has to be used to me always turning down her offers of doing more.

I wrap up editing last night's sunset surf session photos and move on to the interview of Harley who I finally convinced to test the waters in Maui. She's working on a research project on some local subjects and I'm writing up a bio on her to help her make contacts in the area. It may be a bit selfish, but I'd love to have her out here permanently.

A text notification bombards my screen, completely breaking my focus. I don't need to read any further than Mom, to fling it away. I move on to editing the drone footage of Biovandal's latest escapades. This one involved a truck bed stocked with compost and an empty lot on the corner of Kahili and Melia in Nalu Kai.

Finished with work for the day, I pack up my bag and walk my bike, Kermit, through the yard. With our usual perfect timing, Ryder sails through his front door as I close the side gate.

"Off to teach those tourists how to murder the poor little fishies who are perfectly happy living their lives not hurting anyone?" I tease.

"You mean those murderous big fish who have massacred more poor little fish than I ever will in my entire lifetime?"

"One fish is one too many."

"I'll be sure to tell those monsters that Billie's looking out for them."

Laughing, I command, "Okay, but you have to dunk your head under the water when you do."

He laughs off my plea.

I shoulder my bag and hop on my bike to spin off to the Kaulike Hanai offices.

"Hey, Mandy. Piper said she wanted to chat today. Is she available?" I ask the receptionist, hoping to get out of here as quickly as possible.

"Let me check for you, Billie."

I flop onto a couch in the waiting room with a panoramic view of Lanuipoko. Even though it can't be more than a foot high, the lineup is crowded with people enjoying the sun and warm water.

The young lady in the chair opposite me barely notices the seascape, she is so wrapped up in whatever has her fidgeting nervously in her chair. She pulls herself away from those thoughts long enough to start studying me.

Not a moment too soon, Mandy tells me Piper is free.

"Thanks," I say as I make my way towards the Koa wood door that leads past the open workstations to Piper's office.

"Wait." The girl looks to have found her answer. "Are you related to those pro surfers, Brent and Izzy Styles? You look just like Izzy."

"Nope. Just a coincidence. Sorry," I say over my shoulder without missing a step. Not the first time I've been asked that.

Piper is halfway down the hall when she captures me in a giant hug. Even though she started this company and technically is the CEO, she isn't the type to sit behind her desk and make you come to her. And maybe it helps that she's a cousin who's always felt more like a sister, but I suspect she would stop everything she was doing to greet everyone like this.

"When are you gonna start owning up to that, Billie? It was five years ago," she says quietly, respecting my privacy. If anyone heard her, they might make the connection between me and *the* Izzy Styles and that's not something I want to deal with right now. Or ever, really.

"Not any time soon. So, what's up Boss?"

When we make it down the hall, Piper closes the door behind us and sits behind a terrifyingly neat desk with a view through the glass office walls to girls scurrying about. She slides the two computer monitors to the side to get a better look at me. "I had lunch with Tracy Nichols yesterday."

I can tell she's going somewhere with this. "Oh yeah? How's she doing?"

"She's really good. She's working on this incredible project using AI to track and interpret shark behavior data to increase their survival rates."

"Sounds awesome." That has got to be fascinating work tagging sharks and then tracking them. And knowing you're helping more of them to survive. Damn, she's a lucky girl.

"She's looking for a programmer who knows computers and sharks."

I swipe the tiki statue with a stapler for a mouth from her desk and flip it around a few times. "You don't like the work I'm doing for you?"

"I do. You know I love what you're doing for us, but don't you want to do more? I mean what's the point of getting a degree in computer science and marine biology if you're not going to use it?"

I settle the stapler back in place facing backwards, smiling at the thought of watching Piper try to shove a stack of papers into its bum instead of its mouth several times before figuring it out. "I'm happy here."

"Then do something bigger here. I could really use a new UI for the app."

I shrug it off.

Piper lays her finger on Tiki's head and spins him around slowly while her face switches into serious mode. "You know, when Brent—"

"Don't."

"It's just, ever since then, it's like you stopped living. Or maybe..." she struggles for a way to say it with kindness, "you just stopped trying."

"I'm living a dream life. I have no responsibility. I don't waste my life sitting in a cubicle at a job I hate. I have a boyfriend and I surf every day. How is that not living?"

"You longboard, Billie. That's not surfing. Not for you. You haven't touched a shortboard since that day. And a boyfriend? You barely like the guy."

"Whatever. I'm doing just fine."

"Billie." I can see the genuine concern in her eyes when she says, "It wasn't your fault. You know that, right?"

And that pushes me way past the limit of what I'm willing to hear. I shoot to my feet. "So, is that it?"

"Yeah." Piper's known me long enough to know my limits for anything sad or serious or uncomfortable. Knowing she just sailed way past it, she is quick to let it die.

She stands to walk me out. "You know I love you, right? I just know how much you have to offer this world and I'd hate for everyone to miss out on that."

"I know."

Piper raises her hand as high as it can go. I lower mine close to the floor and we commence the same handshake we've been doing since we were ten and saw Corey and Shawn in Boy Meets World perform theirs and knew we were just cool enough to have a handshake of our own.

"I'd rather die while I'm living," Piper starts.

"Then live while I'm dead," I finish.

And then I hug her to let her know I won't hold her trespass into lands-not-to-be-trodden against her.

After stopping for some plate lunch at Hawaii Five Ono, cruising back to my place, and showering off the day, I make it to JJ's just in time for Monday Night Football, though out here they really should call it something else. No way it's night at 2:45 in the afternoon.

JJ's car isn't in the drive, so I settle into the front porch swing and bring out my sketchbook to work out more details for Biovandal's next installation. Spooner lays down in a heap beside my feet.

I've been trying to think of a way to rig up my bike so I can chalk up huge portions of road without having to bend over and draw everything by hand, but I can't figure out how to make it swing back and forth as I ride to form the shape of a rainbow.

Twenty minutes later, JJ rolls up in his brown El Camino. He kills the motor and rubs his face, not making a move for the door. If he's trying to wipe off the day, he must have had a pretty bad one judging by how long he's been at it.

I stand up and wave while I toss my belongings back into my messenger bag.

He rests his head on the steering wheel, clearly miles away. When he finally looks up, he plasters on a smile and hops out of the car.

"We said two-thirty right?" I ask. I can never remember what time these games start.

He brushes past me. "Sorry, I can't just paddle in whenever I want to. People actually depend on me." He plows through the front door.

"Wow." I stand in the doorway, Spooner by my side, not sure if I should even go in if he's in this kind of mood.

He dumps his gun and badge on the table and returns to me, reticent. "I'm sorry, babe. Look, I didn't mean anything by that. You know how important work is to me." He gives me a gentle kiss on the cheek.

"I know it is but, sometimes people are more--"

"Oh, shoot. The game's already started." He bolts for the remote and flips on the game.

I settle into the couch as he disappears into his room before returning in shorts and a Rams jersey, looking totally out of place for this town.

He settles in next to me, wrapping his arms around me, and touches a quick kiss to my cheek. "Hi," he hums, back to Relaxed JJ.

"Hey."

"Watch this. Long pass to McDaniels," he says to no one in particular.

The Rams score and JJ springs to his feet. "Yes. I told you. Long pass to McDaniels for seven. Didn't I predict it?"

"You predicted it. I really think you missed your calling as a fortune-teller, JJ."

When he's not stressed about work, JJ is always quick to bring a smile to my face. I think it was one of the first things I liked about him.

That day we met on Ryder's boat, I don't think I've ever laughed so much. And when he busted out his own lyrics to that classic Tiffany song, I Think We're Alone Now, I spent the rest of the day singing, "I'll stick it in slow now." He had the whole chorus worked out, a new crass line for every cheesy 80's teen-bop lyric Tiffany bellowed, but the only one my brain held onto was, "I'll stick it in slow, now."

So, of course, at the end of the day, when he leaped from the boat to the docks and asked me out, I wanted nothing more than to forget the nightmare of a morning I had and continue laughing as long as I could. I keep waiting for him to be good for more than a consistent laugh, but in the meantime, I know he'll keep me entertained.

Chapter 3

RYDER

I only had one charter on the books today, so I could make it to JJ's by three since his Rams finally had a Monday Night game. I headed back to shore a little early to make sure I would have enough time to make a special trip to Shaka Pizza to pick up JJ's favorite New York Style pizza. I don't really mind because they make a decent gluten-free pie, too.

I swing open the screen door, holding the pizza, beer perched on top. "Pizza's here. Beer's here. And.." *Shit*. I try to hide the hesitancy in my voice. "...Billie's here." I should have figured that out when I saw Spooner asleep on the porch.

I plant the pizzas and two beers on the table and bring the rest to the kitchen.

"I'll grab the plates," Billie offers and is in the kitchen before I've had a chance to gather myself.

I was hoping to hang with JJ to ease my conscience for my slip-up earlier today. Not sure I was ready to face Billie yet, let alone the two of them together.

Billie digs in the cupboard as I stare into the fridge, cold air pouring out and swirling around my feet.

"I'm not bringing it up..." I start. Grabbing a water, I muster up the strength to close the fridge and face her. "...and we don't need to talk about it, but you're not gonna tell JJ, are you?" I'd much rather we pretend it never happened.

"Tell me what?" JJ slides out a drawer and grabs the bottle opener.

Or I could tell him myself without even realizing it. I might as well perfect my day of infringing on JJ's relationship.

"That I beat Ryder to the buoy and back today," Billie deflects.

JJ opens his beer and throws the opener back in the drawer along with the cap. He wraps his arm around her waist, just like I had earlier, but he has every right to do so. "You guys swim together enough. It's about time you got faster," he teases.

As he heads back to the living room, he bumps my shoulder. "You really couldn't catch her?"

Billie shoots me a mischievous smile. "For a minute there, he was close. But I don't think he has the guts to do it."

It has nothing to do with guts, babe. I'm simply smart enough never to make that kind of mistake again. No way I'm putting my wants above a friend's ever again.

When the game is finished, beers and plates sit empty on the old oak coffee table with the exception of mine which is littered with pizza crusts. I may suffer through gluten-free pizza when it's doused in cheese and veggies, but I'm not about to torture myself with the barren crusts.

JJ pushes to his feet and makes his way to the bathroom. I follow his every move until I know he is out of earshot, then look to Billie for some sort of reassurance that she is not going to reveal my stupidity to the guy it will hurt the most.

She seems to take pleasure in my discomfort but ultimately acquiesces. "Don't worry, there's nothing to tell."

My body finally goes slack with relief.

When JJ returns, Billie swipes the remote off the table before he has a chance to nab it. She sits on the remote and pulls out her phone, pulling up a movie to cast.

"Please, none of those crappy movies you always watch."

She turns an eye on JJ. "Hey, I sat through four hours of crappy Rams football, I deserve to watch something decent."

"You watch how you talk about my Rams, girly."

"Yeah, yeah." Fully relaxed now, Billie settles back into the cushions and starts the movie.

Halfway through *Big Daddy*, JJ is still wrapped around Billie, though he is so enthralled in his Instagram feed, he's barely aware the movie's even on.

No matter how many times I watch Rob Schneider misread Hippopotamus as Hip Hop Anonymous, it still gets me. Billie and I both bust up laughing.

"Look at you two. Two peas in a damned pod," JJ sneers.

Billie stands, and grabs the empty beers. "Who needs?"

"I'll take another," JJ says without even raising his head.

I lift a hand. "Me, too."

She wanders into the kitchen and throws something in the microwave. While it cooks, she lifts her arms above her head, stretching out her shoulders, which lifts her shirt to reveal tight, tan abs beneath. Not that I was watching her every move.

She returns with her arms full. She delivers a bowl of pretzels and chocolate chips to JJ, a bowl of popcorn to me, and sets her own popcorn bowl on the table.

"You forgot the beers," JJ mutters.

I shoot him a look.

"Sorry. Do you need me to grab the beers?" he asks like a scolded child.

Billie grins as she pulls two beers and a cider from the pockets of her jean shorts and hands them out.

"No opener?" JJ reverts to ass-mode. Will he ever learn?

"I can grab one," I offer.

Before I have a chance to stand, Billie takes back JJ's beer and pops the top on the edge of the table. She does the same for her drink and my cider before retiring to the couch.

I toss a handful of popcorn in my mouth, a little surprised by the unfamiliar fruity nuttiness of it. "What exactly am I eating here?"

"You like?"

Shit. I have no idea what I just put into my system. Trying not to freak out about the fact that I could have just guaranteed a sick day in bed tomorrow, I beg, "Is it—"

"Of course. You think I would ever let gluten slip into any of your food?"

I take another handful and enjoy the flavor a little more this time. "Parmesan?"

Billie smiles in agreement.

Prison Bound by Social Distortion plays out from JJ's phone. "I've got to take this." He waits until he's in the kitchen to answer, before traversing the distance to the back door in just seconds.

Billie studies him as he paces in front of the windows, her hand frozen in her popcorn bowl.

When Adam Sandler uses his adopted son to pick up girls, I try to distract her. "Maybe, I need a kid to help me with the ladies."

She doesn't take the bait.

JJ stuffs the phone into his back pocket and continues pacing, while she shakes her head, obviously wanting to shake off the dark thoughts invading it.

Done with his pacing, he lumbers through the kitchen, snagging another beer on his way to the living room.

Billie follows his every move until he sits on the couch a good foot from her.

"You okay?" she asks sweetly.

"Yeah. Just work stuff."

His phone now put away, JJ tries to distract himself with a movie that moments ago he was mocking. When the credits roll, he grabs the remote and shuts off the TV. "Thank God that's over."

"It wasn't that bad, JJ," Billie nudges.

He looks at me. "Kinda late, huh?"

Message received, buddy.

"We swimming tomorrow?" I ask Billie as I stand.

"Full-mile buoy?"

"Sure thing."

Billie gives JJ a peck on the cheek. "I should probably go, too. Early morning and all."

JJ walks her to her bike, Spooner following close behind. I can still overhear their conversation and hate that I can.

"Sorry, I was being awful tonight." JJ starts. "Just got a lot on my mind with this case."

"I get it."

She is far too understanding.

Billie picks up her bike and he kisses her. "I really wish you'd use that car of yours once in a while, at least at night. Not every part of this town is Paradise."

"I think I can take care of myself. And Spooner's the perfect guard dog."

"Yip," Spooner warns.

"Yeah. Spooner's gonna do a lot of damage against the gnarliest guys on this island." JJ bends to rub Spooner's head. "At least let me give you a few self-defense lessons."

"If it will get you off my back."

"Friday morning then? We can do it over here?"

"I can do that."

JJ practically skips back to the porch.

I don't bother trying to hide that I was studying their whole interaction. "Shit, JJ. You could be nicer."

He stops dead on the bottom step. "Hey, I know we've been friends forever, but you need to check yourself. This isn't your relationship. Besides, I've never heard her complain."

"She's not gonna. She'll just keep putting up with your shit."

"Well then, there doesn't seem to be a problem, does there?"

Chapter 4

RYDER

So, she calls me. Out of the blue. Hadn't seen her in probably three years." Billie's in the middle of telling us how she came to work for Piper at Kaulike Hanai while we wait for a table.

The Coral Reefer is halfway between a dive bar and a pub. The service is decent, pool tables line the back room, and we come here enough that they've started carrying bottles of Glutenberg Blonde Ale just for me.

"And she has this offer for me to—"

JJ steps into her story. "Table's empty. Who's up for a game?"

"Billie's right in the middle of a story." Sometimes I think I have to teach him how to be a normal person.

"If we don't move now, we won't get a table." JJ jumps up, grabs the table, and we begrudgingly follow. He finds three cues, handing them out excitedly.

"Okay. Settle down there, JJ." I look to Billie for her opinion.

"I guess I could play."

"One game of knockout," I concede.

"Alright. You rack 'em. I'll take one through five, Billie you can have six through ten, Jax eleven through fifteen?" JJ breaks and sinks the three. "Ha. Jax's down one."

"Don't think so, man."

"That's yours, JJ," Billie laughs and lines up her shot.

"So, Pipers got an offer?" I really want to know how a girl with dual degrees in computers and shark biology ends up making a living by surfing all day and posting about it on social media.

"Yeah. She's got this start-up. It's kind of like Tinder but for building an all-female surf and business network.

"What? An all-chick Tinder?" Oh, now he's interested in his girlfriend's work.

"It's not like that. If you want to make a business connection with someone, you can set up a surf session. It's a chill way to begin the conversation and feel it out."

I knock the four into the side pocket. "You lead all the surf meet-ups?"

"No. It's more of an awareness-branding lifestyle thing. I meet up with the new customers and cover our surf session and then write up an unbiased bio and what they—" JJ's phone interrupts again. She watches him check the number as she continues, "—are looking for from the site."

"I've got to take this." He walks outside before answering.

Billie's face sinks as she tracks him out the door, before turning to me. "JJ's not the type of guy to cheat is he?"

"JJ, cheat? No way. Once you're in with JJ, he's loyal to the end." I should know. I've given him years of crap and he's stood by me the entire time.

"And I'm in?" she asks quietly.

"He's crazy about you."

She drops into a stool at a high table nearby. "But these calls. The second he sees the number his whole body tenses up. Like he's hiding something. And he never answers until he knows he's out of earshot. If he's not cheating, then what is it?"

God, I hope it's not old addictions coming out to play again. But that thought won't help Billie right now. I drop into the stool next to her. "Probably just work stress."

"Work? Really?"

"Yeah. Work stress sucks."

"You still remember what work stress is like?" She nudges my shoulder.

"Hey, I work."

"Taking tourists out fishing all day is hardly what I call stressful."

I flash her a grin. "Yeah, I do have it pretty good."

She starts to spin the ring on her finger, pink chalk dust still under her nails.

"They have pink chalk here now?" I point to her hands.

She hides them beneath the table. "They must."

"Funny, I only saw the blue chalk. Maybe I didn't look hard enough."

Yeah, so, I might push her a bit, but it's fun to watch her squirm. She thinks she's so covert, but I know where that pink chalk is from. I've known that secret for a while.

This morning, the people of Nalu Kai woke to find a two-mile-long giant chalk rainbow along the stretch of Pi'ilani Highway that passes through town with the words to *Rainbow Connection* spelled out beneath it. It was signed with her Biovandal signature. Not that she needed to sign it. Most people around here can pick out a Biovandal original with their eyes closed. Always happy and encouraging. Sometimes it will bring just a smile to the community, sometimes it will feed the homeless.

That was the one that tipped me off. I overheard her ask to borrow Finn's truck one night. Never gave him a reason. He never asked for one. Turns out she filled it with compost from the dump and built an entire raised-bed garden in an empty lot back on Kahili over the course of one night.

When I came to meet her to swim the next morning, I found her asleep on the edge of my yard, hands still covered in soil. When the garden showed up on the @hibiovandalism page the following day, complete with a hand-painted sign overrun with rainbows that said, "Water me and eat my fruit," I put two and two together.

Never told her I knew, though. I didn't want to ruin her fun. The way her face lights up when her art gets brought up in conversation is phenomenal. I think a little piece of that happiness would be gone if she thought her secret was out there.

"How does that happen?" her voice pulls me from the joyous memory.

I stop spinning the coaster on the table. "How does what happen?"

"How do you go from being," she lowers her voice, "in the Navy," before finishing off her question at full volume, "to a fishing boat captain?"

"It's not all that interesting." I take a sip of my beer only to see her staring face when I lower the bottle. "Oh. You really want to know."

Billie nods.

"Well, after having bullets fly at my head every day in Afghanistan, something changed in my brain. I was drinking. A lot. Getting in a lot of fights."

"I can't imagine you in a fight."

I raise my brows. "You know what I did, right?"

"But that's different. I mean, like, fights here, with a normal guy."

I pick at the label on the cider until I realize she's not moving on in the conversation. She actually wants to hear the rest of the story.

Detaching from my unit had been more than I was expecting. I always thought I would go out on my own terms when I had peaked, spent my time as team leader, taught a few years at DEVGRU, not five years into my time with the teams, and certainly not taken down by something so fucking pathetic.

"A couple months after I was out, I was on the other side of the island at The Shanty looking for something." That thing that made all my senses focus and light up. The only place I knew I was created for. And if the teams couldn't give that to me anymore, I'd find it somewhere else. "This one night, I'm a dozen beers in and I'm beating the shit out of this local guy in pool, taking all his money. I sink the eight ball and decide it would be a brilliant idea to taunt him a bit."

She leans forward like this is the most interesting story she's ever heard. If only she knew it was par for the course.

"So, I rub it in. 'Even drunk I can wipe the floor with you.' I jab. He steps into my space, but there's no need to stop him. I simply keep provoking him, just laying into him. Next thing I know, we're outside, and I'm letting him beat the shit out of me. He's got me on the ground and he gets in a few solid kicks to the gut before the bushes around the parking light start flashing red and blue."

I take a long draw from my drink. "The bar owner must have called the cops because two patrol cars show up. Some guy yells, "Maui PD. Break it up.' And I know that voice instantly. It's exactly what I didn't need."

"JJ?" she asks, always on the money.

"Yep. Up walks JJ. His partner cuffs the huge dude and JJ cuffs me and throws me in the back of his car. The back. He starts driving in the opposite direction of the station, not that I know precisely where the station is after a few too many trips there."

"You were a frequent flyer?"

"Pualani Elite Status."

I take her laughter as a good sign she is not totally disgusted with me after hearing about my dark days.

"JJ drives me down to Makapu'u lookout, you know, the cliff with the two islands in the distance. He opens the door and drags me out, shoving me towards the cliff's edge. 'Go,' the only word he said since he cuffed me. I'm bloodied and bruised and limping in that direction, thinking he's gonna push me over for being such an ass, but he points to the bench instead. So, I sit. He sits on the far end and I swear it must have been a solid twenty minutes before he spoke. Then he tells me, 'You let that guy beat the shit out of you, Jax. You let him.'"

I have no idea why all this is pouring out of me. I could have wrapped it up in some noncommittal line about fishing being calming. But each time I look up, Billie is looking at me like everything I'm saying, every screwed-up, completely insane thing, makes perfect sense. So, I go on.

"JJ lets another ten minutes of silence pass. I spend that whole time running my finger over the swelling quickly concealing my cheekbone, the pain, not entirely unwelcome. Then he says,

'Look, I know it's been hard since you've been back, but you can't keep doing this to yourself. I'm not going to tell you to go to AA—I don't know if that'll work for you—but you've got to do something. Cause this? This only ends badly for you. I should know.'"

I move the coaster I've been spinning to the edge of the table and begin flipping it and catching it to get out some more of this nervous energy. Even years later, simply talking about this time gets my gears moving way too fast.

"The next week, I took a delivery job returning a boat from the Transpac to the mainland. Fifteen days alone on a boat, fishing for food, shouting at the wind. And, I don't know, there was something about the rhythm of it. It started to put back together some of the pieces that had fallen apart. When I got back, there was more to repair, so I bought my own boat." I don't tell her that the boat was only the beginning of that journey. That it gave me just enough headspace to look into all the other things I would need to heal my brain, like meditation, tai chi, loads of talk therapy, and even TMS therapy.

Billie digests my confessions as I wait for her to recoil in disgust.

I run my finger along my eye's orbital. "You can still feel the fracture from that night, never healed quite right."

She reaches out and gently runs her thumb over my cheekbone, letting her hand rest on my face, and I'm unable to stop myself from leaning into it.

She smiles when she feels the slight bump from the misaligned pieces of bone. "So, why do you think you let that guy beat you up? You think you were trying to even the score with someone?"

How did she come up with that?

She lifts her hand. "I'm sorry. I didn't mean anything by it. Look, I don't know what I'm talking about."

I think she knows more than she realizes.

JJ steps behind Billie. "Whose shot?"

"Yours, buddy," I say, struggling to break myself from this moment.

Billie is still studying me, like she's putting together things I haven't had the guts to for years.

JJ still can't read a room. "Oh, you've set me up. Just the ten and twelve. I got this." He misses an easy one.

Billie gets up to shoot. Her insight still has me plastered to my seat.

JJ catches her with a quick kiss as she moves past him.

I force my gaze elsewhere remembering whose girl she is.

Billie puts away the last two balls with authority. "Who's up for another?"

Not sure I can handle much more of watching those two together, I reply, "I think I'm gonna head out. But you two should stay. Enjoy the night."

Chapter 5

BILLIE

hat do you do?" JJ prods. He has his arms wrapped
around my shoulders like he's attacking me, but he's so
gentle it feels more like a giant hug.

Our "self-defense training" began thirty minutes ago on JJ's
front lawn with a breakdown of the criminal structure of Hawaii
that felt more like the first class of Criminology of Hawaii 101
than self-defense. I swear he would have pulled out a whiteboard
and pictures to diagram it all if he could have.

I can now tell you which towns to avoid, what to look
for in someone looking for a victim, and which local used car
dealerships, construction, and termite companies to avoid using
because of their extensive involvement with Kavika Kinske
Enterprises, the "legitimate" business arm of the scariest criminal
group on Maui.

But even if I have to go through with this charade, at least
I get to enjoy the cool morning air and the sound of the myna
birds serenading me.

JJ tightens his grip on me. "Come on, Billie. I surprised you
and am pulling you into a dark alley. What are you going to do?"

I turn my head and plant a kiss on his cheek.

He drops his arms. JJ is so easy to goad.

"I need you to take this seriously, Billie. I need to know you're gonna be safe when I'm not around."

I throw my hands on my hips and turn up the sass. "I've been just fine for the twenty-four years I've been alive before I met you."

"That doesn't guarantee you always will." He puts on his best hangdog look, which is more pathetic than endearing. "Please, babe."

He spins me around and squeezes a little tighter. "Now, what would you do if I had you like this with your arms pinned down?"

Ryder's green truck barrels up the driveway until he's parallel with the patch of grass that is acting as our sparring mat for the moment. He reaches over and cranks down the window. "Sorry. I didn't realize I was interrupting your afternoon delight."

"Perfect. Get over here, Jax. I could use your help."

Ryder hesitantly approaches.

"Can you grab Billie from behind, wrap her up?" JJ asks.

Ryder looks to me for my approval.

I shrug. "Whatever gets this over with faster."

Ryder handles me like I'm radioactive, his arms barely connecting with my skin. But his breath is lighting up my neck and, as he struggles not to touch me, his pecs flinch from the tiny adjustments he keeps making.

It's not like I'm into him, I'm with JJ, I know that. But, I mean, come on, a hot guy wraps his arms around you and you respond. It's simple human nature.

Not that JJ notices. He has now assumed full teacher mode. "You're walking your bike home from my place late at night and all of a sudden someone grabs you. You know what he wants to do to you. What do you do?"

If this were some stranger, I'd know what to do. But since it's Ryder holding me and not some Mafia villain trying to coerce me with violence, I'm going to do as little as possible to make sure nothing cuts this moment short. "You want me to tell you or just do it? I really don't want to hurt Ryder."

From behind me, he whispers, "I can take it."

The shivers that sound sends down my spine convince me I

may have to cut this moment short after all. Besides, this is just silly. I don't need self-defense lessons. I don't go hanging around druggies and I know what towns to avoid at night.

"Go on, Billie. Show me," JJ instructs.

Fine. Easiest way to get a guy off you? I dip my chin and lick Ryder's hand.

He pulls away. "Damn, that's so gross."

Coach JJ steps in close. "I know you think that this island is paradise and you live a life of peace and tranquility. But I have to walk this island day in and day out. And the shit I see would shatter you. So, please, let me teach you a few things."

Looks like the fastest way to end this is to just do it.

Ryder wraps me up again a bit tighter this time.

"You want me to just walk you through what I would do?"

"Just do it. Show me. He wraps you up and then..."

"Like full speed? I really don't want to hurt anyone."

"You know what he did right? You're not going to hurt him, sweetie."

I look back at Ryder. He nods in agreement. If he wants it...

I secure his hands against my sternum, pop my hip back into his, and twist to the side as I let my entire weight fall. The surprise lets me pull him so far off balance that he is on the ground as I collapse onto his ribs. Once we hit, his arms unfurl as the air is forced out of his lungs. I roll off him and run a couple paces.

Now, I know in a real attack, there would be no way I'd ever get the jump on Ryder. With his training, I'd be lucky to be conscious more than a split second after he started. But I'm guessing he wasn't truly in fight mode. More like, 'Let's go easy on this poor weakling while we teach her a few moves she probably would be way too scared to use in a real situation' mode.

"Damn girl. That was sweet," JJ boasts like it was his coaching that was responsible for it.

Ryder is still laying on the ground. He's not gasping or clutching his ribs, so I know I didn't do any actual damage, but he's still down there.

"You all good, RyGuy?" I ask.

He shakes his head.

I kneel next to him, checking his side for injuries, not that I actually think I might have inflicted any.

He moves my hands off him. "Just getting my air back."

"Ha. She knocked the wind out of you. Who knew I was dating a girl who could take down a—"

"I just wasn't expecting it. That's all." Ryder sits up. "How'd you learn to do that?"

"Oh, you know. The Navy," I mimic Ryder's usual line downplaying his military history.

JJ plops down on the grass next to Ryder. "Babe, why didn't you just tell me you'd taken self-defense classes?"

"Because I didn't?" Not really. It was more self-defense by necessity.

Prison Bound plays in the distance and JJ is on his feet, sprinting to snatch his phone from the porch steps before I can even locate where it's coming from. He takes the call as he wanders around the backside of his house.

I might as well sit. Our lesson surely is on hold for a while if this one is anything like the last few.

Ryder picks at the overgrown grass. "Where'd you really learn that?"

"When I was a kid, I was always tagging along with my brother and his friends. They were surfing and that's what I wanted to do. But he didn't want his sister cramping his style, so he made me earn it."

"He'd fight you for it?"

"Or he'd make me do the crazy stuff, you know. I'd be the one in the shopping cart that they'd push down the hill first to make sure it was safe. They'd make me swim into the sea cave first to make sure we could get back out. The usual stuff."

I laugh at the thought of how insane I used to be. "Insane Izzy. That's what they called me."

"Izzy? How'd they get Izzy from Billie?"

"Isabel. It's my full name."

He tosses the grass clippings aside. "So, they taught you a bunch of moves?"

"Taught me? No way. He wouldn't take the time to teach me

anything. Growing up, I was always a little bigger than him, so I had the upper hand. But when he turned fourteen, all of a sudden I didn't have the size advantage anymore." I lean back onto my elbows, the early morning sun heating up my face. "That fight had a different feel to it. Like his entire self-worth was on the line. Like it would be the last fight we would ever have because he'd finally prove to me and all his buddies that he was the man now. He got me on my stomach, one knee between my shoulder blades and he shoved my face into the grass with all his might. Forced me to say he was the biggest and strongest. And that I was just a silly little girl."

"He really did that? To his own sister?"

"You know, I get it now. It was his moment to separate himself from me. Natural part of growing up and all that. But back then? Shit. It burned me. I spent the next year learning how to outmaneuver someone bigger than me. Use my speed and leverage, fighting in close to overpower him. Elbows, knees, my head."

"Did you ever get to use it?"

I can't help the smile that dawns on my face at the memory of kneeing him in the balls and shoving him, doubled over, into the river at the edge of our property. "Let's just say, I evened the score."

He tosses his head back laughing. "I bet."

I check the porch for any sign of JJ. He's still wrapped up in "work."

"What's his name?"

I can see Brent's face, tanned to a deep brown, flipping on his charming smile, whenever a cute girl would ask his name. "Brent, baby." It was always Brent, baby.

Ryder raises his brow.

"It was something he used to say."

"Is he older or younger?"

That shouldn't be a tough question, but that one answer would open a box I would like to keep tightly sealed. The sincere interest in Ryder's eyes almost draws out the real answer. Almost.

"He's the same age." Although that's not exactly accurate anymore, is it?

By the time I have convinced JJ I can defend myself, it's well after lunchtime. When he heads into work, I bike to Hawaii Five Ono. The owner, Kaimana, used to run catering for the set of Hawaii Five-O. When they wrapped the series, he moved to Maui and opened my favorite food joint on the island. He has only five options on the menu, three basics and two rotating specials. It has all sorts of memorabilia and the cast has been known to stop by when they're in town, so it's become a popular place. But, it's after the lunch rush, so I have no problem finding a table in the sun with a clear view of the waves at Westies out front.

I remember the days when Brent and I used to scrounge for all the spare change in the house, in the couch, next to the washer, our dad's change from the counter until we found enough for a single Shave Ice. We'd ride our bikes here and ask Kaimana to split a small one into two dishes—Brent would devour my half if we shared—and instead, he'd give us two large cups. At ten years old, we thought it was the greatest gift on earth.

Maybe that's why, whenever I have a chance for a longer lunch, or just need a place to think, I end up here. It doesn't hurt that the view is unbeatable, the breeze off the water is just enough to cool down the blazing Hawaiian sun, and they let the grass grow so tall that it brushes along your feet with each gust.

Is it any wonder what Brent would have thought of JJ. Not that I would have asked if he were still around. JJ and I aren't anything serious. Not sure I would have even introduced him to Brent. But if I did? He'd love JJ's crass sense of humor. And his over-protectiveness. And they'd walk at the same speed.

I know that sounds weird, but whenever I was with my brother, I would always feel like I had to keep up, to trot at his super-speed. Most of the time I wanted to stroll. To meander. To cruise. When I walk with JJ it's the same way. He has left Ryder and I in his wake so many times when we all are walking around town, and he doesn't even realize it until no one is there to answer when he finally stops telling his story.

But Brent would hate how JJ bails all the time for work.

You know what? I do too.

The shadow from the row of sugar cane at the far end of the grassy field has stretched over my legs, so I scoot down along the picnic table to stay in the sun.

I know we're not all that serious, but I still don't want to be an afterthought. Whenever we're talking, I can see that he's got his mind on work. Even from my friends, I expect more than that. And he takes those calls all the time. He's never off the clock. Is that really what I want from a partner long term? I can't imagine having a husband who was never around or always had to bail.

Not that we're anywhere near that serious. Which is part of why I like it. He's never pushed to be more.

But if it's not that serious, why am I putting up with feeling this way? Maybe this thing has just run its course.

The wind picks up the napkins from my plate and flings them onto the grass. I hop up to gather them and toss them along with my plate into the trash can, replacing the lid tightly so nothing else blows away.

I sit back down at my table and realize it's entirely encased in shade from the sugar cane. It couldn't have gotten that late. I tap on my phone. 4:35. How the hell did that happen? Game Night starts in two hours and I don't even have a game picked out, let alone finished prepping it, setting it up, or figuring out a food theme to go along with it.

And honestly, I don't have the energy to do it tonight.

Some days, I wish I could call in a closer. You know, like in baseball. The starting pitcher has pitched a solid seven innings and has nothing left in the tank. So, they call in a closer to pitch the last two. I've put together I don't know how many of these Game Nights with games that are both fun and secretly designed to bond people. And the themed foods? Always perfect. So, where's my closer? Just for tonight?

Accepting that one isn't coming, I whip out my phone and bring up the doc with all my Game Night ideas and scroll through dozens that would take hours to do right until I see the solution. Sardines. No setup. Everyone has played it before. And I'm really good at hiding.

And, as an added bonus, I can go hide in silence so I won't have to sit across from JJ all night knowing that I'm going to break up with him as soon as our friends leave for the night. And he won't be able to pick up that something's wrong and try to get it out of me in front of everyone.

Sardines it is.

Chapter 6

RYDER

After a shit night of sleep where I spent more time awake and attempting to calm myself down than actually sleeping, this half-day charter is dragging on. I sometimes wonder if this is all I will be doing for the rest of my life. Taking tourists out to fish. Can I really be satisfied with just that?

It's certainly not helping the day go by any faster when every quiet moment is invaded by that look on Billie's face when she was begging to hear my stories of being so fucked up.

Or her damned question. *Was I trying to even the score?* How the hell should I know? And even if I was, not sure a single beating could ever make up for what I did over there.

The engine is running rough on the trip back into dock, so after getting everyone back on land and lining up for the pictures they always ask to take with me and their catch, I head back down to give it a look.

Grease up to my elbows and sweat down my back, I finally finish replacing the carburetor and pack it up for the day. The only thing I want to do right now is take a long hot shower and drop into bed.

I guide my truck between the Royal Poinciana trees that form an archway over my driveway to find it filled with cars.

Shit. The very last thing I need right now is Game Night.

After slipping in the side door, and taking a quick rinse, I wander into the kitchen to open an ale. It's nights like this that I painfully miss beer.

Finn's voice cuts me from my daze. "Sorry. Didn't mean to interrupt whatever this is."

"Pouring beer?"

"Dude. You stopped pouring minutes ago. And she's standing there arranging and rearranging the same four crackers on that plate."

Somehow Billie had walked in and started plating food without me even noticing.

"Damn. Sorry, Billie. I was so wrapped up in my lousy day, I didn't see you. But I know the rules. Only good times at Game Night. I'll leave it behind."

She looks at me like she might be seeing me for the first time, too. "Huh?"

She was somewhere deep, and if her face is any indication, not happy in the least. It's way too much emotion for Finn. He's out the door.

"You okay?" I ask.

"I think eventually I will be. But I have to do something tonight I really don't want to do and trying to do all this," she waves her hand over the bags of food and drinks on the kitchen island, "with all of that on my mind, is like—"

JJ bounds through the front door. "So, what miracle of fun does Billie have in store for us tonight?"

And that little glimpse of the real Billie gets slammed behind her chill exterior, which is probably a good thing. The last thing I need is a bigger view of her heart.

"I thought we'd go old school and play a little Sardines tonight." She shoves that fake smile a little higher to sell it.

From the blank stares on JJ's face, he must have had a few too many video games as a child because he was never so bored that he had to play a game that involves massive amounts of time sitting perfectly still and silent. I never understood the draw of this particular game, but Billie needs a little support, so I'm all in. "Sounds perfect for tonight."

The gratitude in her eyes makes it well worth it.

I lift the still-full box of crackers and a couple bags of chips. "Since we're going old school, no need for fancy dishes. Come on, let's go show these civilians how to find people."

After explaining the game a few times to looks of bewilderment—it's hard to accept a library-like environment when Billie usually has the craziest games planned—we all decide she should be the one to hide first.

"Anywhere on the property is fair game," Billie starts.

"Anywhere except the second floor. The second floor is off-limits," I amend.

"Right. Anywhere except the second floor is fair game. You'll count on the sand to one hundred. Then come look for me."

We take our drinks with us to the sand. It's going to take a few more than usual to redeem this night. Finn empties his first beer and steps back towards the fire pit at the edge of the yard to retrieve another.

Charlie grabs his arm as he passes her. "You're cheating, Finn. You can't go looking yet."

"Believe me, Charlie. I really don't care enough to cheat at this one."

I don't bother telling either of them that I've been tracking Billie by sound since she left to hide. It's the highlight of Game Night when I get to beat her at anything.

"Still," Charlie prods.

"Fine. I'll cover my eyes." He lifts a hand over his eyes that only stays up until he is past Charlie.

"What number are we at?" Greyson asks.

"Number?" I look to anyone to fill me in.

"No one's counting?" Charlie asks. "Billie's gonna hate us."

Just what she needs. To be stuck, alone, with whatever is draining her of her joy tonight. "Let's go," I command.

I let Charlie and Greyson dash inside while JJ heads up the side yard. Finn makes another stop at the cooler before wandering around aimlessly.

I follow the sandy path a few meters in the direction I heard her head while scanning my yard, looking for anything out of place. The Kiawe shrubs leave no room for hiding without being stabbed by a thousand thorns and though, typically I wouldn't put it past Billie to slither in there just to win, tonight the usual spunk she'd need for that was nowhere to be found.

The canvas cover to my twelve-foot wooden boat has been pulled back a couple inches. I subtly make my way over there, knowing Finn is still lingering near the fire and not wanting to alert him to her location.

The weird part about Sardines, the thing that elevates it above the game of Hide-and-Seek that you played when you were three, is that as soon as you find the person hiding, you have to stealthily climb right into that hiding spot without alerting anyone else nearby. Finally, everyone else finds them and hides in what is usually way too small of a space with bodies piled up high or sprawled out into places they really can't be hidden. The last person to find the group is the loser and is punished by becoming the next person to hide.

As Billie's cute face peeks out from under the tarp, I school my face to disguise the smile threatening to break forth any time I see her. I make a show of checking the boat while Finn watches. He's not invested enough to check for himself if he sees me doing it. I shrug and turn to find my next search location.

Once he's satisfied, I whisper, "How'd you get in there?"

She's laying on her back on the floor of the open sailboat I built a few years back. It sits on a trailer on the east side of the house. Whenever the noise of the charter boat motor gets to be too much, I pull out *Come Monday* and listen to the sound of the wind through her sails, water lapping against her hull.

"I took out the step. I hope that's okay." I see the small bench seat laid gingerly aside the hull.

"You realize we're not going to all fit in here without breaking this thing to pieces."

"I know. They can hide on the rocks between the boat and the Kiawe. That's their punishment for not being the first one to find me."

I sling one leg over the side of the boat and slide down on my back next to Billie, my arms wrapped tight on my chest to keep as much distance between us as humanly possible while sitting in the hull of a boat not more than forty inches wide.

The overripe guavas lying on the ground at the bow of the boat fill the air with the smell of the tropics, sweet and fruity.

"You realize it would have been better to pull the tarp back over you, right?"

"I didn't know if… someone… is claustrophobic and I didn't want to set anyone off."

Someone. She's too kind to say that would be me. But she's not wrong.

"Plus, this way I get to stare at the stars and contemplate my lot in life while I wait for people to find me."

Above our heads, in the still darkness of my backyard, the whole Milky Way is laid out and it shocks me how rarely I take the time to look. The magnitude of its enormity and our frail tininess in comparison settles in over us.

I let my arm fall to my side and it brushes against hers, still warm from the sun beating down on her all day as she absorbs every bit of joy from her life. Or at least that's how I picture her when my days get dark and stormy, lounging on a sunny beach with not a care in the world, her sunniness lightening me.

I don't immediately pull my hand away when our fingers touch ever so slightly. We're packed into a tiny dinghy playing a kid's game after all. How scandalous could it possibly be?

I can hear the justification in that, so I try to distract myself. "You out here hiding from something more than this game tonight?"

I roll to my side to gauge her reaction. The heaviness I saw in her from earlier returns to her face briefly before she tucks it away. "I don't hide." She follows it with a cheeky grin.

"Clearly. It took me all of two seconds to find—"

Billie rolls towards me and slides her hand over my mouth. "Shh."

Eyes green as the deep jungle convince me to comply. If there's anything Billie takes seriously, and there's not much she does, it's Game Night. She is like a woman possessed when it comes to winning.

ERIN SPINETO

"We already looked there," Charlie whispers to Grey as they walk right by us without even a glance in our direction.

Billie lifts her hand slowly, but doesn't roll away, and we're captured for an instant, gazing at each other, neither of us moving.

She finally breaks the moment with a whisper. "So, does it? Bring stuff up for you?"

No. Say no. Being this close to you brings up nothing for me, Billie. Never even thought about it. Because there's no way in hell I could ever do that to JJ.

Others First.

It's the mantra that has kept me from ever repeating the chaos and hurt I caused in the Congo.

"I didn't know if it was a particular space or just any small space," she adds.

Oh. That.

Thank God.

She has no clue what is really on my mind. "This is fine here. In fact, it's kinda nice." My gaze drops ever so briefly to her lips before I drag it back to her eyes, but she notices.

She notices and deflates, twisting away from me onto her back. And now I've made it awkward.

Shit. I'm making her rough night even worse. I should not be laying under the stars with my best friend's girl and thinking about the way her fingers drew across my lips as she removed them from my mouth. My body should not be reacting to her nearness. I should be better than this. I know what happens when I let my selfishness make decisions. And it's always those around me who pay the biggest price.

I roll to my back trying to give her as much room as possible in this confined space that is getting more claustrophobic by the minute. When I dare turn my head back to check the magnitude of destruction I have wrought, she's watching me, smiling. "Thanks for finding me first, RyGuy."

I return her smile but keep my distance. "Always."

Finn tugs back the tarp. "No way I'm climbing in there."

"Shh." Billie, always protecting the integrity of the game. "You can just crouch down behind the boat so no one sees you."

50

He slides down the side of the boat and takes a long drag from his beer. "I like this game."

Considering it's one of Billie's less emotionally revealing games, that's probably true. She has a way of picking games that get you confessing things you never thought you would. But it has bonded our little group of friends in much less time than it usually takes. It's been kind of like Billie's little emotional boot camp.

I'm not sure Finn has adjusted to all the emotional prodding, though.

Soft plodding brings Charlie and Grey to the boat, with JJ following close behind. "No Jax or Billie yet?"

Finn points a finger over his shoulder to us.

JJ considers us. "So, you two in the boat and all them out on the dirt." He takes another long look between Billie and me, and I swear he is scanning a printout of what has been running through my head. Which is exactly why it has to stop.

When JJ takes his punishment and hides for the next round of the game, I keep my distance from Billie. When she searches inside, I scan the yard. When she heads my way, I duck into the garage. When I'm trapped between her and the edge of the side yard, I climb up to the second-story lanai before she finds me.

After twenty minutes of searching, Charlie, Grey, Billie, and Finn gather on the grass just below me.

"Dude, he's nowhere," Finn starts.

"We can't just stop looking, guys. Come on. One more round," Billie rallies the troops.

"Fine, but this is the last round," Greyson says what's on everyone's mind. "After this, we drink around the bonfire."

JJ comes walking up the driveway. Billie spots him first and her face is a cross of anger and horror at the fact that JJ broke the sanctity of the game by leaving the in-bounds area.

"I've got to go. Work." He gives her a quick hug before disappearing through the back door.

I wait to see how badly Billie will take it, but her mood immediately lightens. "Guess this round's over," she hoots. "To the bonfire."

Chapter 7

BILLIE

The next morning is an unusually overcast day. Shadows from the clouds sweep across the windblown water. It's a rare moment that I ever put on a wetsuit out here, but with the wind popping up like it has, I almost wish I did today.

A couple hours ago, when I paddled out at Natties, it wasn't too bad. But somehow, as my mind spun with whether or not to follow through on my break-up with JJ, the clean head-high waves turned into a walled-up crashing mess. The clouds are darkening by the minute and the waves are jumping up in size with every set. The last few guys out here paddled in with the last set that rolled through, leaving me alone out here with my thoughts and waves that are almost more than I can handle.

I was so ready last night to break up with JJ, but the weight of it was unreal. I hate knowing that I'm going to cause so much strife. I mean, how is that even going to work? Our lives have become so enmeshed that to split them now would be miserable.

Do I stop doing Game Night? Does he stop coming? Or do we both come and end up ruining it for everyone with the tension? I know Piper will stick with me, but what about Charlie and Greyson? They might end up siding with JJ.

And the way Ryder was looking at me last night? I nearly

melted. He was barely a heartbeat away from kissing me. Then what? If Ryder and I ever got together that would make things so much worse.

Oh my God. What am I saying?

This is so incredibly bad.

JJ's a good guy. Sure he has a shady past, but who doesn't? He's kind and sweet and really funny. Why am I being so picky?

I look out to the horizon, hoping it might have the answers I'm searching for when a huge outside wave appears. It's a solid five feet bigger than most of the set waves have been today, which means it is going to break farther out.

I sprint for the outside, praying I make it over the wave before it breaks, but that's not going to happen. It's going to unleash all its energy right on my head. I start taking in long deep breaths to flood my system with oxygen and lower my carbon dioxide levels and to slow the pounding in my chest. It should let me stay underwater for a few more seconds and sometimes that can be the difference between a great story and people telling stories at my funeral.

I watch the lip of the wave tumble over as I shove the nose of my board as deep into the water as my strength will allow. Before I even get a chance to force the tail of my board under, I take the full force of the wave on my back and it drives me to the ocean floor.

Knowing my board floats much better than I do, I feel for my leash around my ankle and follow it upwards to my board tombstoning above me. When I clear the surface, I spin around to locate the land, then back out to sea to check for the next set.

It's coming quickly, but I find the strength to climb on my board and begin paddling for shore. The wave closes in and surrounds me in a veil of spray. I seize the rails of my board and hold on tight as the wave drives me towards the sand, finally spitting me out as it dies out in the depths between the inner and outer reefs. I drift a minute, thanking God I just made it out of another stupid situation.

There's not a soul on the beach now and if I had gotten knocked out or held under a bit longer, it might have been really bad. I should have paddled in with the last group of guys, but that would have required my attention to everything going on around me instead of wasting my energy deciding the future of a relationship that I know I will just continue anyway. I mean when was the last time I did anything but cruise along?

As I walk up the beach, I realize that the ocean was not the only place I should have avoided while alone today. Fourmile Homestead was on the list of towns JJ gave me to avoid, but with the swell coming in from the Northwest, this was the only beach breaking with any ridable shape. And it was fine when there were tons of guys out with me in the daylight. But my surfing buddies have left along with the light and this is not the picture-perfect Hawaii of Ryder's backyard. This is the crusty underbelly of Hawaii, the part they don't ever show the tourists.

Not sure I want to take the time to fully change, I throw on my T&C Da' Boys T-shirt and a pair of black and white checked trunks over my bikini. I don't need to ring the dinner bell for the land sharks around here.

I usually ride Kermit among the trees between the beach and the road, but the road will be way faster and I need to get out of here as quickly as possible. The last thing I need is another lecture from JJ about my risky behavior. And, after that lecture from him about all the things going on beneath the surface here, I'm more hesitant than I'd like, envisioning all of the horrible things JJ was sharing.

Dragging my bike along the sand path to the road, I look up to find two local guys leaving their crap shack. It's time I get out of this place.

I turn away from the road to give them as much space as I can when I hear a truck pull up. I check to make sure they haven't noticed me.

And out steps JJ.

Way out here where he makes me promise I won't go.

And he's not in his police cruiser. He's in his El Camino.

He steps out, slides a backpack onto his shoulders, and looks in my direction but doesn't react. Maybe he doesn't know it's me or, more likely, he's mad at me, which would make sense. Last night when he showed up to Game Night, I told him we needed to talk. He knew it was something bad, he's trained to pick up on that kind of stuff. I don't really want to give him any more reasons to be pissed at me, so I head toward the house.

He does one of those hug-back-slap things with the guy clearly in charge and it almost seems like they are old friends. But JJ doesn't have friends like these guys and coming from LA, there's no way he grew up with a couple of local boys.

The big guy is a solid six-two and, in just a pair of black trunks, has more ink than skin visible. His second in charge, dressed in the same uniform but in blue trunks may be smaller in height, but he looks like he could rip the head off a pit bull.

There's something about JJ's body language that is off a bit. More languid, maybe.

When I'm twenty yards off, I call out, "JJ."

He doesn't even acknowledge me.

I try again. "Hey, JJ."

He waves, but I can't tell if it's a 'hi come talk' kind of a wave or a 'hi, now go away' kind.

There's no way he's that pissed about last night. I have to go smooth things over, especially since there's no way I'm breaking up with him now.

All three of them turn and walk towards the house and JJ looks just like one of them. Shirtless, low-slung trunks, barefoot. They stride through overgrown weeds that make up the front lawn. Past the chain link fence with so many holes, there's no way it could keep the German Shepherd lying on the porch contained.

The dog jumps up at the sight of the three men closing in on him and sprints at them until he hits the end of his chain and yelps.

"Fuck off, Kai," the big one yells at him.

The short one stops at the bottom of the stairs and points me out.

I freeze.

JJ says something to them that I can't hear before the big one waves me over.

JJ's whole body tenses up. It's a small difference, but I can feel his anger.

As I get closer, the smell of barbecue chicken drifts by probably coming from the backyard as some sort of bad rap music hangs in the air. I walk past the lawnmower abandoned mid-mow and flip down my bike's kickstand. When I join JJ, he doesn't bother introducing me to his friends, he simply wraps his arm around my shoulders, pressing me to his side.

On the porch, a nasty couch that is more dirt than orange holds up some other guy napping in a weird angle that looks more like he's passed out than enjoying a post-surf siesta.

The big guy, Kavika, his name emblazoned on his collarbone tattoo alongside spiders dripping from each letter, herds us into the hovel where cockroaches take up more space than the furniture, before disappearing out the back door. There's no way he's the Kavika JJ was telling me about, but he looks scary enough to be him.

The room is black when we step through the door—blinds pulled on all the windows—the only light blaring from the slim door on the back side of the shack. My eyes slowly adjust to the dim light. The rundown exterior is a palace compared to the inside. Bottles and trash cover the floor, bodies in various states of dress and consciousness litter all horizontal surfaces, and all the vertical surfaces are the color of a dripping ashtray. A small camera stands on a tripod in the corner next to a pile of zip ties. I don't want to imagine what those are for.

I look to JJ to explain what kind of alternative reality I just stepped into. He doesn't return my gaze. I knew he had a past, but I thought it was just that, the past. I search his face for some confirmation that he hasn't gone to the dark side. That he hasn't become a criminal. But he won't make eye contact.

My gaze drops to the coffee table where some sort of white drug is splayed out next to stacks of money and a few guns.

Guns?

Shit. They *are* guns.

Where the hell am I?

I know JJ says there are places like this, but how did I just end up in one? I only wanted to go for a quick surf, get some dinner, maybe chill on my porch.

And why the hell is JJ in a place like this anyways?

He's supposed to be the one arresting these idiots, not acting like they're his best friends. Or worse yet, his business partners. I guess I should have figured out with all the phone calls that's what this was. I was so stupid to think he was just cheating on me.

Chapter 8

BILLIE

JJ, what the hell is going on?" I plead.

JJ drops his arm from my shoulder, steps back, glancing briefly around the room, and barks at me, "Why are you freaking out?"

"You have to get us out of here. This is—"

Kavika returns with another guy following close behind who's as scary as the first two and twice as big.

"Is this how you do business, Kavika? Product all over. Everyone in your shit?" JJ demands.

"Settle down. They ohana. Dass why." Kavika nods towards the body on the chair in the corner who reflexively wanders out the back door. "You got it or not?"

"Relax. I have it." He nods to the backpack.

I try to get JJ to look at me, give me some signal that this isn't the real him. That he is playing some sort of awful joke on me. That maybe he's undercover. But the only thing I find in those eyes is pure unadulterated hate.

Holy shit. He's in bed with *the* Kavika Kinske.

I'm on my own. And in way over my head.

"Grindz done," a voice calls from the back of the house.

Kavika turns to look and I take the opening to get the hell

out of this place. Two steps towards the door and Blue Trunks slams me against the doorjamb. "Where you going? The fun is just about to start," he snarls.

I look up and silently beg JJ to do something. To step in and arrest someone. To pull his gun and shoot everyone so I can escape. But he does nothing.

"Noa, make sure she doesn't move." Kavika nods for JJ to follow him out the front door.

The big guy, Noa, shoves me back into the hovel. Blue Trunks is right next to him.

I strain to watch Kavika and JJ over their shoulders.

"She gonna be a problem?" Kavika demands.

If Kavika thinks I'm a liability, there's no telling what he'll do. People have disappeared for less.

"Don't worry about that bitch," JJ spits out. "I'll take care of her so that no one ever hears anything from her ever again."

Shit.

"Mile marker twenty-four off Kahekili. Three hundred yards mauka. Put her there," Kavika instructs.

JJ nods and hands over the backpack.

I'm so fucked.

Noa pitches me against the wall and stalks up to me, trapping me. The stench of sweat mingled with stale smoke envelops me. Inked spiders crawl over every inch of his skin.

"You think she'll be a screamer or a crier?" Blue Trunks asks Noa.

"Sorry to disappoint, but I'm not much of either, so... I'm gonna go." I push against his chest, but he doesn't budge.

His smile flees like I wish I could, a scowl taking its place.

Doesn't like a smart mouth. Got it.

My hands shake as I drop them to my side. My heart beats wildly. I force in a long breath to slow the pounding in my chest. Not working like it does in the lineup.

Couch Guy is now at the alert next to Blue Trunks. Was he even passed out or is that just their security system?

No talking your way out of this, Billie. Just don't be a threat.

I cross my arms across my chest and stare down at the blowtorch laying on the floor beside the door.

Kavika steps in beside Noa. "You gonna keep your damned mouth shut about this?"

I try to nod but it comes out as more of a tremble.

Don't incite him. Just sit here. Ride it out. He'll get tired of it. Let you go once he's made his point.

"I'm not telling anyone anything. Ever," I plead.

Kavika puts his hands on the wall behind me on either side of my head as he fixes me with a sick smirk. "Let's show her what we do to snitches."

He drops one hand to the fly of his trunks.

No way in hell.

I'm not riding that out.

No way around it now.

I have no choice.

I'm gonna have to...

I slam my forehead into his nose before he has a moment to react.

Rush past them out the door.

Jump off the porch.

Sprint towards my bike.

And crash to the ground.

Lawnmower.

I pull my legs under me and take off again.

Before something barrels into me, taking out my legs from under me.

I roll to my back.

Kick the dog.

Scramble back beyond the range of his leash.

Hop up.

Rush to my bike.

And put as much distance as possible between me and that hell hole.

Bursting through my side gate, I drop my bike in the yard. I sprint around to my back door and smash through it, locking it behind me. Slam all the windows shut and close the blinds.

They'll be here any second.

I scurry into my room and lock the door. Shove into my walk-in closet. I wish I had more than a bunch of beads as a door. This is the first place they'll look for me. I have to hide better.

I scoot the dresser forward a foot, split the clothes hanging on the rod above it, climb on top, and lower myself into the gap I created. I slide the clothes back in place and hunker down.

They have to be right behind me.

I draw my legs up to my chest.

You're breathing too loud. They'll hear it. Slow down.

Why did I have to attack the scariest guy on this island?

You remember when your stupid ass did something like that in Peru. What happened? You idiot.

Rivers of sweat roll down my back, but I can't wipe at them. This space is far too small for any but the smallest of movements.

I tried so hard to stay Chilly Billie, to not go aggro. But Kavika. He wouldn't let me.

Streams of tears leak from my eyes. At least those I can wipe away with shaking hands.

Chink.

Oh, God. Is that a window breaking? They're coming in through the windows. I should have left the doors open. I chose the worst place to hide. There's no escape. No retreat. I'm a sitting duck when they come for me.

I hold my breath while I scan the house for the next sound. Nothing.

They have to have followed me.

I spin my ring around my finger over and over, waiting for their attack.

How did I end up in that house in the first place? Did JJ ask me to come? Did I follow him?

I rub my forehead trying to relieve the building tension.

He was going to…

Shit. He was really going to…

Buzz. Beep. Buzz. Beep.

Damn. They're totally going to hear that. I reach for my

pump in my back pocket to cancel the high alarm. But it's too tight in here. I can't get it. Not without standing up.

But I can't. They see me and I'm done. But when it goes off again, they'll find me for sure.

I slide my arm up the wall, hoping the clothes hanging from the rail will provide some cover, and reach around for my pump. Pulling it from my waistband, I silence it and slide my hand back slowly in front of me.

I screwed up everything. I had to shoot off my mouth. Piss him off. I couldn't just go with the flow. I had to go insane.

Just like Peru.

Fuck.

My throat tightens and my tongue gets hard as my stomach threatens to empty right here.

What the fuck was I thinking even dating JJ?

I let the bad guy in. I *let* him in. How did I not know?

I should have left that beach when everyone else did. I would have been perfectly fine. But I had to get distracted with whether or not I was going to dump JJ.

Well, at least that question has been answered. If only I had followed through with it last night.

The pain in my stomach begins to spread to my shins, as waves of exhaustion start to wash over me.

I lower my head onto my arms.

They had chickens in that house. Wild chickens. In the house. That place must have been covered with chicken shit.

Why couldn't I just have kept my cool?

I wouldn't be hiding in the back of my closet waiting for my death right now.

I wouldn't have a dirty cop as a boyfriend.

I wouldn't be feeling like this.

Again.

Chapter 9

BILLIE

lank.

My eyes pop open and I scan for the source of the sound in the darkness. Seeing nothing, I close my eyes again and listen as the silence carries me back to sleep.

Thud.

I turn my head, but it's stopped by a solid wall. The dresser. From last night. Hiding.

The hallway creaks, announcing their arrival.

I tip my head back to see over the edge and prepare for the onslaught. I'm trapped. There's no way out. With no weapons. I'm gonna have to fight with my fists.

Elbows.

Knees.

Forehead.

God, I headbutted him.

The door swishes open.

Here we go. Breathe quietly. Don't move. Maybe they won't look.

I feel the dresser bump into my hip and can hear their breath.

This is it.

Yip.

Yip?

Spooner. I look up to see Spooner's face. Happy.

"Yip."

I shimmy to my feet and draw him back down with me into my hiding spot. "Aww, Spooner. I missed you." I pull him tight into my chest as I rub my hand down his back over and over. "How'd you get in here, pup?" I could have sworn I locked everything up.

Spooner begins to whine for food and I realize the space is filled with more light than before I drifted off. It must be morning.

They didn't come for me. But they will. JJ's a dirty cop and I saw all of it.

Shit. I saw all of it.

And Kavika told JJ where to bury me. Fuck. And JJ knows where I live. I'm a sitting duck here.

I can't go to the cops because he'll probably make something up about me to cover his tracks. Tell them I'm crazy or stalking him or something. He can find me anywhere on this island. I've got to get out of here.

I park Spooner on the dresser so I can climb out. The moment I'm on my feet, searing pain shoots up from my shins. Sleeping in a one-foot crawl space is not such a hot idea.

I lift my leg to climb over the dresser and the pain is multiplied. I turn and scoot my bum onto the surface instead and inspect my shins. Crusted burgundy rivulets fall from giant gashes on each shin. Where the hell did those come from? No one slashed my shins.

Lawnmower. That's right.

I stumble into the bathroom and pluck a towel from the rack. After dousing it in the sink, I try to scrub off the dried blood. Standing as soon as I finish, I look down at my shorts and tank. I feel naked.

I return to the closet and wrench open my bottom drawer, retrieving a navy pair of sweats and hoodie. On my way out of the room, I pluck my ball cap from the back of the door.

I always suspected there was something JJ wasn't telling me, but I would never have guessed that he was dirty.

By the time I make it into the kitchen, I have no idea why I'm here.

I have to leave.

Get out of this house right now.

JJ's promised he'd take care of me and put my body in some gang burial site. He's going to come charging through that door to clean up the mess I made last night.

Ryder. He'll protect me. But would he believe me? He's been friends with JJ for years. How does he not know?

Or does he know? He was so quick to cover for JJ with all of those calls. All of that "Once you're in with JJ, he's loyal to the end" shit. Ryder has to know. That's why he was covering for JJ.

And even if he doesn't, would he really be able to hide me from JJ? JJ's probably already in his ear about finding me.

I have to get off this island.

I fly back into my room and nab a bag from the top shelf of my closet, filling it with whatever I can find in my drawers. Clothes, shoes, socks, underwear, all by the fistful get stuffed in the bag.

Back in the kitchen, I search for vials and pens of insulin. Bag almost full, there's no way I can fit pump supplies.

I snatch the Amazon box next to the trash and dump the recycling into the can. I open the hall closet outside my bedroom which I converted into a diabetes pantry and fill the big box with smaller packages of cartridges, infusion sets, syringes, strips, collection of old meters, and Dexcom sensors. It'll only hold a few week's worth of supplies like that.

What if I'm gone longer? Who am I kidding? I'm not coming back.

I rip open package after package and empty the individual pieces into the box. Four times as many fit this way.

I scan the room for anything else. A picture tucked into the warping chair rail molding in the hallway catches my eye. JJ, Ryder and I standing on the docks after my one and only day fishing on Ryder's boat. I pull it from the wall and tuck it into my Bible sitting on the side table, and stuff both into my backpack, followed by the tactical knife from the junk drawer in the kitchen.

Spooner follows me to the front door.

I drop my bags and box and rush back into the house. Coming back through the door with an armload of food, I load up Spooner's bowl before leaning down and wrapping my arms around him. "I'm not gonna be able to feed you anymore, Spooner. You're gonna have to take care of yourself from now on. Be careful. It's not safe out there."

With my backpack on my back and my box of pump supplies strapped to the rack, I'm off.

They'll be able to track my cards. Cash. I need cash. All of it in cash.

Once at the ATM, I hop off my bike and push my card into the machine. Withdrawal. $5000, I type in.

"The maximum withdrawal is $500. Please try your transaction again," the machine replies.

That's it. Five hundred? Fine. Five hundred.

With cash in hand, I shove my only other card in and withdraw another five.

Where else can I get cash? The store. I need food anyway. I take off towards the supermarket.

And sugars. I forgot to bring sugars. Shit. What's my blood sugar?

I yank out my Dexcom and check. HIGH.

I pull over to the curb to fix it and flip the screen to a twenty-four-hour view. It's gone from a level ninety straight to HIGH without budging since last night.

Dammit. 180. 240. 300. 360. 420. That's five units. But biking's gonna drive me lower. Shit. I don't know. If they find me and I'm low, I won't be able to defend myself. I'll have to reduce the correction. Three units not five? I dial up a bolus and then continue toward the store.

Once there, I lock up my bike, pull up my hood, and tug my hat down on my head before heading to the granola bar aisle to clean them out.

Throwing twenty bars on the conveyor belt, I try to contain

myself so I don't scream at the cashier. "How much cash back can I get?"

"Two hundred," she says with a genuine smile.

"Great, I'll have two hundred." I toss the granola bars into my backpack.

Twelve hundred may not be enough. And once I'm off island, everything has to be in cash or he'll know where I've gone.

On my way out, I pass the self-checkout. I swipe a bag of M&M's from the stand, run them across the scanner, and pull out another two hundred dollars. Then I do it again at another scanner with Skittles. Sixteen hundred is going to have to do.

I shoulder my backpack and point my bike toward Maalaea Harbor before I have to make the long, hot ride across the island to the airport. For a long stretch of the Honopilani Highway, there's no bike lane, so gusts of wind try to push me off the road with every car that passes me.

Heading into the tunnel halfway to the Harbor, it is almost impossible for drivers to see me in the darkness, so I ride in the center of the lane, knowing I'm going to piss off a couple of them with my speed. A truck decides he doesn't want to wait, so he pulls around me nearly hitting a Jeep coming the other way and then swerves back towards me. Slamming on my brakes, I veer into the wall, searing a colossal stripe of road rash up my arm.

Once out of the tunnel, I pull into the small overlook just south of the tunnel, unearth my phone, and swipe open the Hawaiian Airlines app. Where do I fly? I want to be as far from here as I can. Florida? It's been nearly twenty years since the last time I was there, but it's the only East Coast state I've been to.

First flight out to Florida? Three hours. Perfect. I click on the link and begin to fill out the reservation.

They can trace my card. They'll know where I went and just come get me there. I flip back a screen.

Where else? Long Beach? Opposite coast? I can find my way to Florida in a way that's untraceable once I'm on the mainland. That'll do. I book the ticket and hop back on my bike, dreading the hottest part of my ride.

By the time I make it to the other side of the island, I have sweated out every ounce of moisture in my body. I buy a gallon of water at the gas station and take in as much as I can, then strap the rest to the top of my diabetes box and head to the UPS store.

The blast of cold air greets me when I open the door. It feels so refreshing, I think maybe I can just hide here forever.

"How can I help you?" the UPS guy asks.

I slap the box down on the counter. "I need this to go to the post office in Key Largo. They can hold packages for a while right?"

"Three weeks." He grabs the tape from beneath the counter and starts sealing the box for me.

"Perfect. Send it there."

The UPS guy fills in the address. "Who is it for?"

My pump screams at me again. Pulling it from my back pocket, I expect a low after all that riding. But it is a solid line for the last three hours at HIGH.

No movement? There's no way. I run my hand along the tubing and come up with the entire infusion site in my hand. It must have pulled out of my leg at some point. Who knows how long I have been without insulin? That's not good. And I have no extra sites with me.

I rip open the box this nice guy just sealed and dig in the pile for an infusion set. He probably thinks I'm some sort of freak druggie with all this. "Sorry. I'm done." I fold the flaps back down and he begins to seal them up again.

I should have backup with me. It's gonna take me a while to get to Key Largo. "Wait." I stick my hand under his tape. "Sorry, I need more." I snatch a few handfuls of supplies and shove them into my already crammed backpack.

He waits for me to meet his gaze. "You good? Don't need any more?"

"Yeah. I'm good. Sorry."

Ding.

I spin around to look toward the door, and scan the guy who walks in, but I can't make out his face because of the sun coming in from behind him.

"Hey, Mike. In for that package?" The UPS guy's voice is relaxed, but he's not the one they're looking for.

I search the room for an exit. The counter is open at the end. Light is streaming in from a clear door in the back. I spin back to the man who is now only a few feet from me, but his face is finally lit. I don't think it's one of them.

"Miss? Miss."

I pull my gaze from the intruder and turn to the UPS guy.

"Who do you want me to have them hold it for?"

"Billie..." JJ only knows me as Billie. "Wait, no. Izzy Styles."

———

At the airport, I realize that leaving Kermit locked up here would be like sending off a flare that screamed I left the island. And there's no mistaking that this bike is mine. I spent three weeks designing and hand painting it with smiling sea turtles chasing Myna birds along the frame under one skinny rainbow the entire length of it. JJ would know it in an instant and I have to delay him figuring out where I am for as long as possible.

The only other place I can think to hide it is at the bottom of the ocean. It's not like I will ever be back here to need it again.

Kahana Beach Park sits just beyond the airport runway. I can walk back after sending Kermit off to a watery grave. I hop back on the bike and ride the dreadful mile to the sand.

How could I have been so completely wrong about JJ?

When the dirt path ends, I drag him toward the water until his front tire hits it.

Maybe I don't have to leave. Maybe I can just hide.

And not go anywhere.

Or see anyone I know.

Shit, he already could have the whole force looking for me and he knows everyone on this damned rock. There's no way to stay.

I slip off my sweats and roll Kermit into the water a few feet.

I might not even make it off this island before he figures it out.

Waist deep in the water, Kermit is now submerged.

Let go. Take your hand off the handlebar and let it go. Now.

I release the last thing tying me to this rock, watching it sink until it lands in the sand, throwing up a cloud of silt around it. With the final trace of me washed away, I exit the water ready to start my new life. As long as he doesn't know I've left for a while, I might be able to get away.

Tomorrow. Our swim. Ryder will know I'm gone and he'll tip off JJ without even knowing it.

The glare of the sun dancing on the water over the grave of my bike overtakes the dam wall and the tears begin to flow. I wipe them with the back of my hand, forcing myself to turn from the water. I need more of a head start than that.

Back on the beach, I fish the phone out of my sweat's pocket, but I can't bring myself to hit call. I have to get this right. As I wander back up the beach to the street, I practice my declaration. *JJ's dirty and he tried to... And those guys...*

Sobbing disrupts my rehearsal, and I sink into the sand.

They're gonna come find me. He was gonna... He almost...

I lift my head enough to see the phone still in my hand.

Pull your shit together, Billie. You have to do this. Facts. Just tell him what he needs to know.

I dial and hit call.

"Billie! You're not bailing on tomorrow are you?" Ryder's voice removes what little air was left in my lungs. "You too tired from yesterday's little swim?"

Just the facts, Billie. "I'm alive. I'm leaving. Please don't look for me. And don't tell JJ."

I don't wait for a reply. I hang up and stomp on the phone, before dousing it in the beach showers and tossing the watery pieces into the trash can.

My final task complete, I take one last long look at the sea, knowing it will be the last time I see the Pacific from these shores, before I begin the slow walk to the airport.

Chapter 10

RYDER

One of the best things about this house, besides the backyard with views of the sunset each night, is the front porch. Wide enough for a pair of rocking chairs, ceiling painted a crisp aqua, propeller-style fans blowing a cool breeze to cut the heat. And the morning sun hits just right.

On mornings when I don't have a charter, I love to spend hours reading out here. Today it's *In Memory of Bread,* one of the few celiac memoirs I've seen written by a guy. For some reason, it feels like celiac is a woman's disease. Maybe it's because only thirty percent of cases are in men, or maybe it's because celiac takes away all the things we consider manly, burgers, beer, and being strong. Either way, it's encouraging to connect with another guy dealing with it, even if it's only through a book.

On the table next to me, my phone lights up with Billie's goofy face. I swipe to answer. "Billie! You're not bailing on our lunchtime swim, are you? Too tired from yesterday's little workout?"

Her flexible schedule leaves her open to fit in swims around my charter trips. Lunchtime swims are my favorite. Sure, there's nothing like waking up to Billie's sunshine, but lunchtime swims usually lead to long lunches at Hawaii Five Ono and Afternoon Billie gets chatty and deep. Okay, maybe not deep, but her mind wanders into the strangest of places. We've been known to discuss the merits of the movie *Clueless* as a tribute to the climate of women's rights in the 90s or why the gorilla on her beloved 80s T&C shirt is truly an accurate representation of Dane Kealoha, or why Thursday is the greatest day of the week.

"I'm alive. I'm leaving. Please don't look for me. And don't tell JJ."

"Wait? What?" I look at the phone to make sure it's really Billie. But I know her voice. It's her.

My screen turns black. What the hell was that?

I'm on my feet in seconds. I open my phone app and call her back. It just rings and rings.

Just as it goes to voicemail, JJ's El Camino pulls up. He gets out, shouting, "Is Billie here?"

This isn't good. "What the hell is going on, JJ?"

He crosses the porch and looks in the front door. "Is she here, Jax?"

"No. Why am I getting calls saying she's alive? What the hell happened?"

He turns back to me. "Jax. Shit, Jax." He runs his hands through his hair as he steadies himself. "She ran into us at Kavika's."

Why the fuck did he let her anywhere near Kavika?

He paces back and forth in front of me. "They made me leave."

Fuck, no.

I step into him. "You left her with Kavika?"

"I had no choice. They had a gun to my head."

With both my hands gripping his shirt, I slam him against the door frame. "You always have a choice. She'll do whatever you ask. You should have told her to leave or follow you out. You shouldn't have left her there."

"Let me go. I have to go find her."

The moment I release him, he's halfway down the front steps. I call out after him, "You're not going to find her. She left."

This stops JJ dead. "What? Left where?"

"I don't know." I look down at my phone like it could tell me. "Shit, man. I don't know."

JJ jogs to his car.

I shout, "You're a dead man if anything happens to her."

Fuck. *I'm* dead if anything happens to her.

My joy is gone. The only thing holding me together and filling in those dark holes in my brain has left and I have no way of bringing her back. And, fuck, if I can't find her, how am I supposed to protect her from whatever drove her away in the first place?

I slam through the door, pacing from room to room like she is going to somehow materialize.

"Like hell, I'm not going to look for you," I say to her or no one or myself. I don't know. This island is only so big, I will find her. I pocket my keys and fly out the door.

When I arrive at Billie's house, Spooner is asleep next to his bowl on the porch. I push the front door open. Not much is different, but there has to be something here that tells me where she went.

There's a pad of paper on the counter. I run my fingers over it trying to see if anything was written there. There's some texture to it so I scrub a pencil over the top.

Don't cross the midline. Fully extend the stroke. Hip to opposite shoulder.

It's only notes on swim technique. No intel there.

I charge into her room. Complete chaos. Clothes still dangling from the dresser. Her diabetes pantry is in total disarray and almost empty.

"Dammit, Billie. Where'd you go?"

───────────────

I have ways to find people. I have people to help me. But I'm not sure we're at that point yet. There's no need to go breaking dozens of laws if Billie is just holed up at someone's house somewhere. I run through my phonebook for anyone who Billie might turn to for help. And I should be the first name on that list.

Why didn't she just ask me? Come to me? She knows I would do anything to protect her. And that I'm damned good at it too.

I dial Piper. "Hey, have you heard from Billie since last night?"

"Uh. We chatted at Game Night on Friday. I know she was in a funny mood for some—"

"Piper. Have you heard from her since last night?" I bark into the phone.

"No. What's going on, Ryder?"

I hang up. I'll have time later to smooth things over with Piper. Right now time is much more important than manners.

I call Charlie and have nearly the same conversation. Greyson and Finn are next but have nothing to add. No one has heard from Billie since Game Night a few nights ago. No one except JJ. But he's the one who got her into this in the first place.

I'd love to call Billie's parents or her brother, but we aren't at that place where I would have their numbers.

I take another pass around Billie's place to see if anything stands out. It doesn't look like there's been a struggle or like the place has been ransacked, that's good. The only things missing are the things Billie might take if she were planning to leave in a hurry.

I'm alive. I'm leaving. Please don't look for me. And don't tell JJ. There's got to be something in what she said that will lead me in the right direction. She's alive. Does that mean she thought she might not be? With Kavika involved that is a definite possibility. Maybe I should go over there and knock the answer out of him.

Not that he would tell me. And that's just going to stir up a hornet's nest.

And don't tell JJ? You'd think she'd at least want her cop boyfriend to help her escape whatever it is she's running from. Or is it him she's running from?

There's no way she'd do that. JJ might not be the most sensitive guy out there, but he's good people. He'd never hurt Billie. Or hunt her down. That's nuts. She's way more likely to be running from Kavika. That guy is crazy.

There are rumors that he runs the Hawaiian mafia, that he's a human trafficker, that he's a murderer for hire. He's most certainly at the center of a lot of drugs and plenty of violence, though, at this point, nearly all the violence that surrounds him is carried out by other people. If he is anywhere near Billie, I can't blame her for wanting to get as far away as possible.

Maybe it is time to call in my people.

Chapter 11

BILLIE

I lock the bike I hastily purchased at Walmart into the back of a train car, slide into the seat in front of it, and prepare for a neverending blur of trains and buses and even more trains that will obscure my trail to the other side of the country.

When my third train finally makes it to Miami, I unstrap my ride and step out into a mass of tall buildings, the exact opposite of the flat land and ocean views I was expecting. Sure, the streets are lined with palm trees, but this place looks just like LA.

Oh shit, did I screw up the route and end up coming right back to where I started?

I turn back to walk into the train terminal and see, among the ads for some bar and some gorgeous model with a fancy purse, a black sign that says Miami Central Train Station. I slide my hand into my back pocket to pull up Google Maps and come up empty. Without my phone, I am once again in the late aughts when a person could actually be lost.

I look to the sun, tipping towards the horizon over land in the afternoon, point my bike in the opposite direction, and ride to where I think the coast will be waiting.

The tall trees lining the road give me some relief from the blazing sun, but it is only moments before I'm forced to remove my protective shell. I stop to tuck the navy sweats into my backpack before hopping back on my ride in the pair of compression shorts I had on underneath.

An enormous green sign announces that I have made it to A1A as I get my first glimpse of the Atlantic. Just a small channel that works its way into the city, but it's enough to unfurl the tension in my muscles that has been there since...

I shake off the thought. Fifty miles till safety. I turn right for the double marathon to Key Largo.

After forty miles through the same suburban sprawl that could be any town in the US, the road leaves behind all traces of settlement and winds its way through the lush overgrowth and I'm finally greeted by the Florida I remember from my sailing trips with my dad so long ago.

The sun blasts the sky with wistful pinks and hopeful oranges as it runs away and spins toward home. My old home.

The scrub brush that lines A1A breaks for a brief moment as the Florida Bay crawls right up to the highway. I pause from the perpetual motion I have been in since I left Maui to wish the sun farewell and pray that he takes a message home to Ryder for me. I don't know exactly what that message is though.

I'm safe? I'm sorry? Not sure of either, I race against the darkness creeping in.

Off the side of the Jewfish Creek Bridge, just past mile marker 107, stands a little green sign that says, Key Largo. I look up to see a huge island and am overwhelmed by what to do now.

I picked Florida because, even though it was far away, I had been there before. When the UPS guy asked me where to ship my things, Key Largo was what popped into my mind. But now that I'm here, faced with an entire city, I have no idea what the hell I'm doing. I don't even know if there are hotels here. And the cash I have won't last long at a hotel, anyhow.

When we came here seventeen years ago, my dad had planned the whole trip. We sailed *Incommunicado* into Hammerhead Key one hundred meters off Key Largo, hopped out, grabbed the best burger I had ever tasted, and slept on the boat before we set sail the next day headed toward our final destination, Key West.

I don't know why I thought I still knew this area when I had spent a total of two hours on dry land here.

But I can't just sit here on the side of the bridge kicking myself for being so stupid. I hop back on my bike and coast down the incline. A mile into town, I see a sign for Mango Bay Marina, Hammerhead Key. Could it be the same marina we sailed into so many years ago? It's worth checking out and I could really use a hearty burger right now.

At the far end of a gravel-lined parking lot stands a thirty-foot tall gray boat barn with one entire side open. Inside sit layer upon layer of boats in dry dock, like some sort of toys in a child's Hot Wheels carrier. At the other end of the lot is a bright blue restaurant with a sign above that says, "The Salty Dog. Locals Welcome. Tourists Tolerated." In between the two is a repair shop with a Help Wanted sign in the small window.

The gravel crunches under my feet as I move a little closer to the repair shop to get a better look.

"Go grab a burger at the Salty Dog and we'll have it done by the time Sally brings you your check. I'll have her ring you up for both," says the weather-beaten man in charge.

That's all the convincing the younger customer needs. "Sounds good."

Bossman shouts to one of his workers, "Topher, come give this engine a quick oil change," as he heads towards what looks to be his office. When he catches me staring, he tosses me a warm smile.

I spin on my heel and pretend like I'm doing anything besides creepily watching these normal people going about their normal day.

Money's going to run out pretty fast down here and I bet they wouldn't care if I didn't give them a real name. Bossman doesn't seem like the type of employer to ask for ID. Maybe a little side job is just what I need.

Even by beachy standards, I must look like a lunatic, hair tangled by the wind and a full three days of stink packed on me. I slip into the bathroom between the restaurant and the little dive shop to freshen up.

The zombie who greets me in the mirror is almost unrecognizable. My kiwi eyes are still there, but they are surrounded by so much puffy blackness you can barely see them. The darkness fades into a dirt stained face, evidence of my sweaty skin picking up road dust as I made my way into this new oblivion.

Dipping below the mirror, I splash my face with cool water, pressing it into the bags under my eyes, attempting to press some of the inflammation out of them. I dry my face and gather the strength to reassess myself.

My cheeks aren't dirty anymore, but my eyes are still dreary. Without any makeup, I'm left slapping my face, hoping to add some color to this ghoulish appearance and make myself look less undead.

I'm grateful for the single stall bathroom, so that I can whip off my shirt and take a paper towel bath without scaring anyone trying to use the facilities. Once the stench has been adequately removed, I head back toward the shop.

Bossman is working on a 45' Benetau with a few of his employees scattered around, busy with their own projects. I know I should walk right up to Bossman, exuding confidence, and introduce myself. That's the best way to make a good impression. And a good first impression is the only thing I have going for me since my resume has no formal experience working in a boat repair shop. But I can't pull myself from the doorway. I'm locked into it.

"You need somethin', darlin'?" Bossman asks.

I point weakly. "The Help Wanted sign." Fantastic first impression, Billie.

He wipes his hands on a rag as he approaches with a sincere apology. "Sorry, it's for a shop grunt."

"A what?"

"Shop Grunt. You know. Sweeping up, sanding, running out for lunch. Grueling work for hours on end."

"That sounds great."

This confuses him even more than my inability to move must. "You ever work on boats?"

"I restored a 22' Catalina with Captain Jack when I was fourteen."

This seems to impress him a bit. "Captain Jack?"

"My grandpa."

He tucks the rag into the back pocket of his overalls as he weighs the need for extra help against the potential lawsuit for sexual harassment from the boys who have lined up behind him to size me up. He points over his shoulder. "There's a broom over there."

After a short two hours of sweeping and taking out the trash, Bossman sends me home telling me to come back tomorrow for more. I head out the door making my way toward the center of town. When I'm certain no one is looking, I double back around to the boat ramp visible through the shop's back window. I spotted a long dock along the channel below a screen of mangrove trees while I was cleaning. At the east end, an empty jet ski platform rests under the dock creating a perfect sleeping nook.

I stash my bike in the trees before scanning the spot that is fully protected from the wind and out of the water. Crawling into my new bed for the night, I desperately hope I haven't mistakenly claimed the nest of an alligator who will come home, drag me into the bay, and spin me underwater until I have lost all air and consciousness.

I lay my head on my backpack, but cannot for the life of me convince myself to close my eyes. Instead, I stare at the small fragmented picture of my former life. It's wrinkled and discolored along the folds from being stuffed into the bottom of my bag. Folded in half. I just couldn't look at the other side after what he did. He incinerated the life I worked so hard to build after Brent. And I was blind to the whole situation.

But the good half? It is the only thing I have left. A three-by-three picture on a scrap of paper. Sure my arm holding that little baitfish is hidden along with the piece that contained JJ, but in the small part that remains, Ryder gazes down at me, arm wrapped around my waist. And I was happy.

On October 7th, the worst day of my year, the day I'm forever reminded of the devastation my actions spawn, Ryder somehow found a way to give me hope. Staring at the photo now, maybe I am just deluding myself, but I have been trying to suck out every last ounce of comfort, praying it will sustain me through the newest devastation my fury has once again forged.

Chapter 12

RYDER

Three days later and it's still radio silence from Billie. Since the instant I met her on the Lahaina docks, I have never had to face three successive days without seeing her or hearing her voice or at least reading her words to me.

Even though it was JJ who pursued her romantically, we seemed to run into each other constantly. Two days after we met, I nearly ran headfirst into her. Quite literally.

I was just rounding the half-mile buoy on my morning swim when I heard an enormous thud in the water. I popped my head up to scan for the source of the thump and was greeted by Billie's smiling face. Without her spanking the surface of the water to warn me, I would have punched her in the face with my next stroke.

"Can you believe someone put this buoy out here? It's like exactly a half-mile out and back. What are the chances?"

I didn't tell her that I put it out there myself about a week before. "Crazy, huh? Exactly a quarter-mile from my backyard."

"What?" She spun towards land, her excitement practically propelling her out of the water. "Which one is yours?"

I leaned in over her shoulder, pointing out my place.

"The one with the blue chair?" she squeals. "Do you spend every single minute in that chair? I swear, if that were mine, I would never leave." She whirled back around to me. "Well, except to swim to the perfectly placed quarter-mile buoy. You live a charmed life, Ryder."

Running into her like that was the first time I felt like maybe that was true. I don't know what possessed me to ask, but I heard the words fall out of my mouth. "Want to swim back together?"

"Can you hold on?"

Hold on? What was she going to take a call real quick in the middle of the ocean?

She sprinted around the buoy and then right past me. Three strokes later, she pops up, "You coming?"

We raced to land, not sure if I was trying to prove something to her or her to me, and then we spent a few hours chatting on my back lawn, her legs hanging over the side of the aqua chair, mine sprawled out on the grass next to her. I went out that afternoon to buy another Adirondack just in case she ever swam by again. Now, that same pink seat screams a reminder that I might never swim with her again. Or wile away the hot Hawaiian afternoons talking about everything and nothing at all.

After her distress call, the last three days flew by in a blur, calling and recalling everyone she knows, searching her place for clues, sometimes just driving around to all her favorite spots, hoping I would run into her. Now, I've sunk into the Instagram black hole, wishing that she has been leaving me some sort of coded message in her Biovandal account.

It's been a week since she posted pics of the chalk rainbow that she named Lovers and Dreamers. She usually posts a few different angles or videos of the making of an installation periodically until her next one goes up, but there has been nothing added since four days before she fled.

I've even gone so far as to read every one of her old posts, looking for edits in the captions, or random comments in the string of hundreds she gets on each post. There's no compelling code that I can make out. No breadcrumbs from a girl who actually wants me to locate her. So, I'm left with no other avenues to find her except for slightly illegal ones or those avenues that are completely illegal.

And for both, I need Savage.

Savage agrees to meet me by four at his place on the west side of the island, but when I pull up to his house, the driveway is empty.

Savage was my team leader during the five short years I spent with the teams. Since then, he has filled the gigantic hole my own dad should have occupied. I think he even tried to solidify that position by setting me up with his daughter, Harley, but she was way too much like a mini-Savage. I guess when you're raised by your SEAL dad and his team and without a mom, you end up an emotionally sealed-off mini-warrior.

Savage still has access to the kind of tracking technology necessary to find out where Billie went and he and I have the type of relationship needed to ask something this significant from him.

I text him to let him know I'm around back as I wander through the side yard. Savage lives in a small bungalow halfway up the Pu'u Kukui peak on the West Side, just above Napili Bay. From the front, his house is barely visible, camouflaged behind the colossal Uluhe ferns that grow beside the rivers that wind their way down the mountain. But in the back, he has a sweeping view of the West Maui coastline, from Nalu Kai to Hawea Point, and a clear sight to the tiny Kapalua Airport. I swear he bought this place so he could keep an eye on his Piper Warrior plane in the hangar next to the airstrip down there.

"Read me in on the situation, Jax. What's going on?" Savage is one of the few people who can sneak up on me.

"I have to find someone. You can still do that, right?" I plead.

"Can? Yes. But I'm going to need more intel. And it looks like you're going to need a beer."

We head inside and I lay it all out for him, Kavika, JJ, the phone call, and what I've done since to track Billie down. I fiddle with the plastic cup of ice water he dropped in front of me while I rack my brain for more details.

Savage is reclining on a bar stool at his kitchen island sipping casually on his beer while I pace, adding specifics as they come

87

to me, completely out of order and disjointed. When I think I have given him every piece of intel I have, he takes a slug of his beer and sets it down on the counter, spinning it while he contemplates his next words. "So, how long?"

"I got her last communication seventy-four hours ago." And those have been the hardest seventy-four hours since I left my team.

He chuckles. I know Savage is the guy who can handle any situation thrown at him with grace and ease, but he's sitting there laughing.

"Not since she bailed out, dumbass—not that you're counting or anything—I meant since you've been in love with her?"

I chuck the water cup into the sink. "Can you help or not?" I bark.

"Let's work the problem before we go blowing everything up. It sounds like she probably just needs a little time to herself. Once she calms down, she'll come home. Maybe she has some friends on the mainland that she went to stay with?"

"You sound like JJ." He's been spouting that theory to anyone willing to listen to assuage his own guilt. I don't know how much validity there is to it.

"Have you checked with Harley or her roommate? Blue or Cloudy? She's got one of those artsy names from hippie parents who wanted to use their kid to make a social comment."

"Indigo."

"Yeah, that's it." He shoots off a quick text.

"There. I filled Harley in on the situation. She'll reach into her networks in San Diego. What is JJ doing on his end?"

"I have no idea." I haven't talked to JJ since throwing him up against my porch that first day. I've only heard what he's been telling our friends to pacify them.

"You guys have a little dust-up when he realized that you're into his girl?"

"You need to let that go. She's a friend. Period. I'm only over here because no one else seems to care that she disappeared in the middle of the night without a trace." I know her friends are getting worried—Piper called me yesterday for a status update,

Charlie has been texting me, too—but they are all managing to go about their days normally. I haven't been able to function since that phone call. "Can you help or not?"

"Let's give it a little more time, Jax. If you don't hear from her in a week or so, we can talk again and make a new plan."

I'm pissed that he won't help, but I get it. And I guess I shouldn't break all sorts of laws if, in fact, she's just visiting the girls in San Diego.

But I can't get my mind to believe that. If she were simply cooling off, she would have returned at least one of my calls. Or texted. There's no way she'd be that cruel.

Knowing that once Savage decides something, there is no convincing him otherwise, I thank him and leave.

I throw my truck into gear looking forward to taking these narrow roads at top speed; there's something relaxing about the focus it takes to do it well. Most times, I love the little island roads. No one is in a rush to do anything. The streets are tiny and sail right along the edge of the coast. But tonight, I absolutely despise them.

Savage lives in the middle of nowhere, but, of course, I end up behind the only other person out at this time of night who ends up being the slowest driver alive. I could get out and run faster than this guy. I try to pretend that the wheelman is my grandpa in hopes of garnering some compassion, but instead, I can only see his car as a Humvee patrolling the sand traps. Slow. Slow enough for someone to walk beside it. Or for it to creep inch by inch over an IED. And all I can do is watch as it happens.

My phone buzzes. I pull over to read the text since I'm not making any progress behind this idiot anyways.

SAVAGE: Harley's on it.

A screenshot of another text comes in a second later.

HARLEY: Contacted Indigo, Sonny. Will do some research. Does she have a bugout plan? Can he check for her go bag to see if it's still in place? Her hide sites? Do we know if she's still on island? Will reach out to Billie myself in case she is simply avoiding those two boys. But if I had a run-in with a guy like Kavika, I might have gone off-grid too.

Chapter 13

BILLIE

"I had no idea we even had floors in here," Rusty calls out from across the shop.

Giving up on my quest for sleep well before the sun came up, I headed in to see if I could get started. No one was there, but the back door was open, so I thought I'd get a head start. Last night, I realized that manual labor was the first thing that has helped quiet the constant stream of thoughts that have been attacking me ever since... I shake it off. I wanted to get back to it as soon as possible.

By the time my new boss showed up, I had already swept the floors again, cleaned the tool racks that were covered in a layer of sawdust and grime, and reorganized all the tools by size and use.

"Did you do all this Sam?"

So, I may have lied when Bossman Rusty asked for my name last night. I wasn't sure he even had the Internet, but I couldn't risk him filling out any sort of official paperwork with my real name. "You take care of your tools and they'll take care of you," I forced a smile on my face before looking up at him.

"If you're as good with a broom as you are with those tools, I could use some help with the Coronado."

We spend the next three days fixing the engine on the

Coronado. The owner brought it in complaining of a rattle when he accelerated. We inspect the torsional coupling and the tooth flanks of the transmission to try to fix it. We finally figure out that the propeller shaft was not aligned correctly, so I start on that.

While we work, Rusty and I chat about where the fish are biting, why I should buy a 25' Coronado for my first sailboat, and how I came to stop in his shop, though Rusty does most of the talking. When Rusty has to take care of the office drudgery that keeps this place afloat, I keep laboring on the propeller shaft, until someone taps my shoulder.

I drop the wrench.

Scramble to my feet.

Spin to face my assailant.

Rusty stands there with a handful of papers.

He says something I can't hear over the hammering of my head.

I try to focus on him as he holds up one of the forms. "You forgot to fill in your social security number?"

I look closer at the paper. It's the application I filled out when I got the job. I was hoping he wouldn't bother reading it. "I figured you paid a grunt under the table."

"You're not a grunt, hon. You got more skills than half my guys."

Shit. I can't give him my social. *No phones. No Internet. No trace of me.* It's the mantra I keep repeating to make sure I stay off JJ's radar. Trying to stay invisible in a world where no one is invisible. And filling out paperwork with my social security number would definitely be a trace of me. "I can go back to being a grunt."

Rusty still looks confused.

"I can't use my social. He'd..." How do I explain when I can't even say the words in my head? "He can track it. No phones. No Internet. No trace of me. I..."

"An ex?"

I nod, hoping I haven't lost the only thing that is keeping me tethered to reality here. And my only hope of continuing to feed myself.

"I don't care what was in your past, Darlin', as long as you keep working like you do, I'd pay you in squid if that's what you asked for."

Holding back the tears his kindness threatens to pull from me, I breathe out a weak, "Thanks."

Rusty glances out the back door to my bike piled high with my bag. "You found a place to stay yet?"

I nod to the end of the dock. He gapes at me.

"It's getting warm." I'm not sure if I'm trying to reassure him or me that it's fine to be staying out there.

"You can't be serious."

"It's all I got, but I get it if you have to kick me out," I say sheepishly. I didn't even think about the fact that he owns that dock and that it would be more than enough reason for him to fire me.

"My sister's got a place. I'll give her a call. It's not much, but it's got to be better than sleeping on the dock. And a lot safer, too."

"I won't turn that down. Thank you."

"And food's free at the bar before and after your shift."

Rooster snaps his head up from under a speedboat. "Since when?"

"Since she can finish sanding a whole boat in a day without having to do it twice cause you missed so many spots."

"Fair enough." He ducks down and resumes yet another oil change.

I glance down at my insulin pump. The reservoir is almost empty. And despite all this physical labor, my appetite hasn't really returned since… "I'm not too hungry right now. Next time?"

"Sure, hon. Anytime you want. I'll let Sally know."

———————

The next day, with a pump full of the last of the insulin I brought with me, I head out to the far end of Key Largo where Topher, one of the shop guys, said the post office was located to pick up my box of insulin and pump supplies. It should have arrived by now and I can't guarantee they won't leave it out in the sweltering heat and destroy my final batch of insulin.

When the postman tells me they don't hold packages and the office I want is on the other end of the island, the one right across from the repair shop, I pedal another six miles in the oppressive humidity only to discover that my package hasn't turned up yet. After that long and fruitless diversion, I barely have time to make it to meet Rusty's sister in what might be my new home.

Down a shady side street, well off Highway 1, houses become harder and harder to find. Address markers that might at one time have been a broad declaration of home, have since been grown over with creeping vines and shrubs. I pedal down the crushed shell drive and hope I haven't gone too far. 1082, weathered away on a stone at the base of a driveway comes into view. I'm close.

The buzz from the insects that grow by the millions down here drowns out the buzz in my head. My right shoulder, tight from sanding all day, draws my mind from the thought that renting an apartment means I am settling in here.

The chain link fence lies open at the foot of the next driveway which must be mine, but an actual apartment is nowhere to be found. I follow the ever-shrinking drive as it becomes a cave of overgrowth over a floor littered with fallen trees and dead leaves.

I lean my bike against a bushy-tree sort of thing and realize it's probably time I start learning the name of the plants in my new home state.

Damn. Florida has somehow become my new home.

Looking to distract myself from that horrible thought, I look up at the structure that I suppose down here could be considered an apartment. More like a deserted cage. I look for an address on the building but only find a lonely six.

"Sam? Glad you found it," a cheerful voice pulls me out of my despair. Jenny appears in the front doorway in a pair of jean cutoffs and flip-flops. "Come on in."

I step on the bottom porch tread, testing it before applying my full weight.

The door barely shuts, but the view out the dirty back windows more than makes up for it. The low-lying scrub brush turns to marsh grass and then to water. Water to the horizon.

Jenny shows the one room shack to me. It's barren, but it's got a roof. "The utilities are covered. You can use anything in here. And feel free to make whatever changes you need." She pushes a kitchen drawer as close to closed as it will get.

"Thanks. It's great."

She continues to give me the dime tour, which all happens from that one spot. "Dishes are in the cupboard. There's some linens in the closet over there."

"Got it."

"Alright. Well, I'll leave you to it. If you need anything else, have Rusty give me a call or you can stop by the Shell Shop. I'm there most mornings."

She closes the door behind her and silence rushes in. I'm standing in a barren house in the middle of nowhere. No one knows I'm here. Or would know if I were gone. No one would be close enough to hear my screams.

I twist the deadbolt on the front door, but it won't budge. Shoving my shoulder into the door, I move it enough to allow the lock to engage. I yank it to double-check.

Windows. I fasten the latches on the two beside the door. The back windows that just seconds ago held an enviable view, now hold far too easy of a view inside. One they could use to hunt me down.

I secure the latch on one, but the other one is missing. There's no lock. I'm a sitting duck here.

It's way too dark to go anywhere. No way I'm going out in those woods, so I tear through the kitchen drawers searching for anything I can employ to fortify the loose one. A long pair of metal tongs looks to be the right size. I shove them into the sill and test it. The window opens but not far enough for someone to fit even a hand in.

Returning to the front door, I test it one more time before reassessing my fortress. They may not be able to get in, but they sure as hell can see in. And once they know I'm in here, it wouldn't take more than broken glass to get in.

The lack of curtains forces me to improvise. Pulling sheets from the linen closet, I secure them over each window with tacks from the kitchen drawer.

I check the front door lock again and push the small dining table in front of it just to be certain.

Standing in the center of the room, for the first time, it hits me. This room, this house, this place is now my life. I have nothing. No one.

Devoid of strength, I sink to the dusty floor, crushed by the magnitude of the wreckage, unable to cry tears with enough might to lighten the anguish.

This is what I am now.

This is my life.

Nothing.

One movement, one choice, and I lost it all.

Why couldn't I have just not done anything?

Eyes burning and scratchy from crying, fatigue washes over me in waves, but I fight to stay awake. Too heavy to hold my head up any longer, I lay it down on the splintering floorboards,. Fighting against the pull into oblivion, I force my eyes open one more time and find a phantom Ryder sitting at the table. He leans back in his chair, arm resting on the table, relaxed and smiling.

My head lightens. My shoulders ease. My smile returns.

"I got first watch, Billie. Sleep. I'll wake you when it's your turn," he says.

Knowing he is there to protect me, I fall into the first deep slumber since that night.

Chapter 14

RYDER

on't Worry Be Happy fills the air above me. Without opening my eyes, I feel around for my phone to shut off the alarm. Unable to locate it blindly, I drag my eyes open, turn my head towards the sound, and am greeted by the words, "Swim With Billie." My chest swells with sunshine, throwing off the fog that has filled me since... she left.

Shit. I won't swim with Billie this morning.

Or any other morning.

After pressing myself upright on the couch, I polish off the warm cider abandoned on the coffee table, tear my goggles off the rack, and stagger out to the waterline. My feet hit the water, but I cannot propel them any further. A swim without Billie is unthinkable.

Going back to my regular day without her is just as unimaginable.

And so I stand, paralyzed, an idiot at the waterline, goggles dangling from my limp hand.

Throwing in the towel on my swim, I stumble backward a few paces, still staring at my foe, the ocean. Giving it another attempt, I step forward, but stop, unable to get any closer.

A turtle breaks the water's surface a couple meters out, and it's too much. I collapse in the sand, studying my friend as he swims off as if he could somehow lead me to Billie. When he takes one last breath and plunges to the depths of the sea, I'm left alone with only the little waves to wash over my feet and retreat down the incline.

Again and again.

Even the water won't stay with me.

For all the hate I've thrown at JJ, the frustration towards Savage that he won't just use his resources to find her, I've been too scared to be pissed at the one person who is really to blame here.

If I had just surfed with her when she asked that night. If I could have put aside what I needed, to blow off a little steam with the boys, to put her first. If I had just done what I swore to do every time after Emma.

Others First.

But I failed. Just like with Emma.

Once again, too weak to protect those I love.

After what must be an hour, I break from my trance to get ready for today's charter. I canceled all my charters for this week, thinking it would be easier and better in the long run to avoid too many bad reviews for snapping at my customers or quitting early to go cry in the cabin. But too much time off the water has only made things worse. So, when Greyson suggested we get the boys together for a trip, I jumped at it.

As I prepare the boat, Greyson, Finn, and Riley head up the docks, arms loaded with supplies. JJ follows close behind.

Shit. They thought that putting both of us on a forty-three-foot boat in the middle of the ocean was a good idea?

No promises one of us won't be going over the side at some point.

"Hey, Jax." Greyson sets the cooler down on the deck. I push it out of his way before he steps onboard. "I'm ready to catch my first Hawaiian fish."

"We'll see what we can do," I reply.

Finn simply nods as he makes his way through the swing door.

"Hey, Jax. You've been MIA lately, haven't you?" JJ pokes.

I barely manage to muffle the "fuck off" that slips from my mouth. He looks like it's just another day on the boat instead of another whole day where Billie is still missing. I don't know how I'm going to manage going the whole day without putting my fist through his face.

I tug my phone from my side pocket and give it a quick check for any missed texts. Still nothing.

"Permission to come aboard, Captain?" Usually, Riley's uber-politeness is comical, but for some reason, I appreciate it right now.

"Permission granted, Riley." I close the swing door behind him and latch it, before heading up to the cabin to get us underway.

The boys stow their gear and hang out on the back deck giving me much-needed space from JJ.

It takes us nearly an hour to get to the place where the Ahi have been biting the last couple of days. They've got JJ trying out some new tongue twister if the Naaaaaah's and Feck's and hysterical laughter are any indication, but I don't envy the joking going on down there. The solitude up here is welcome, the hum of the motor doing a fine job of drowning out the white noise in my head.

I still don't know how JJ can be so mellow when his girlfriend just bailed. Shouldn't he also be freaking out? Maybe he has his cop friends keeping an eye out. Or maybe he put out an alarm if she uses any of her credit cards? I know he cares for her, but it sure doesn't look like it right now.

I check my phone again, but it's not pulling much of a signal out here, so I stow it under the fish finder. Nothing to do now but focus on the three feet ahead of me.

When we get to our spot, I set the boat to drift, make my way down to the bait station in the middle of the back deck, and nab two 'Oama out of the live bait tank. I slip one on my hook and hang the other one over the side, letting it return to the sea unharmed. *That one's for you, Billie.*

Once my pole is in the water, my mood improves. I forgot how much fun it can be to fish for myself as opposed to setting up everyone else, teaching them, and making sure they don't do anything stupid.

We drift through the spot I hoped would produce a catch without so much as a nibble, so I head back to the bridge to motor to another position that the fish finder is pinging on. I pull my phone from under the fish finder and check it while we motor. I navigate to Billie's Biovandal account, praying that this time there will be a fresh post. Maybe a new installation in some faraway state that will explain why she left without telling anyone. And as soon as it's up, she'll return home with some wild story to cover the fact that she is one of the most popular street artists in the nation.

But the latest post is still the drone footage of a hooded figure riding her bike along the Pi'ilani Highway. The motion of the chalk rig on the back rhythmically swinging from the top of the frame to the bottom over and over again in sync with the music, drawing out a life-sized rainbow on the road, repeating on a loop, lulls me into a daze.

When the finder beeps, I slip the phone back into my trunks and set the boat to drift again. Maybe this time, we'll get more than a nibble. I could really use a win out here today. Something to remind me that there is good in this world.

After another thirty minutes, Greyson hooks what looks to be a big one, but I let JJ handle helping him figure out how to reel it in. It's Greyson's first deep-sea fishing trip and there are a few things that he might need help with, but I'm not in the mood to deal with the commotion.

Or to deal with JJ.

I head to the bow deck. Once out of sight, I slip my phone out of my pocket and flip to the deleted photos where I store a copy of the pic Billie, JJ, and I took the first day we met, though it was mysteriously cropped to cut out JJ. That smile on her face, so different than the pain that was etched there earlier that morning. And thinking I had something to do with putting that grin on her face? It fills me with delight. I hope that wherever she is now, I still do that for her.

A pair of dirty slippahs comes into view behind my phone. I

pocket it, but don't say a thing. If he wants to come over here to smooth things over, he's gonna have to do the work. After twenty minutes of silence, I survey his face to see if he's come to mend things or make them worse. Maybe he's not worried because he honestly thinks that she went to go see family or someone on the mainland and that there's no actual threat to her. Or that he really doesn't need her in his life. She is a grown woman, she is free to move wherever she wants. Sure he's a little sad, but he understands why she wouldn't want to talk to him anymore.

"You getting anything up here?" he asks.

"Nope," I reply, hoping he leaves. But he stays. I don't think he'll leave until we fix things between us. He's not the type to avoid hard conversations. If we're gonna do this, I might as well dig in and get right to it. "You remember that op I told you about?" I give my reel a few spins. "The Congo?"

"Emma?"

Emma. So weird hearing her name out loud again. The only time I hear it is in my head, middle of the night, when I'm recalling all the shit things I've done in my life. She's top of that list. "Yeah, that one."

I reel in my line and cast it back out. And then again.

"Jax, you okay?"

"I'm slipping back there, JJ. I can't lose anyone else."

"I know, man. I know."

It's never taken many words for him to understand me. Or many for me to understand him. Or to forgive him.

The clouds begin gathering on the horizon, drowning out what would have been a striking sunset. Winds will be picking up in about an hour, making for a choppy ride back in, a fitting return for a shitty day fishing.

Reeling in my line, I get right to the point. "I'm fighting off the temptation to take the toaster into the bathtub, JJ. Except I have neither toaster nor tub."

After a long pause, he rests his hand on my shoulder. "Should I worry about you buying one?"

I have too much to do here now. Too many who depend

on me. And I have a Billie to find. "No man." Dismissing the thought, I cast again.

JJ stays, having nothing else to offer besides his presence.

Chapter 15

RYDER

The sky now streaked with reds and purples, I drag my grocery store contraband to the living room. I crack a beer and set it next to the open bag of Rold Gold Pretzel Sticks. The real kind. Not the shitty gluten-free substitute. After a day on the water, with my skin crispy and salt-beaten, the only way to end this day is with a real beer and pretzels. Fuck the consequences.

I flip on the Padres game and hope it fills the empty air with the buzz of the crowd enough to silence the buzzing in my head. After twenty minutes of trying to watch, I give up and pull out my phone. Scrolling through Billie's feed in reverse chronological order, I can see how each installation series builds on the one before it. Or how a particular moment inspired a standalone piece.

My favorite was her first series that starred little green army men dressed up in Hawaiian shirts hanging in tiny hammocks or laying out on the rocks by the ocean. She must have sewn the shirts by hand and built every single miniature hammock. I can't imagine the work it took to string up dozens of pygmy hammocks. Her captions read, "If anyone deserves a life lived in a hammock, it's our warriors," or "After giving us their all, it's time they found some rest."

It wasn't the last time she used little green army men. She modified them—probably melting them and reshaping them into new poses—to create little scenes around the city. A group of them standing in the gutter, helping each other scale the insurmountable height of the curb. A trail of little soldiers marching along the outstretched branch of the banyan tree in the center of Lahaina. All of them permanently affixed.

There were also moss paintings on walls around town. Reverse graffiti images of happiness blasted into dirty walls with a power washer. Rain-activated hydrophobic messages of joy. Every one of her installations was focused on reminding people about how amazing life could be, of the delight that she so easily shined around her. I still don't know how anyone who knew Billie wouldn't immediately know the only girl capable of such pieces of artistic elation had to be her.

She has posted a pic of her work at least every week for the last three years. So, when she didn't post last week, speculation began about what had happened. I study the comments for any sign someone has seen a new piece. But instead of finding anything useful, I have to wade through some pretty intense conspiracy theories already starting to gain momentum. Her last post, the video of her rainbow, seems to be gathering the most speculation.

@LunaticArt ten days. 10!!!!!!! @HiBiovandal's gone. Never has he not posted at least once a week.

@ArtsHearts Maybe she faked her own death so that the price of her art will go up

@streetartsavestheworld You brain dead @ArtsHearts? He never made a dime off his work. HiBiovandal only wanted to bring joy to people. You must be some sort of corporate whore to think he could ever do that.

@MauiSandy @HiBiovandal was really Alicia Silverstone. Have you seen any of her work since Alicia died??? I think not. #proof

@rainbowdonutsNaluKai In her video where she is stringing up the cellophane in Waikiki, you can see a small mole on her left wrist. Alicia has the same one showing in Clueless #seriousproof

@ArtsHearts DUDE!!!! Alicia Silverstone is alive dumbass!!!!!!

@banskyrules128 you guys are crazy. He probably just got thrown in jail for all his crimes.

@ADmittedADmirer What crimes?!?!? The crime of providing food for people struggling to eat? The crime of spreading joy during hard times? I wish we all committed more of those crimes. Hawaii might actually be a better place to live.

@hashburrito I think @biovandalhoodiefan killed him

Now that one I can guarantee is not true.

When I found out Billie was Biovandal, I wanted to go see every installation. When I found each one, I would take a picture of myself with my hoodie drawn low to hide my face in the spirit of her anonymity. Leaning up against a bigger one, or sitting on the curb next to a smaller one, I would shoot a quick pic. Since I couldn't congratulate Billie without letting her know I knew it was her, I made my own fan account to express my admiration. Soon other people were finding her creations and posting their own fan pics in front of each one. It became a thing to photograph yourself with a Biovandal installation.

@truestreetartstories and why would he do that?

@hashburrito to take over the @HiBiovandal account. You ever notice how he's always there like 20 minutes after Biovandal posts? How does he know where Biovandal is unless he's stalking him?

When her work began to get more temporary, chalk art that would wash away with the next rain, or a mural cleaned into a dirty wall, I knew I had to get to each one rather quickly before it vanished.

@generationart42 I think @HiBiovandal is really a tribe of Menehune who are taking care of the Hawaiian people and bringing them joy in tough times and now they are waiting for us to pick up the torch and keep spreading joy.

At least that one is in the spirit of Billie's work.

With nothing useful there, I run a search on Billie Styles and HiBiovandal. Four pages of results later, I come across a Patreon account she must have set up years ago but never publicized. If she won't send me some breadcrumb of a hidden message, maybe it's time I start sending them her way so if she ever does look up, she'll know she is missed... and loved.

By her followers.

Loved by her followers.

I get the link to the page and begin to blast it everywhere, in comments on every single one of her posts, in each of my @biovandalhoodiefan posts. I even search for the hashtags people have been using to discuss her or her work, #hibiovandal #Mauistreetartist, #whereishibiovandalnow. On any caption that mentions her, I share the link with a short message, "Let's give @Hibiovandal the tools she needs to accomplish her next big installation. If you have ever gotten any joy from her artwork, now is the time to pay her back."

I have to go back and change all the she's to he's and her's to him's before I post. It's the general consensus that HiBiovandal is a guy, and if that's another layer of protection for Billie, I'm not going to be the one to rip it down.

Feeling a little better being able to actually do something to help Billie, to send up a flare, I put my phone away and wait for sleep to overtake me.

Come on, Billie. Look up. Find the signal. Come home.

Chapter 16

BILLIE

My swollen eyes drag open in the early morning light to find Imaginary Ryder still stationed where I left him last night, safeguarding me from all the sinister forces in the world. A smile washes over me as the tension in my back eases slightly.

"What happened to waking me for my turn?" I ask.

"You've been on watch plenty lately. You needed some rest. Besides, it wasn't a major difficulty sitting here watching you sleep."

I pull my ragged body up to sit. "RyGuy?" I tuck my knees into the oversized sweatshirt I haven't taken off since I left. "Why couldn't I just stay chill for a little bit longer? He would have let me go. I could still be at home with you right now instead of out here all alone pretending."

Ryder answers with a charming smile.

The corner of the makeshift curtain drops, the tack not strong enough to secure it for long. Sun streams in through the windows promising another roasting day in the sweltering shop. By the time I look back to Ryder, I only find an empty chair.

My Dexcom blares out the dreaded five beeps. I pull up the Alert Screen on my pump. Sensor Expired. There's no way. I just put this one in the day before Kavika…

Has it really been ten days?

Thinking back to when I inserted the last sensor, it almost feels like it was an entirely different person doing it. I was sitting on my bed in my pink striped bikini trying to decide if wearing my black and white striped trunks, the ones that made me feel like Greg Noll taking on Waimea in *Ride the Wild*, would be too many stripes.

That was my biggest care in the world. Too many stripes.

And now?

I dig through my backpack looking for another sensor so that I won't be flying blind. Especially now. My entire insulin regimen has changed. The stress has driven my sugars higher, but the random biking and physical labor is counterbalancing that a bit. And my lack of any real appetite has made dosing so much more difficult than normal.

Normal.

It's been so long since I even thought about normal.

Not finding anything, I dump the whole bag onto the floor. I scatter all my worldly possessions trying to locate the one that may ensure I continue living. But there's nothing.

When I snatched some extra pump supplies out of the box at the UPS store in Kahului, I forgot to take a few Dexcom sensors. Now every one of them is on some plane or truck somewhere between Maui and here. With my luck, they decided to put them on a sailboat that would have to sail around Cape Horn to make it to Key Largo in about six months.

Gathering up my possessions, flung across the room in my haste to find a new sensor, it's probably time to take a full stock of what diabetes supplies I do have until my box arrives.

I used up most of my final vial of insulin last night when I refilled my pump, which should sustain me for around five days if the insulin doesn't go bad from the heat before then. I have two infusion sites remaining, which could survive ten days if I stretch them out and my unrelenting sweat doesn't make them slide right off.

So, that's it. Five days and I'm out of insulin. Maybe seven if I ration it. Once my insulin is gone, I have forty-eight, possibly seventy-two hours until it gets really serious. Much longer than that and I probably won't have to worry about JJ finding me because there will be nothing left to find.

Well, shit.

If my box arrives, I will be fine for a while, but what about after those are used up? I can't stay off the grid. I'll have to go see a doctor. Get insurance. I'm pretty sure Rusty doesn't carry medical coverage for shop grunts.

Am I going to have to assume a new identity? How does a person actually do that? And wouldn't that put me on the police radar even more than JJ probably already has me?

How has diabetes made it nearly impossible for me to go off the grid?

I'll have to worry about the long-term later.

Or not. I may not be around long enough to worry about it if I can't figure out a way to fix the short term.

First stop is to go back to the post office and suss out where my supplies went. And exactly when they'll be here. They must track that sort of thing.

Or maybe they don't.

After twenty minutes of arguing, screaming, and eventually crying to the post officer—is that what they are called—I'm convinced that things are done a different way down here. I thought business moved slowly in Maui. Here, it's not the speed, though it isn't any faster than back home, but the general incompetence is stunning. He cannot find any record of the package that I sent.

And I'm left with nothing.

Absolutely nothing to sustain my life past the seven-day mark.

There has to be some way to fix this.

Back at work, I must have been taking my frustration out on the skiff I was sanding because Rusty demands I take a lunch break at The Shanty. Since I only have seven days to live, I might as well enjoy one last meal.

I nab a stool at the outdoor bar overlooking the marina. Most of the slips are empty now, their boats somewhere out on the ocean showing tourists a marvelous day of sun, fish, and far too many beers.

When Sally comes by, I order a barbecue burger, fries, and a diet Dr Pepper, which they have on tap here.

Where am I going to get new insulin? And extra pump supplies? And more Dexcom sensors? I can do without the Dexcom if I have to. I did shove a couple hundred strips into my backpack, but I hate not having Dexcom watching my back. I'm already alone out here and the flashes of panic that have been hitting me since Kavika feel just like a low. I'd have to test every single time I experience that.

There may not be a backup for insulin, but I can make my insulin needs go down with a lot of exercise. Biking has been helping, but I should probably start swimming, too, if I want to outlive my one-week dead-line.

When Sally lays down my plate, I reconsider my decision to pig out. It doesn't look as tasty as I thought just a minute ago. Not that it isn't a great-looking burger, but nothing has looked appetizing lately. I try a French fry as I watch one of the charters return.

Pelicans gather on the edge of the dock in front of my feet, oblivious to the fact that I am here. Soon fish are popping their heads above the water. There has to be some sort of bait ball beneath the surface, but the water is clear enough that I can tell that's not what is causing all this commotion.

When the deckhand walks to the stern and dumps a huge bucket of chum over the back, I figure it out. The sound of the returning boat is like ringing the dinner bell for these scavengers. I wish there was an insulin chum boat I could find. Somebody with no need for the extra insulin of the day.

That's it. The last time I was at my doctor's office they offered me a free vial of a different type of insulin to try. I bet all doctors have samples to hand out. I reach into my back pocket for my phantom phone.

Damn. No phones. No internet. No trace of me.

I take a huge bite of the burger. I can't leave this free food uneaten. That would be a total slap in the face to the nicest people I've ever met.

With no cell phone, I'll have to go old school to find a doctor. But that's not a problem. Old school is the only school I like.

How would Rick Kane have found a doctor's office? And yes, I know *North Shore* was a kooky movie, but what 80s surf movie wasn't?

So, Rick Kane. 80s...

Payphones. They have phone books. Maybe the fact that this island is still decades behind can help me after all.

How is it that a doctor's office five thousand miles from home looks exactly the same as every other office I have been in? Same dirty beige waiting room chairs. Same decade-old magazines on the tables. Same overworked girl behind the desk.

I thumb through one of those ancient periodicals hoping to distract myself as the receptionist has disappeared into the mysterious back room to ask a doctor for some samples of insulin for me.

"What's your name?" asks the girl scribbling all over the Highlights magazine.

"Billie. What's yours?"

She puts down her cerulean crayon, her full attention on me now. "I'm Molly. Do you have diabetes? Is that why you're here?"

"I do."

"Do you have a Dexcom? I put mine on my arm right here." She pulls up her sleeve and spins to show off her hardware.

"I did. But I ran out."

"Is that why you're here? To get a rescipshun?"

Her mom leans in. "Sorry. We're working on polite boundaries. Looks like we have a little more work to do."

"Sorry for being..." She looks to her mom.

Her mom prompts her. "Im..."

"Impolite." She grins at getting it out correctly.

"That's okay, Molly. What are you drawing?"

The receptionist materializes from behind the secret door. "Billie?"

I stand and make my way to meet my fate.

"I talked with the doctor. And without seeing you first, he can't give you any samples. And you said you don't have insurance to cover the cost of the appointment?"

In truth I do, but there's no way of using it and not creating a paper trail. "Not right now."

"I am sorry."

All that time. Biking fifteen miles here and another fifteen home in the blazing thousand-degree heat for nothing. "Thanks for checking."

I shuffle to the front door when Molly's mom calls to me. "There's a group on Facebook that gives away surplus supplies; pump sets, Dexcom, insulin. They may be able to help. It's called Orange County Diabetes Extras."

My first dash of hope for extending my life beyond a week. "Thanks."

Now, I just have to figure out how to get onto Facebook without a phone or the Internet. Looks like I have to bend those rules a bit to stay alive.

Chapter 17

RYDER

The third riser of my stairs lets out its signal squeak, telling me someone is on their way up. I'm laid out naked on the bathroom tile, sucking in any cool I can find. The pizza and beer I "splurged" on last night didn't take long to turn my insides into mist and blast them out like squirters from an enemy target when our boys kick in the front door.

I gather all the energy I can muster to pull a towel from the rack and let it fall over my bare ass. Don't want to be found dead *and* naked when that intruder does me in.

"Duuude." Finn's voice hits my ears before I can draw my head back enough to focus on his face. He slowly studies what's left of the bathroom. "You okay?"

Okay's not even on my radar. "Water?"

"I'll be back." The tap of his footsteps down the stairs is followed by his muffled voice. Multiple faint voices reply. Who did he bring over when I'm like this?

Oh, damn. Game Night.

How the hell did it get to be Friday night?

Heavy footfalls return. "Don't know what kind of rager you threw last night, but this was the only clean dish left." He hands me the bowl of water. "What happened?"

I only take a sip. No need to anger the stomach infidels. "I was in the mood to make really bad decisions."

He takes a step out of the doorway. He hasn't had the past twenty hours in here to get used to the stench. From a safe distance, his glance moves from the towel covering me to the bathtub which served more than its purpose when one orifice became too few for the escaping legions of hell. "So, did it work?"

"Did what work?" I reply.

"Is the pain gone?"

I let my head fall to the tile. It's not gone. I've only added physical pain to the emotional. And the emotional pain won't ever be gone.

"No sense in beating yourself up now. Looks like you've already done a damned good job of that."

I shrug. "If you're gonna do something, you might as well do it well."

"You have enough in you to get into bed?" He moves towards my trunks on the bathroom floor.

"Not those!" He freezes. He knows why.

"Red shorts on the chair in my room."

He disappears, then returns to toss the trunks on my face before disappearing again, leaving me with one last shred of dignity.

I slip them on and slide my back up the wall waiting for the churning to return. I guess with nothing left in my system, I'm safe to resume normal human movements. I stagger out of my cage and collapse into bed as Finn flips the light switch and pulls the door shut behind him.

The late afternoon sunlight floods through my bedroom windows. I wake, famished and thirsty, like I haven't been since I first got sick. There's nothing like expelling every ounce of moisture from your body through every single orifice and pore you own.

I roll over to pick up my phone and spot a full glass of water on my nightstand. I sip it hesitantly, testing the stomach waters. When I don't purge, I sit up and take in some more. I check my

ANYTHING ANYTIME ANYWHERE

phone for any messages I might have missed as I slept nearly an entire day away. Still nothing.

At least nothing from Billie. Work emails, charter reservation requests, and spam offering me eternal life from a single supplement all crowd my inbox, but I don't have the bandwidth to deal with any of them.

I crawl downstairs to find it spotless. When I was forced to leave my splurge-fest to grapple with the aftereffects two days ago, my living room was the rancid aftermath of a gluten grenade. All of my favorites I've had to avoid for the past four years—the West Coast IPA, Hawaiian-style pizza, Cheeze-Its, and Mother's Iced Oatmeal Cookies—were consumed with a vengeance, packages and crumbs tossed aside.

Now the room is sparkling, not a remnant of my bad decisions. If it weren't for the residual pain in my guts and the pounding headache, I might think that it was all a strange nightmare.

I head to the fridge for something to take away this bottomless thirst and find it, not only packed with Gatorade and Kill Cliff drinks but devoid of all my contraband. The Salted Caramel TWIX bar I had been saving to end my feast, gone. The second six-pack of IPA removed. The box of HoneyComb cereal, nowhere to be found.

I snap up an orange Gatorade and drain half the bottle as I turn around to verify that I'm still in my own home. A scrap of paper sits on the counter. It reads, "Don't make me take you back to Makapu'u."

He doesn't need to sign it. I know JJ will follow through.

My hand instinctively moves to my cheekbone, my thumb snagging on the improperly healed fracture.

Enough of this shit. I'm done with punishing myself.

I finish off the Gatorade before heading upstairs. After rinsing off, I throw on my sweat shorts and hang my towel, smoothing it out neatly. From the bathroom drawer, I pull out a card and I read it out loud, "Take action. Maintain order. Breathe. Your brain will heal," before tucking it into the mirror.

You said you were alive, Billie. I know you're smart and can handle yourself. I'm gonna have to trust that.

Though she is strong enough to take care of herself, that doesn't mean that I can't take another look at her place in hopes of discovering something that will tell me where she is. My mind is going so much slower today, maybe it will find whatever I missed last time when my head was spinning with fear.

When I pull up, some guy is standing on her front porch. He's far too old and well-dressed to be one of Kavika's guys. I jog up to him. "You need something?"

He finishes taping a paper to Billie's door. Across the top, it reads, "5-Day Pay or Quit."

Her landlord. Shit. The last thing Billie needs is to lose her home and all her belongings.

"Crap. Billie went to visit some friends on the mainland and she asked me to make sure you got her rent this month, but I totally flaked. Can I pay you now? Check? You have an address? Or can I Venmo you?"

He looks me up and down but probably decides money is money, no matter who is paying him. "I take Venmo."

He gives me his account and I pay him on the spot. "Thanks so much. I'm so sorry I forgot. Promise it won't happen again." I shake his hand and hurry him toward his car. I have to get inside as soon as I can.

I wave from the lawn as he drives off, before slumping down. That little jog and pretending to be respectable took way more energy than I have right now.

On the porch, Spooner wakes from his nap next to his empty bowl and licks my hand as I bend to pet him. "Come on, boy. Let's get you some food and water."

Pushing through the unlocked door, I nearly trip over the mail splayed out on the floor before heading to the kitchen. After filling Spooner's water dish, I dig around in the cupboard for something for him to eat. Can of tuna and some bread will have to do.

I return to gather the mail and lay it in the little basket on the entry table where Billie usually keeps it. Then I pick it up again to skim through it looking for clues. Coming up empty, I wander to Billie's supply closet. It's practically cleaned out except for a couple boxes of test strips and the box of old pumps and meters that are currently scattered all over the floor. The amount of supplies she took doesn't look like a short trip to visit a few friends. She took nearly everything.

I clean up the spill and tidy the remaining items before closing the door when the pictures in her hall catch my eye. Billie at the top of Machu Picchu with a guy that looks like he could be Brent. Billie with three other blond surfer girls on some tiny boat with a wave that can only be Teahupo'o in the background. A five- or six-year-old Billie ten feet up in the air with a swing quickly retreating behind her. Must be Insane Izzy.

Thirst drives me back to her kitchen. The fridge is barren except for one Dr Pepper and the container of what used to be strawberries but now is simply white fuzz. If Billie does come back she'll need much more than one Dr Pepper for her lows. I make a mental note to bring more the next time I'm here.

The strawberry fuzz gets tossed into a trash can overflowing with empty pump cartridge boxes. I drag the bag from the can and take it to the outdoor trash can before the stench can take over the whole house. Then I pull both to the curb for trash day this week.

This is exactly what JJ must have done for me last night. I have to remember to thank him.

When I return, I fill a cup with water before collapsing on the dusty orange couch. After polishing off the water, I rest my head on the back of the sofa. I know I said I was coming over here to look for clues, but to be honest, the only comfort I can find is to be in her space, near her things. I can almost pretend that she is simply running late and forgot we were going to meet up. "The surf was too good," she'd say when she finally came back.

I'm in no hurry to leave.

Spooner, finished with his feast, jumps up on the couch next to me and snuggles his head on my lap. I run my hand down his back as I breathe in the sweet pineapple oils Billie always has out. I miss that scent.

I continue to pet Spooner as heaviness beats me again.

I wake to a dimly lit house. I must have been more tired than I thought. Spooner hasn't moved. Still snuggled up to me. "Come on, boy. You're coming with me." I struggle to my feet, taking a minute to make sure I'm steady before heading out the front door and pulling it closed behind me. I should probably lock it.

Billie, I know you think everything is safe, but, believe me, it's not all rainbows and sunshine.

But, I guess you know that now. Don't you?

I shuffle to the end of the porch to retrieve the small ceramic turtle perched on the edge. Sliding the secret door underneath, I remove the hidden key.

After locking the door, I pocket the key, planning on making a copy for myself and returning the original to the turtle. I don't want to lock Billie out of her own place if she ever does return.

Once at my car, I open the passenger door. "Load up, Spooner."

He jumps high enough to get his front paws on the footwell, but it will be a few more months before he is grown enough to make the jump himself. I lift him the rest of the way and shut the door behind him, before rounding the truck and hopping in.

Chapter 18

BILLIE

A light in the office on the far side of the boathouse is the only sign of life this late. I've been working away on the inboard diesel engine dropped in between the seats of a Cheoy Lee sailboat. My arms are marked with engine oil up to my pushed-up sweatshirt sleeves and sweat blurs my vision as it drips into my eyes.

I stop to wipe my eyes on the grease-free part of my sleeve, stretch my back, and find Imaginary Ryder perched on top of the cabin, staring back at me. Barefoot, in trunks, he looks as relaxed as if he were on his boat back home waiting for a sea turtle to pop up above the waterline. "You making any headway with that thing?" he says, nodding to the mess of an engine.

"I'm starting to, finally." I rub my hands on a shop rag, more than ready for a distraction from the engine, and there's no one I want to chat with more right now than Ryder. "I can take a break, though. I'm in desperate need of one of our famous, post-swim chats. I know it's not the chairs in your yard, but this could work, too."

He taps the top of the deck next to him. "Think she'll be seaworthy again soon?"

I hop up beside him. "After the beating she took in Dorian? I'm not sure."

The boat's owner was out of town when warnings of Hurricane Dorian first came in. She wasn't able to dry-dock her in time so she took quite a thrashing during the storm.

I lean up against Ryder wondering what it would have been like to come back after that storm and find your boat in shambles after spending so much energy restoring it. After struggling to get the engine running this time, I'm beginning to understand what must have gone into it the first time around.

Ryder leans back on his hands as if he was trying to capture even more of the sun's rays, and, for a moment, I'm out on the water with him, drifting under a gentle breeze, no place to be, not a care in the world. He looks down at me. "What's with the hoodie, Billie?"

When I first slipped into his blue sweatpants with NAVY scrawled in bold yellow letters on the hip, it became a layer of armor. I had a small piece of Ryder with me, protecting me, shielding me from all the misery this life had in store for me.

The matching sweatshirt was even better. I could pull up the hood and nothing could touch me. From the second I pulled it on, it provided me with the comfort I needed so badly. The Florida heat drove me out of the sweats, but I haven't taken off the ultra-soft pullover since I got here. Rusty must think I'm nuts.

I look down at the grime that has piled up on my security blanket and shrug.

Ryder smiles knowingly. "You think, maybe just for now, it might be easier to work if you weren't sweating buckets?"

I get it. I should have abandoned the garment the moment I hit Florida. Back in Maui, I didn't even own a hoodie, which is the reason why I had to borrow this one from Ryder during one especially cool Game Night. But knowing I'm probably one minute from passing out in this heat, I slide it over my head, wipe my face with the clean interior, and toss it onto the seat.

I hop off the cabin and stride back to the engine, ready to take another stab at it. "You know, it would go twice as fast if you'd help."

Silence.

I look up to find an empty boat.

I consider the sweatshirt, but resist, going back to the irreparable engine instead.

"Sammie? You still up there?"

Though quiet, Rusty's voice shocks me into spinning around and further contorting myself in the confined space. I slam my head into the cockpit bench and knock my elbow into the carburetor.

Rusty's head pops over the deck above me. "I scared you again, didn't I? So sorry, hon."

"It's not you. I'm just jumpy." I reach for my hoodie and slide it back on. "What's up?"

"I was looking for the torque wrench. Have you seen it?"

"Last I saw, Rooster was using it on the Starcraft."

"I should start calling you the tool whisperer." He laughs at his own lame joke the way that only old men seem to do. He descends the steps before popping back up. His face softens. "Sammie, you can let fear happen to you or you can take fear by the balls and beat the hell out of it. You just have to make the decision. And if I've ever met a fighter, it's you."

I pull the hood up over my head. "I wish I knew how."

"Take care of your tools and they'll take care of you. Captain Jack taught you that, right? You just need to get a hold of the right tools."

The right tools? Where do I get those, the Scared Little Girl Tool Store? The Never Will Be Normal Again Tool Store? Not sure they have one of those down here.

"We're out of here, Rusty." Rooster, Topher, and Danny head for the door.

Rusty nudges me. "Why don't you call it a night? Join the boys for a drink."

Maybe it's time I stop talking to visions of friendships past and try some real humans. I step out of the engine cavity and nod to Rusty.

"Hey boys, hold up. Sammie's gonna join you."

"And he's feeding Gwendolyn pizza and Chips Ahoy, and cooing, 'You like that, baby, huh? You're excited now,'" Rooster says.

Hidden away at the far end of Key Largo, The Forgotten Anchor is wall to wall with locals tonight, dotted with the few tourists who have managed to find it. Rooster, Topher, and Danny are treated like local celebrities here with people all around listening to Rooster's tall tale.

"The gator's thirteen feet now, so the authorities are trying to take him away from the guy. But he's had it as a pet for fifty years, since he was nine. He even took it to college with him. So they can't figure out what to do."

Sitting at a picnic table beneath a palapa wide enough to shade an entire village, the evening breeze off the water makes the heat almost bearable.

But that doesn't mean that I'm not sweating buckets.

Or that my heart is not racing.

Or my hands shaking.

Dammit. I'm low.

I try to retrieve my AWOL Dexcom from the pocket of my jean shorts, until I realize it died three days ago. Instead, I unzip my kit and pull out my meter. Seventy. Without my Dexcom, I have no idea if that's seventy and stable or seventy and plummeting.

"He should just dress it up like that lady in Lakeland does with her gator, Rambo. Then he could just call it his wife and they'd have to let him keep it," Topher jokes.

If the speed of service is anything like all the other places around here, it is going to take a good thirty minutes to get a waitress and another thirty to get our drinks. I can't wait that long for some sugar, so I make my way to the bar.

Though it's fairly packed in here, there's an opening at the end of the bar. Under the Swamp Head Brewery sign is a handwritten note that reads, "Breathe in, Breathe out, Move on." Solid advice for the customers who come in here before resetting their expectations for quick service.

At the other end of the bar, the barkeep is slowly making his way toward me and I hope my sugars won't dip even more while I wait.

A pint glass clangs against the bar. My head spins to assess the situation and the only thing I can see is the colossal faded spider on the back of the hand gripping the glass, a spider that I've seen before.

Shit. They're here. Has he recognized me? Does he know?

I drop my head to hide, and whip around, my back now to the man.

My gaze flicks to the front door. Kavika takes up the entire doorway, light flooding in behind him.

They found me. The computer. You stupid moron. You touched a computer to find supplies.

The exit out to the patio is blocked by Couch Security Dude. I can somehow hear him mutter from across the room, "You think she'll be a screamer or a crier?"

No exits. Can't run.

Hide. You have to hide.

I scan the crowd. No one has noticed these two. They seem to pass by them in slow motion as if they weren't even there.

"Hey. Do you need something or not?" a deep voice demands my attention.

I turn to find the bartender leaning over the bar towards me. "Huh?"

I study the spider tattoo wrapped around the pint glass to my right for a second time and follow it up to a kind face, weathered by the sun and topped with a mess of white hair.

The old man smiles at me. "I think he's trying to get your attention, dear."

I pivot back to the bartender.

"You need a drink?"

I struggle to get words out. "Dr Pepper?"

"We only have Mr. Pibb. It's pretty close."

I nod.

When my liquid sugar comes, so do my tears.

"Here you go, hon. Take my chair."

I shake my head. "Thanks, though."

"My doc says all this sitting is killing me. You'd be doing me a favor." He gets up and slides his stool over to me. "A guy?"

"Kind of."

"Well he's a fool, that's what I think."

I return a faint smile, the most I can muster at the moment.

Chapter 19

BILLIE

After signing up for a new email and Facebook account, I managed to track down the diabetes group that illegally saves lives. Though I suppose there is a reason, it's crazy that sharing life-saving medicine is considered a crime.

Connie lives near Key West and was offering the extra insulin pump supplies she had because she changed pump manufacturers. We made a plan to meet today to exchange the black-market goods.

When the bus lets me off on the corner of Front and Duval Street, I head straight for the water. Of course, everywhere you head on this little island is toward the water, but in some directions the water is closer than others.

The narrow, one-way street is empty this early, as most everyone is still sleeping it off. A mama chicken leads her four baby chicks along the sidewalk in front of the Conch Tour Train stand, looking for breakfast bugs.

Just one block later, the water comes into view. Across a small channel the little Sunset Key, littered with two-story white villas, seems like just a short swim away.

A monstrous cruise ship is pulling up to the harbor, sending crew scurrying around like crabs on the dock, struggling to tie her fast. It looks like a gargantuan skyscraper moored to the landing, its mammoth size dwarfing the tiny shops and restaurants.

I stroll along the water trying to absorb as much strength as possible before meeting a total stranger in a strange land. A few blocks later, I wander up a brick-lined alley towards Salty Frogs.

Across the street, a shop owner is lifting the security bars on an open-air market that reminds me of an ABC Store back home with its collection of all the usual liquor store items plus enough touristy souvenirs and sunscreen to stay in business.

When Connie shows up in her yellow and green floral print dress, I spot her immediately. I wait to see if anyone else looks to be with her, checking the eye line of all the other customers. When no one makes eye contact, I approach her.

I told her she could recognize me by my pink sweater and matching pink heels. More like a dirty hoodie and jean shorts. But it will give me a chance to check her out before I make contact to make sure this isn't some sort of crazy ruse JJ has set up to unearth me.

"Sorry, I couldn't find my sweater and heels. Laundry day. What can I say?"

"No problem," she says with a friendly smile. She lifts a loaded reusable Winn-Dixie bag. "I'm so glad these could go to a new home."

I peer down into the life-sustaining bag. "I can't thank you enough."

"You want some lunch? It's on me."

Free lunch on top of free pump supplies? Wow. I guess there still are big-hearted people in this world.

I check my insulin pump. Six units left. "I'm good. Thanks."

"Trying to stretch your insulin?"

I tuck the pump back into my pocket. "Kind of," I admit to this complete stranger.

"Do you have any more?"

"After this, just a vial I got from Walmart."

Some thoughtful people from the same Facebook group where I arranged this exchange also told me about Walmart

Insulin. It is like stepping back into the 80s with this technology, really hard to control and super inaccurate. I can't use it in my insulin pump, so I'm forced to shoot up six to eight times a day, but shooting up is better than the alternative of not shooting up, which is not doing anything. Ever again.

After these last six units in my pump, I will have to make the change. Which makes the pump supplies I'm about to get almost obsolete, but you never know.

Connie checks her purse, pulling out two Humalog pens. "Here."

"I couldn't."

"Take them. I have a huge stash back home. I wish you would have told me you were short on insulin, too. I would have brought more. Come on, breakfast is on me."

After a leisurely meal, I hug my new friend Connie and watch her leave. I pack my windfall into my backpack and prepare myself for a few more hours of buses to get back to Hammerhead Key.

To get back home.

In the last hour, this place went from a sleepy little town to the streets of New York City. The sidewalks are packed with people looking every which way but where they're going. I guess the cruise ship finally let everyone off to explore. Once I step out, someone zips by and bumps right into me.

I retreat behind the black fence separating the restaurant patio from the sidewalk and take a breath.

My hood goes back up and I pull my hat down low over my eyes. Tightening my backpack straps, I shuffle into the pulsating crowd.

You can't see anyone.

They could be anywhere.

You can't get a good view.

A group of guys hurls into me, knocking my backpack from my shoulder.

I scoop up my bag and hold it to my chest.

Get out of here. Go. Find someplace.

I spot the restaurant gate, but the throng of people has pushed me too far to go against the flow back there.

Shit. Not an option.

In the other direction, an alley. Not more than ten yards ahead. I tuck into my respite, which turns out to be more of a short driveway, blocked off by a grimy yellow fence ten feet in.

I put my back against the dirty brick wall, looking left and right. It reeks like they wash out the trash cans here each night after every drunk in town decided to take a piss in one corner and hurl in the other and then it sits around all day roasting in the Florida heat.

There's no way I'm going to make it back to the bus station.
And this driveway is a dead end.
I have to get back out there. To my bus. Four blocks away.
Might as well be four miles away at this rate.

I push off the wall and approach the sidewalk. The hurried crowd won't stop.

There's no break.
There's no way I'm going back out there.
I won't make it.

I retreat to the safety of the delivery driveway. Another chicken comes pecking my way with her little babies in tow.

I'll never make it out of here.
I can't even make it across the street.
No way in Hell I'll make it to the bus station.

I lean my head back against the brick wall.

You're stuck.
You went too far and screwed yourself over.
There's no way out of this.

I let my head fall to the side as I check my escape route. My eyes come to rest on the Floridian ABC Store.

They'll have a burner cell phone in there.
I could call him.
If I could just hear his voice, I'd have the strength to make it to the bus.

I look back to my current prison.

Get up.

Stand up.
My body complies.
Wait for a break in the crowd. A break. Wait.
I survey the street for my opening.
I glance behind me. Back to the crowd. Behind me.
A gap finally appears.
Go. Go now. Go.
My feet move.
At the curb, not wanting to let the momentum slip, I bolt into the road, barely missing a pedicab.

Once under the tin roof of the convenience store, the disposable cameras and phones aren't hard to locate. I snap the cheapest one off the rack and take it to the counter.

Returning to the safety of the alley, the package is challenging to pry into; it slices my finger in the process.

Avoiding the dripping blood, I dial the first three numbers with my ring finger, then slam the phone shut.

No phones. No Internet. No trace of me.

In the curtailed driveway, dingy asphalt covers the five yards to the other side of the dead-end. Weeds push through the crack running down the center of it.

I take a deep breath and dial again, this time succeeding, and await the sound that will hopefully give me the momentum to leave this cage.

"This is Ryder."

A hushed whimper escapes my lips as I slide down the wall into a puddle.

"Billie? That you?"

Tears slip from my eyes. I tug my hat over my eyes and pour every thought into listening to his voice.

"Please don't hang up," he pleads. "Where are you? I'll come meet you anywhere, anytime."

I cover my mouth to quiet the sobs threatening to break loose.

"You name it, I'll be there. Billie?" he begs for a response from me.

Don't do it. You can't do it.
You just needed to hear his voice. Don't you dare talk to him.

His voice grows faint. He breathes out, "I miss you, Billie."

My head drops.

His voice breaks everything inside me.

Shatters it.

All my resolve, my self-preservation. The only thing I need right now is more of this man.

I find my voice. "End of the Wilmington Pier. One week from now. Exactly."

I slam the phone off.

No phones. No Internet. No trace of me. I can't even do that right.

I stomp on the contraband and chuck it across the alley as the tears flow.

Chapter 20

RYDER

*E*nd of the Wilmington Pier. One week from now. Exactly."
I'm instantly wide awake. The voice I had craved for so long was gone before I had a chance to even register its presence.

I slide down the railing on JJ's porch and pause, letting the phone fall from my ear. I inspect the screen to confirm she's hung up before redialing the last number. It rings repeatedly.

Come on, Billie. Pick it up. You were just there.

She doesn't answer.

But she's safe. Or at least alive.

And in Wilmington.

And, better yet, willing to see me.

I turn my head to see JJ through the front window enjoying another game. I bend down to scratch behind Spooner's ear. "He's gonna kill me."

But she asked me to come. How can I say no to that? To her?

And I'd only be going out there to protect her. It's not like I'm going out there to hook up with her so I'm not betraying anyone. Only doing my duty to protect.

I slip back through the front door, Spooner at my heels, staring at the phone like I can summon it to call me back.

"Aw, come on Blue, that was higher than a t-shirt at Mardi Gras!" JJ yells at a ref who will never hear him. Without taking his eyes off the game, he asks, "Who was that?"

I turn the phone over and over in my hands. "Uh, just a charter. Have to do a three-day next Monday. So, I've got to bail on surfing Secret Spot on Tuesday. Sorry, man."

"I get it. Work comes first."

The irony of that is not lost on me, but I'm too tired from worrying to fight. I flip on my phone to book my plane ticket while the game continues to play.

And JJ continues to yell like it matters.

Chapter 21

BILLIE

Six days after making a mistake that will likely give me up to an incredibly violent drug cartel, I am, for some reason, still planning on going through with it. At least I gave Ryder a location far away from here so I still have someplace to run.

If I can run.

If I'm not walking directly into a military-level ambush.

You do know what I did for a living, right?

That should scare me, but Ryder's voice, the humor in his eyes every time he said that, not only serves to encourage me but draw me toward my demise. Either way, I will be able to see him one last time before I'm "taken care of."

I'll be there at most for a day, so I pack four day's worth of supplies. Cartridge, syringe, four sites, insulin, strips, meter, batteries. My provisions get wrapped in a black case and slipped into my backpack.

I swipe the insulin from the nightstand. Not three days after meeting with Connie, a box overflowing with ice packs, vials of insulin, and Dexcom sensors arrived at the shop. I almost cried at the show of love from a complete stranger. It gave me a little fragment of hope that there still might be some love in this world.

That hope prodded me to go through with this suicide

mission because maybe, just maybe, it won't be the total disaster I'm expecting.

My once-packed nightstand is nearly bare except for...

The knife? I'll need all the help I can get if Ryder turns out to be more loyal to JJ than I predicted. I toss it in my pocket for easy access, and, after slinging my backpack on my shoulder, head out the door for a long night of travel.

When I reach Wilmington, the early summer morning has left the pier bathed in sun, but practically empty. My hood and hat on, halfway to the end, I have at least an hour before Ryder should be here, leaving me some time to scope out the place and plan.

If he comes alone, the restaurant at the end will be a safe place to slip away. I could try to outrun him off the pier and disappear into town, but he's quicker on foot than me.

I approach the rail and size up the drop to the water. Not too high to dive. I was faster than him last swim and I'd have a jump on him. But I haven't been training enough. If it's JJ or *them* who show up, it will work. But, if there's more than one...

Why did you do this? You were fine alone. No phones. No internet. No trace of me. Why couldn't you just do that?

Clang.

I spin to face the sound, bracing myself for a fight. But it's only the old man unlocking the chain on the Ice Cream Stand on the opposite side of the pier.

You've got to get a hold of yourself, Billie.

I head around the back of the charter ticket booth behind me to make sure another escape route isn't cut off. It could work as another way out.

Satisfied with my options to bolt, I take a seat against the ticket booth with an unobstructed view of who's approaching.

You'll see him before he sees you.

A gentle hand on my knee wakes me. "Billie...Babe..."

I lift my head. It's just me and Ryder on an empty, sun-drenched pier. The perfect way to wake up.

"You have a nice sleep?"

"I had the worst dream, RyGuy."

Ryder smiles, reassuring me it was just a dream, his strength filling me with peace. "You're safe now. I'm here."

Another hand on my shoulders shakes me. I'm on my feet in a second, jumping back from the figure in front of me.

The pier is packed with tourists and locals enjoying the weather. A kid screaming as he is chased by his older brother. Seagulls squawking. The Ice Cream Man's register slams open.

With each motion, my head tracks then returns to Ryder.

"It's OK Billie. It's just me."

I try to focus on Ryder. Ryder... and the vast liability he is now.

I survey the pier for anyone who looks out of place. Is the guy with the fishing pole turning around too much? Scoping out the situation? How often is too often to look around? I scan behind me for anyone else approaching.

"How are you?" Ryder pulls my gaze forward again. He steps in to give me a hug.

I take a quick step back. Out of his reach. Was that for a hug? Or to trap me?

He stops dead, not making another attempt to wrap me up. His voice gets gentle and unhurried, "How are you, Billie?"

I can't decide on which of the dozens of emotions to go with, so I shrug.

In the few moments when my glance passes from scanning the pier to him, he looks to be studying me. "It's beautiful here. Is this where you've been staying?"

He's already fishing for information. Not a promising sign. "I can't tell you that."

He laughs. "What do you mean you can't tell me?"

"You'll..."

Damn. I don't know what he'll do with that info. Tell JJ? Tell Kavika and his boys? Track me and send in a drone to bomb my new shack?

"I'll what? What the hell does that mean, Billie?"

"You'll tell them," I blurt.

"Tell who?"

A door slams in the distance. My hands instinctively fly up in front of me, ready to fight, head on a swivel looking for the origin of the sound.

"No one's coming for you. There's no one trying to hurt you," he sounds reassuring, but I don't know.

"You didn't hear them," I argue.

"I know it feels like no one's safe. Like around every corner, there's a threat. But I'm telling you, there's not."

He's lying. He's lying. He wants you to lower your guard. He told them. He brought them. Shit.

"Billie. Did you hear me? Did you hear what I said?"

I train my gaze on him. He appears concerned, but he's been trained to outwit anyone.

"Kinske's been indicted along with eleven of his guys."

That stops the rush of thoughts. Kavika locked up. His boys, behind bars. "Even JJ?" I ask, not ready to believe any of it.

"JJ? What are you talking about?"

"You said all of them."

"JJ's not with—"

Thump.

I'm locked in on the sound, taking a step back into fighting position, prepared to flee or attack.

A fish at the end of a line flops onto the pier. A boy, not more than five, runs up to it and holds it up by the tail for his dad.

I lower my arms.

Ryder, looking for another tack, pulls out his phone and brings up something before holding it out to me. "Here. Read this."

No phones. No internet. No trace of me.

I look from the phone to his face and then back to the phone. I shake my head. No way I'm making that mistake again. That's what got me into this situation in the first place.

"It's just a news article. JJ wasn't dirty, he was on assignment. But he got them, Billie. With the location of the burial site, the FBI got them all." He holds the phone out again, slower this time.

I try to read the article from here, but the glare on it has shielded the screen from me. My hand reaches out for the device.

No phones. No internet. No trace of me.

I pull my hand back.

His face is a blend of disappointment and concern. "You're afraid of me," he stammers, "What's going on with you, Billie?"

Hearing him say my name breaks me almost as much as his confession that he missed me did in that crappy alley seven short days ago. And through those cracks, everything comes spilling out.

"What's going on with me? Seriously? My boyfriend draws me into a trap where guys try to," I can't even say it. "I have to leave the only home I've ever known so they can't finish the job like they promised, and you ask what's going on with me?"

"JJ didn't know," he says solemnly.

That's more bullshit. He's lying. He's got to be working with them.

"You know you can trust me, right?" He leans against the railing, probably a trick to get me to relax. "You have to know I would never hurt you."

"Ha! How do I know you're not just here to bring me to them? How do I know you're not strapped right now, waiting for the perfect moment to point a gun at me and make me go with you?"

I know that he's not. Where would he even get that stuff? Though he might have some leftover weapons from his days as a SEAL, or he might still have some buddies who would lend him one no questions asked, so maybe my suspicions are not that far-fetched.

Yet, even if it is crazy to think he'd pull a weapon on me, it's what my head is telling me—to be careful, not to let my guard down more than I already have when I picked up the contraband phone and dialed his number just so I could hear his voice.

"You really think I could do that?" he laughs. "Fine. Frisk me."

"Frisk you?" Tempting, but no. "I'm not coming within five feet of you."

"Fine." The mischievous grin spreading across his handsome face transports me back to a sunny day on his boat moments before he would throw me into the water. An immediate softening takes my heart from scared to intrigued.

Ryder unbuttons his shirt, slips it off, and tosses it to me. He then takes off his flip-flops and flings them at me. His trunks are next. Standing in only his briefs, he spins around slowly, hands raised. "See, no gun. You can check those for a wire. I've got nothing. The only reason I'm here is because you asked. That's it."

I pretend to inspect every inch of the clothes for a wire, not because I think he has one on, but because I am really beginning to enjoy this view.

He's trying to distract you. Keep your eyes open.

If it is just a distraction tactic, it sure is working. And, damn, if it isn't an enticing distraction. I take a quick glance around me just in case, before letting my eyes settle on Ryder, now helpless in his skivvies. If I can keep him in front of me like this, I may never have to think of another thing on earth ever again.

I look him up and down in slow motion, the first time my world has mellowed out in weeks. His black briefs hang just below his tan line which somehow feels scandalous to see. Although he has slimmed down since his days in the Navy, he is still the picture of a perfect athlete. A small scar crosses the crease along the left side of his abs, drawing my eyes along with it.

My shoulders soften and I bring my hand to my mouth as I soak him in.

He catches me looking and smiles, loving every minute of it.

Satisfied I'm in no danger, I realize I've got the power to keep him in his skivvies.

"You're liking this aren't you?" he teases.

I am.

He spins one more time, slower this time, letting me get a long, slow look.

I toss his clothes back and he slips his trunks on before sitting on a bench placed to deliver a view of the expansive Atlantic in front of us. "Now, come on. Sit down with me. What do you need from me? How can I help?"

How can you help? I think back over the last few weeks. Every moment I have been so strung out, wrapped tighter than a tourniquet on a shark victim. What I wouldn't give to feel unwound again.

"Honestly? What I really need is just one good day, you know, like back home, when we didn't have a care in the world? And we'd be in the sun and the water all day. Like nothing could ever touch us. That's what I need. Because If I can't get that, I'm not sure I can hold on any longer."

"I can do that. Where do we start?"

How have I come so far that I have no idea how to have a normal day?

The bell on the ice cream cart rings out, proclaiming that someone ordered the Super Duper Scooper.

"Ice cream. We start with ice cream."

Chapter 22

RYDER

The past few weeks without Billie have been torture for me. A sleepless nightmare of unending pain and helplessness. I couldn't do anything to help her, to protect her. And, I hate to admit it, but a small part of me was pissed that she did that to me.

What I didn't realize is, that while I was throwing a narcissistic pity party, Billie had been destroyed by what she went through, some of which I don't fully know the extent of. And she has been struggling with it while completely alone in a new place with no one to support her. If there's anything I have learned, you need your team to heal from a brain grenade. And Billie's been trying to recover from hers on her own.

When she called last week, she sounded so incredibly sad. I was certain I could cheer her up with nothing more than my presence. That I would bring her home and everything would go back to the way it was. When I got here, I was expecting her to fall into my arms and fill my heart with the sunshine she always gave.

But the Billie I saw today was a lot more like the Billie I met on the docks of Lahaina. And that Billie is going to need a good deal more than my presence. Right now, all she wants is a perfect day. So, that's exactly what she'll get. Even if I have to die trying.

When the bell rings out after Billie's Super Duper Scooper order, I actually think I see her crack a smile. It was always those simple things that brought her so much joy, so let's see how many of those simple things I can find and fit into today.

We take a seat back on our bench and race to finish our cones before the sun melts them while we plan our next move, first of which is to allay her fears that she is still in danger.

I open my phone to the Nalu Kai Sun's front page article. The U.S. District Attorney stands at his podium announcing the names of all those indicted. The article goes on to describe how the fine people of the Maui Police Department along with help from the FBI took down the longest standing drug ring in Maui's history.

I read that article and any other I could, trying to pull out any details about what happened that night after JJ left. Not that any reporter would have access to those details, but without having Billie around to fill me in, it was all I could do.

I slide my phone on the bench next to her, offering her proof one more time.

She glances at it and ponders. Not ready to give in, she rejects the phone, but at least she starts to talk, a little more like old Billie. "So, how's work been?"

Work has been awful. If I'm not canceling charters at the last minute, I'm barking at customers and generally being a miserable bastard the whole trip. I don't want to throw any more of a burden on her, though, so I'm intentionally vague. "Work's slow. It's been hard."

"The old dockside flirting routine hasn't been filling your boat with tourists?" She wags her brows suggestively.

"My what?"

"You know. You see a gullible girl walking by the docks and you flirt with her until she agrees to take a trip."

"I have never done that."

"You did it with me. You got me on that boat and then didn't say another word to me."

"I left you for one minute to get someone set up. By the time I got back, JJ was doing a fine job teaching you how to fish."

She licks her ice cream while she considers her comeback. "You know I don't fish."

"Sure. Now. But I didn't then. And if you were so opposed to fishing, why did you agree to come on a fishing charter in the first place?"

Her gaze drops to the gray, wooden planks beneath the bench. "I needed to forget about life for a while and I thought you... I thought a boat ride would be a good distraction."

"You at least seemed to enjoy the ride back."

Behind us, a kid squeals with delight as he pulls up his catch. Billie is immediately on her feet and in defensive mode. She is looking around for escape routes and I'm beginning to grasp the full scope of the damage. She looks down the pier towards land, then to the restaurant behind us, before moving to the railing.

I join her as she studies the water below, sliding my hand next to hers. "It was just a boy who caught a fish. That's all."

Billie looks at my hand, focusing on the long scar from my first knuckle, running over the back of my hand. She runs her finger along the length. "Was that from the boat or deploy...."

Not a story I want to tell her right now. I don't think it will help settle her anymore to hear about the knife that fileted my hand. "Billie, you're safe here."

She gets defensive. "Yeah, I know. I'm fine. Let's just go."

"Where to?"

Billie peers over the rail, then back at me. A smile spreads across her beautiful face. "You in?"

"It's your perfect day, Billie. I'm up for anything."

Her smile grows as she strips to her bikini, tossing clothes and her pump onto the bench and, for a moment, we are back in Maui preparing for our normal morning swim. Until we have to dive off this pier to get started.

Looking left and right, we climb the wooden railing before plunging into the water below.

The pier only extends about a thousand feet off shore. It couldn't be too deep here. When we jump, I play the game I always play when I'm jumping into a body of water. I make myself as sleek as I can, trying to hit the bottom if possible. On my way up, I open my eyes so I can pop up right in front of Billie. By the time I do, she is twisting around looking for me.

She relaxes once she knows I'm fine, but she is sure to add a quick splash in the face as punishment.

I spit a stream of water toward her. "Jetty or shore?"

"You still a little sore from our last workout? Is that why you want to swim to shore?"

"Is that a challenge? How about we make it a jetty-jetty-jetty?" I say, pointing back and forth from the jetty before us to the one behind and back. "Or have you stopped training and gone soft here on the east coast?"

That's all she needs to hear. She takes off.

I put my head down and swim. Fifty meters in, I pop my head to see if I've caught her. She's not in front of me. Must have passed her pretty quickly. I turn back, never wanting to miss a chance to taunt her, but again, what I expect to find and what I do find are two completely separate things. Billie is a good thirty meters behind me, head up, doing a shit-poor job of treading. The look on her face rivals the one she wore when I woke her on the pier earlier.

I sprint back to her. "Breathe. You're okay. Remember, humans float."

"Dead humans float, too," she snaps.

"You're gonna be just fine."

"No, I'm not."

"Hey," I shout, trying to pull her out of her head and back to reality. Then more calmly, "You are safe. Just focus on your breathing. Here, breathe with me. In. Out. In. Out."

Her flailing slows as she matches my inhales and exhales.

"We're gonna swim to shore, okay? Nice and slow. Keep your head above the water and just breaststroke in." I tap her on the shoulder to start moving and begin an exaggerated breaststroke like she's never done one before. She follows suit and we slowly make our way to the sand.

After dragging her body onto the sand, she sits silent, head buried in her knees.

I give her a couple moments to sit with it, but I don't really want to let her mind spin out, so I try to get her talking. "What was that?"

No reply.

I wait beside her for a few more minutes until she lifts her chin onto her knees.

Since talking wasn't doing much, maybe distraction will work better. I roll over onto my belly and pick up a fistful of wet sand, squeezing it as tiny bits drop underneath, making a little tower. "Drip castle contest?"

Billie can't turn down a competition. She flips to her stomach and proceeds to build a whole town of towers with a fierce wall around them.

I make a village of shrunken castles while putting most of my attention on assessing Billie's current state. Her jaw clenches as she focuses on her towers, and after each one, she scans the beach for any threats. Every muscle in her back is clenched. When she finally relaxes her eyes, the creases around them are white against the tan of the rest of her face like they haven't seen the sun in weeks.

When she looks content with her creation, I give her fair warning. "Watch out for the oncoming earthquake." My hand dives into the sand under the foundation of her wall and begins to shake.

She fights me off and goes on the attack. I defend my village only to have a wave wash both of our castles into nothing. She lets out the sweetest laugh.

"Showers?" When she nods, I hop up and begin to run, with Billie closing in on me.

Part one of the perfect day? Check. Now let's see what else we can do.

Chapter 23

BILLIE

S o, what's next?" Ryder asks.

Right now, I'm completely content to simply walk with RyGuy down the pier at a pace that is perfect, with no need to hurry to catch up, where meandering along is its own reward. But the pier will soon end, and we'll have to do something new. And he did say he was up for anything. "There is something I want to check out while we're here."

When Ryder said he'd meet me anywhere, the one town on the east coast I have always wanted to visit came tumbling out of my mouth. And the reason is one I don't readily admit. Whenever I had a bad day, or things got tough as a kid, I would stream my one guilty pleasure, *Dawson's Creek*.

When my teachers would give me crap for missing so many classes for surf comps or the meanest girl at school decided that I would be her target for the year, I could come home and escape. I hate to say it, but the thing I miss most about not having a phone right now is not being able to watch *Dawson's Creek* these past couple weeks.

I would never admit this to anyone, but I may have researched this town and all the filming locations over the years, and have made my own little Top Ten list of places I wanted to see. And I think today is the perfect day to knock a few off that list.

After renting boards at the SUP shop at the foot of the pier, and stuffing our belongings into dry bags, we paddle along marshland and waterways rich with history. Tidal creeks wind their way into the tall marsh grass. A flock of birds takes flight as we pass by.

With Ryder paddling ahead, my eyes freeze on his shoulders, a mile-wide, and long, sturdy Viking legs and, for the first time since I left Maui, my pulse quickens in delight.

I point to the narrow inlet leading to a tidal creek that will bring us further inland. "I think it's this one."

"That one right there?" He begins speeding up.

The race is on. And this time, the speed feels exhilarating. As we make the turn up the shallow creek, we slow. I'm not above gloating though. "Looking a bit sluggish, there, big guy."

"You been practicing?"

"It's all-natural talent, babe," I let another of Brent's famous quotes roll off my lips.

This land is a beautiful blur where water meets solid ground. Houses soak up the view behind private docks complete with salt-beaten dinghies for the kids tied up next to untouched boats for the adults.

We tether our boards to a dock jutting out into Hewlett's Creek that runs from the backyard of a white, two-story Cape Cod-style house, and make ourselves at home, sitting on the edge.

"I see why you'd pick this place to move. It's fantastic."

He's fishing again, but this time I can see it's driven by genuine concern for me. "But the sun sets over the land. Over land, Ryder. Not sure I can get used to that."

"Yeah, but it rises over the sea."

"I guess so." It doesn't feel right lying to him. Or even just letting him believe something that's not true. "But I didn't move here."

"What do you mean? Where did you move?"

And it hits me like the buckets of freezing water Brent would douse me with if he ever found me napping in the hammock in our backyard. We're not in Maui anymore. I don't live down the street from my RyGuy. We aren't having one of our famous post-swim talks. Everything has changed. And all because I couldn't keep my shit together and just stay chill. Chilly Billie. I worked so hard to be Chilly Billie. And it all went away in one split second.

"You know, I managed to stop being Insane Izzy for five whole years." I pick at a splinter at the edge of the weathered dock. "But, then it all went sideways."

Ryder taps my thigh with his knuckle. "I like the little glimpses of Insane Izzy you show me. Why did you ever stop?"

In addition to keeping Insane Izzy at bay all this time, I've also managed to keep this story at bay. But, so beat down now, I'm not sure I have the strength to keep it to myself. "I used to be aggro. All the time. Shooting off my mouth. Trying to prove myself, keep up with the guys, be, not only the best chick surfer out there but simply the best surfer."

I chuck the scrap of wood I pull from the dock into the water. "Brent and I were on tour in Peru. Not really the best part of town, but we had both won our heats that day and wanted to go out and celebrate. I was being loud and some local guy grabs my ass, so, naturally, I go full-on aggro. I shove him and start screaming in his face. Next thing I know, there's four of them."

"Peruvian locals? Those are some serious dudes."

"Tell me about it. So, Brent comes over, trying to smooth talk his way out of it, which, of course, pisses me off more. He was always doing that. We'd get caught stealing oranges from Mr. Wellington's tree, and he'd be screaming and ready to call our dad, and Brent would go over and swear that we were just helping him harvest the tree so the oranges wouldn't rot. And the guy would believe him. He was the total Tom Sawyer. I didn't have that sort of charm. I only had aggression."

"You have plenty of charm, Billie."

Looks like Ryder was blessed with the same smooth-talker gene Brent had.

"These guys think he's my boyfriend or something, 'cause they ask him, 'Don't you know how to control your woman?' I don't know how, but Brent somehow manages to push me out the back door into the alley."

While I stall, trying to avoid getting into the gritty part of my story, a dinghy slowly glides up the creek towards us. I pray it's not the owner of the dock we are currently trespassing on.

"And I'm furious. Furious with him for thinking I needed him to step in and save me. With the back-ass locals for having such small dicks that they had to pretend to be ultra-manly to make up for it. So, I am tearing into Brent in the alley, going full Insane Izzy on him when the door opens behind him."

An older guy in a salt-beaten dinghy rows up to the dock we are squatting on. "I suppose you two are looking for a tour?"

My eyes go wide. "Really?" I hop to my feet thrilled that, instead of being screamed at, I might get a glimpse behind one of my favorite fictional places.

"A tour of what?" Ryder asks. So, I may not have told Ryder exactly why I picked this dock to rest on.

The old man ties up to the dock. "You've already gotten a good look at the dock, so, the house I suppose."

Ryder stands and dusts off his shorts. "Wait. This isn't the house from that dumb show with the girl who's always rowing off in her boat while she's crying."

"Not a fan of The Creek?" the man asks. "Neither was I, believe me. When we first bought this place, there was a constant stream of looky-loos trampling my garden and looking in the windows." He ties up the dinghy and jumps onto the dock with the energy of a five-year-old. "But, you know, since my wife passed, I don't mind the company so much."

I know I asked for the perfect day, but I never thought I would get a view inside of this site. This house has been off-limits for years. The last owners even erected an imposing wooden sign out front warning visitors that it was private property and that they weren't above calling the cops if anyone stepped foot on any of their property. And I get to go inside. "We would love to see inside. We won't stay long, I promise."

"Come on in. I'm Midge by the way." He waves at us to follow him up the landing.

We head in the screen door leading to the porch and I'm immediately in another world, one where problems are simple. Where your biggest life choice is to pursue the comfortable boy next door, the one you've always known, or to aim higher and go for the boy who always provokes you and challenges you to grow and chase your dreams.

Although a good portion of the house is untouched, there are signs that new people live there. The front porch still has the same white wicker rocking chairs and table, but the kitchen is entirely redone. And the pictures in the hall aren't of teen actors who are old enough to have kids of their own who could have starred on the show.

Instead, they are of Midge and his late wife, yellowed and worn. Loved, I'm sure, for decades. The two of them at the beach, her in one of those old-fashioned high-waisted bathing suits. The two of them in front of a small bungalow, probably their first home, with a baby swaddled in her arms. With two toddlers wrapped around their legs, leaning up against a huge old car. Him in his dress blues next to her in a wedding gown, simple, white.

Ryder stops to really look at that one. "You were in the Navy, sir?"

"Thirty-two years. Commander of Det. Golf in Vietnam." He looks Ryder up and down. "How long have you been in?"

"Nine years. But it's been a few since I took off my uniform."

"Those first few are hard," Midge says. "I was lucky to have Alice help me find a new purpose. After all my years of transfers and moving around the country, it was good to build a forever home with her and the kids."

Late afternoon has settled on the marshland since we've been inside. Midge walks us to the edge of his porch. "Anytime. Seriously, you two are welcome back anytime you want."

"And maybe I'll give that show another chance," Ryder says. I think all my fangirling has convinced him there must be something redeeming to The Creek.

"Don't torture yourself," Midge says.

I give my new friend a hug. Ryder gives him a handshake.

I overhear Midge trying to whisper to Ryder. "Don't let that one slip through your hands."

Ryder gives him a back pat. "I'll try, Sir."

Once at the end of the dock, Ryder begins untying our boards.

"Where to now?" I ask.

"I bet we could get a pretty good view of the ocean from down-creek a little."

"Sounds like a plan."

A tall grass field overlooks the tidal marsh and beyond that, the ocean. The sun is dipping lower in the sky, heading further over land, letting up on its scorching heat as we paddle on.

Ryder glides for a moment, before turning to me. "You need a little break?"

"Tired so soon?" I tease.

"Hungry is more like it." He points to a food stand just above a sand berm on the edge of the river.

The look on my face is more answer than he needs. We drag our boards ashore next to a locked-up boat launch and hop the fence to get to the pizza place.

Chapter 24

BILLIE

Standing in line at a shack that consists of little more than a kitchen with an attached window for ordering, I pull out my pump. A stable ninety for the last three hours. The constant movement has been good for my sugars. Replacing it on my shorts, I wrestle my wallet from my pocket. I wish it was doing as well.

"Put that away," Ryder orders.

I don't bother arguing. After trying to win that argument the first few months we went anywhere, I gave up trying. And now, with next to no money to my name, the argument is even more pointless.

I order and then swipe a whole handful of sugar packets from the counter and slide them into my pocket. I can't afford the costly energy gels I used to consume when I get low. I pilfer a couple more for good measure and wander over to the huge deck bathed in fading sun to find a table.

Ryder brings our slices and drinks moments later.

I dig into the slice of pizza like a blacktip reef shark in chummy waters.

"It looks like you've never seen food before," Ryder jokes.

And that feels not too far off from the truth. I can't remember the last time I was actually hungry or that food didn't look like more than a necessary evil to keep the Low Monster at bay. But today, after moving my body all day, and alternating between baking in the glorious sunshine and flinging myself off my board into the perfectly cool saltwater, my body is absolutely craving food.

I finish nearly the whole slice before Ryder has the guts to try to stop me with conversation. "You never finished your Peru story."

Horrified that I even started that story, I wipe my face with a napkin from the stash Ryder brought.

I don't know what convinced me to share the one thing I don't talk about, but I am in no mood to continue that stupidity. "What's new in Nalu Kai?"

The corners of his eyes crease in amusement. He recognizes what I'm doing, but he plays along anyways. "You know that artist Biovandal? The conspiracy theories are starting to get really wild."

Of all the things to bring up. I've often wondered if Ryder knows. He loves to mention Biovandal. Like he's giving me an opportunity to spill. "Conspiracy theories of who he is?" I ask.

"No. Where he's gone."

Oh crap. I haven't even thought about the Biovandal account. I typically post every three days with a new view of my latest piece or just a repost of a fan's pic of one of my pieces. And now, in the exact timeline that I disappeared, I let the Biovandal account go dark. I'm sure that was all it took to fully convince Ryder.

I try to cover. "He went somewhere? Did he put up an installation somewhere besides Hawaii?"

"You didn't hear? Biovandal was hired by the old mayor to spread propaganda, so when we got a new mayor, she threw him in jail."

I've always loved how an artist can mean one thing with her art, but as soon as she launches it, it is up to the viewer to add meaning. And some of the meanings they add can get quite pretty insane. "That's crazy. I don't know where people come up with this stuff. Did they have proof?"

"Oh yeah. That one had a list of Biovandals installation dates and the dates of something the mayor did. Remember the one where you, uh, he used the power washer to clean off a picture of bumper-to-bumper frog traffic in the tunnel on the Honoapiiliana Highway Bridge at the edge of town? That was right before Mayor Kaneole signed her transportation bill. And then he did the community garden right after the mayor had her press conference trying to save her own ass because the new numbers came out on poverty and food shortages."

"No way. And they have dates for this."

"Oh yeah. They've done their research. It's almost convincing, but I think Biovandal just has a sixth sense of what is going on in his community. Probably because he's so friendly and chats with everyone he sees. And because everyone knows he loves them, they all open up to him."

Man, I didn't realize how much I miss people. I knew I missed my friends and family. That I felt immediately. But I forgot how invaluable it was to have those other people, my community. Kaimana down at Hawaii Five Ono. The boys in the line-up. All the people around town that I knew even if I didn't know their names. I really miss those silly little chats about nothing.

And it all comes crashing back down on me. Ryder may be here with me now, but it will never be the same. We can pretend to have a perfect day, but when he goes home tonight, I will have to go back to the shop and my depressing one-room shack with every window fully covered and no one to know if I ever left. I grind my palms into my eyes to get them to stop leaking.

Ryder steps into my spinning thoughts. "You know, there's this new movement to convince him to put up another installation. At least the ones who don't think the CIA has him locked away in a dark site because his work has been leaking state secrets to terrorists."

"They don't. Seriously?"

"Yep. Well, really, it's only this one nut, but he has some pretty good data to back it up. He wrote up a whole dossier."

"No way."

"Sure. And you can download it for only $9.99," he laughs.

"He probably makes more than Biovandal with that."

"Not anymore."

I have never made a dime off any of my artwork. The confusion must show on my face because Ryder goes on. "I guess at one point, Biovandal set up a Patreon account but never told anyone. That one guy, @biovandalhoodiefan, found it and has been sharing it everywhere. So, everyone has been donating to get him to put up his next piece. The dude's loaded now."

I can't pull my eyes from this man, even as they fill with tears. I have to blink the tears away to focus. I've always known he had a fan account. I may have even dropped a few hints to make sure he knew about each new installation. But I never thought he would take care of me like this.

When he showed up, I thought he might be there to hurt me. How could I have ever thought that about Ryder? From the first moment I met him, he has always found a way to make me feel cared for. I never even had to say a thing for him to know. He just knew.

That day on the docks, he somehow knew I needed to get on the water. And on the way back, when the ladies were squawking in my ear ruining the moment of solitude I had found playing with the spray from the bow, he shooed them away and then turned up the ride. And now, while I've left without a word, he has been secretly working behind the scenes to make sure I was taken care of again.

A few years back, I got frustrated about not making any money from my art. I signed up for a Patreon account where people can support artists, but second guessed myself when it came time to publicize it. It felt too much like begging and I decided that the joy people get from my work is enough payment.

I may have been able to hide my tears at the thought of being alone, but this show of love is too much. I slide around the circular table and wrap my arms around him, not caring if it gives away my secret. There's no way he did this and didn't know who I was all along. And why should it surprise me that he's once again seen right through me? He always has. "Thank you, RyGuy. You have no idea what that means to me."

He holds me for a drawn-out moment and the touch warms my entire body. When he releases me, I drift back to my side of the table. He leans forward on his elbows and exhales a contented sigh. "What am I going to do with you, Billie?"

We sit for a beat, playing a game of who is caught looking and every time his gaze meets mine, my blue heart grows a little sunnier.

The line of customers has grown while we've been eating. And it makes sense, the pizza here is unearthly. A little girl is pulled out of line by a dog that must outweigh her by thirty pounds. She muscles him into submission and returns to the line.

My face falls as the guilt washes over my whole body. I left Spooner alone to fend for himself. I may have found him on the street when he was only a couple of months old, but, since then, he got used to being pampered by me. He lost all his street smarts. I don't even know if he's still alive.

Ryder turns in his seat to look for what has sucked all the joy from my face. He rests his hand on my arm. "Billie, Spooner is doing great."

My head snaps to him. "What?"

"I brought him home with me. Here." He pulls out his phone and shows me the lock screen. It's a pic of Spooner sitting in my chair in Ryder's backyard in front of the most glorious sunset.

"Hey. He took my chair."

"He's only keeping it warm until you get back."

"He looks so happy."

"He should be. He gets steak and bacon every day. And he won't leave my side." He taps into the photos on his phone. Spooner's hovering over a bowl of bacon pieces and I swear he's smiling. I swipe to the next one. Spooner's splashing in the ocean, a huge stick in his mouth.

"I put his doggie bed at the foot of my bed since I couldn't get him to leave my bedroom when I went to sleep. Check this out." He swipes to the next video and hits play.

Spooner may be in the video somewhere, but I can't pull my eyes from the view of a shirtless Ryder in bed talking so sweetly. "Hey, love bug. You get scared last night? Had to hop up in bed?"

I may have imagined Ryder keeping watch over me while I slept, but my imagination didn't do him justice. I had no idea he could look so hot and sweet at the same time. I can promise my future daydreams will be much more accurate.

He looks into the camera and laughs. "I wonder who spoiled him so much that he thinks he owns the place?"

And I wonder who Ryder was making this video for. It seems like it was filmed to send to someone, not just to record the moment. Has he been talking to an Imaginary Billie too? "You can't blame me for his lack of manners. I never let him sleep in my bed."

"I can't say no to that sweet face." He holds up the pic as proof. "And I think he misses you."

"I miss him too. So much it hurts." *Almost as much as missing you.*

I swipe to find the next video, but instead of Spooner's cute little face, I'm greeted with a picture of a table covered in food and wrappers and half-eaten pizza and beer cans everywhere. And the couch behind the mess looks exactly like Ryder's. So, maybe he hasn't been as sad as I have been picturing him. More like he's been partying.

"What's this?" I turn the phone his way.

He clenches his lips together and forces out a breath through his nose, before turning to look off to my right. "Just an old pic JJ sent to me when I went off the rails. It's nothing." He swings one leg over the bench seat so his whole body is turned away from me.

I know he had a really rough time when he left the Navy, but that picture looks more recent. I mean it's *after* the Spooner pics. He wouldn't have done that to himself because of me. Right?

I study his face, looking for any clues as to what it's been like for him since I bailed, but he is not letting on about anything.

"You want to play?" he asks, finally turning back to me for my answer.

I give him a *what on earth are you talking about* look.

He points to where he was staring moments ago.

I follow his hand toward the covered patio filled with old arcade games. "Sure."

He throws a few quarters into Target Terror and hands me the plastic gun. "Ladies first."

I take the gun and get in my shooting stance, which in reality is more like a tennis stance since I've never shot a real gun.

Ryder points over my shoulder at the screen. "You know not to shoot the kids or old ladies, right?"

I turn my head to give him my best duh look, but when I do, he is so close, my face can only scream, *Holy crap, I want to kiss you.*

I try to throttle the dizzying tide washing over me, but when Ryder gazes at me, I can feel it in the air between us. His whole being seems to be filled with longing.

"You ready?" he asks in a husky tone.

Hell, yes. I have been waiting for you to kiss me since the day I met you.

He leans forward and loudly taps the start button. I force the disappointment from my face, hoping he doesn't see the eagerness that is written all over it.

It isn't until the game announces Round One that I can pull my eyes from his face, but I cannot get the screen to come into focus. The only thing my mind can hold is the fact that Ryder's hand is now resting on the small of my back as he points to the screen and says, "Don't forget that one."

By the time I swing my weapon over there, the bad guy has disappeared again. With Ryder standing so close, there is no hope of me finding a single terrorist with my imaginary bullets. I think in the end, I hit two and kill about twenty-three grandmas and fifty-six kids.

Ryder slides a few more quarters in and I hand the gun over. He immediately falls into fighter mode. Feet spread, gun resting in two hands like it's an extension of himself. He presses the gun forward and with one shot each takes down every single terrorist before they've even fully appeared on screen, avoiding every little old lady and child, not missing a beat when he has to shoot off-screen to reload.

His focus gives me the chance to study him, his biceps flexing as he moves the gun left and right, his core tightening with each movement as I attempt to restrain myself from wrapping my arms around his waist so I can feel each motion in addition to observing it.

As the next level loads, he turns to me and, with an irresistibly devastating grin, says, "You impressed?"

Completely caught off-guard by the confidence of his smile, all I can do is nod.

He smiles as he holds my gaze while taking down four more evil villains without even looking.

I've never really seen Ryder in action. I know he is a highly skilled warrior and is the absolute best at his job, but to see those skills on display, right in front of me is a whole other beast. His lightning-fast reflexes and preternatural accuracy is damned well near the sexiest thing I've ever seen. I now understand why women everywhere go nuts for guys in his line of work.

By the time he is finished, he has earned the third-highest score. When the game asks for his initials he types in BHF. I raise my eyebrows, asking for an explanation.

He just smiles.

And then I get it. Biovandal Hoodie Fan.

Chapter 25

RYDER

I have to admit, I might have been showing off a bit by building a fire from nothing. Well, "nothing" if you don't count the stack of firewood I picked up while ducking into the Bluewater Corner Store before we crossed back over the Intracoastal to this deserted barrier island.

We dragged our boards up a sand pathway that quickly disappeared into shrubs and tall grasses. At the top of a small berm, we dropped everything and I built a fire while Billie tried to sneak a peek into the bag I kept hidden from her since we hit that store. I might have packed in a couple supplies to last us through the night.

At least in my book, it's not a perfect day without a sunset, a few treats around the campfire, and sleeping out under the stars. I'm hoping Billie will agree. She's sitting next to me on the blanket I spread out in front of the fire, staring out to the horizon in silence. And that silence is beginning to worry me.

I wrap an arm around her, and she settles into it, really cozying up to me. Now to get her talking. "Is it story time yet? I'm dying to know how Peru ends."

She hops up and begins digging through her bag.

I try again. "Telling stories is what you do around a campfire isn't it?"

She pulls out a pair of blue sweats and a sweatshirt and puts them on. "As long as you're the one telling the story," she deflects.

Still not ready to talk. Good copy.

She sits back down and snuggles up against me. At least I haven't fully pushed her away. Looks like it's time for a distracting story from me to get her mind off things. "What kind of a story do you want? A scary story? A funny story?"

She tugs her sleeves down over her hands before looking up at me. "Tell me how you became a... well, you know."

"So, a horror story then? Awesome."

"Only if you want," she says sweetly.

How can I deny that adorable face pleading for something, anything, to get her thoughts far away from what's troubling her right now?

"Same old story, I guess. My dad was a real shit. I knew early on that college wasn't an option—not in my family, at least— and the only skills I had were protecting my little brother from that Shit and making sure we both had everything we needed and unfortunately, that doesn't go too far on a job resume. I read this book in my freshman English class, *Men with Green Faces*, and I knew right then who I was meant to be."

"You knew that early what you were meant to do? Damn, I'm still trying to figure that out."

"Yep, fourteen and I knew. I started training right then. I was this tiny kid, no muscle, no skills, so I began lifting weights and swimming. I joined cross country and water polo. I would do these super long hikes on the weekends with a weighted pack, you know, to the top of Haleakala or the Mahana Ridge Trail. I'd train every summer at 0500 and I'd come home from three hours of morning PT and my buddies would still be asleep."

"So, you've always been this disciplined?"

"Not really. Before that, I was the laziest guy around. I barely showed up to school. Spent most of my time screwing around at the skate park. Getting into trouble. But the second I heard about the SEALs, I knew. I was going to be the ultimate protector.

Nothing was going to stop me. The funny thing is, I spent more years training for the teams than I actually spent on them."

Not sure funny is the right word. Maybe fucked up? After all that, the training, the hell in BUDS, and school after school, I was sidelined by something that nearly every human on earth can handle. Hell, even babies can deal with it. But my entire life gets taken away by bread. Fucking bread.

I toss another log on the fire. This is supposed to be a happy distraction for Billie. No need to go all dark on her. I have to change the subject.

I look down at her wrapped up in my arms now and realize, I've seen those sweats before. Hell, I've worn those sweats before. "So, that's where those went." I pull both of the strings to the hoodie.

She ducks her head, and says sheepishly, "You said I could borrow them." She wraps her arms around herself. "Please don't take them away from me."

"They're yours," I say, tucking my hands behind my head as I lay back.

She takes a while but eventually follows, wrapping herself in my arms just as close as before. I run my fingers along her arm, more as a distraction to myself than for her. She rolls over, resting her head on my chest, forcing her eyes open again and again, like a toddler in her high chair refusing to sleep until it finally overpowers her. I've been that toddler, too, never able to get my brain to unwind enough to sleep. Or too terrified of what it would conjure up if I did.

I wonder if she is even aware. I was lucky enough to have a team of guys who recognized it immediately. Who told me what was going on. Billie doesn't have that team. But she has me.

"Hey, Billie, you know you..." I search for the words to bridge this subject with grace. In their absence, I shoot for succinct. "that you have..."

I take in her face, fully relaxed for the first time today. Maybe less direct is better. I technically don't know for sure. "Do you ever think..."

Shit. This should be easier.

I turn away from her, resting my head on my other arm still tucked behind my head. The sun is long gone now, the last dying embers of dusk are quickly receding toward the land.

Billie slowly begins drawing circles on my chest, pulling me back to her. Maybe instead of assuming I know what she's dealing with, I merely share what I've been through.

"When I came back after…" After summer camp? After hell? How do you describe that place? Those places? "After. Things were different. I was different. Loud noises? They'd take me someplace. I'd react to stuff that wasn't really there. Sleep was painful or non-existent. I'd see things, people who weren't there. People who weren't anywhere anymore."

I turn back to her, watching her face for signs of acknowledgment. "It was like the pieces of my head would all tumble out for no reason, without warning, and I couldn't figure out how to put them back."

I trace her arm with my finger while I plan my next tack. "Do you ever feel like that since, uh… since… you left?"

Billie, turning it over in her mind, can only manage a nod in agreement as we both let the weight of it bury us in our separate recollections of our pain.

She ekes out a whisper. "What did… I mean, how'd you fix it?"

"Some people talk to someone, a therapist. I wasn't ready for that right away. So, I learned about it. Podcasts, books, scientific papers, whatever I could get my hands on. And I tried just about everything to see what would work for my physiology. Keto diet, supplements, sleep hygiene, even TMS therapy.

"It?" she asks.

"What?"

"You said you learned about it. What's 'it'?"

I say it slowly, letting each word sink in. "Post. Traumatic. Stress."

She can't stymie the tears any longer. I pull her closer as she melts into a pile of tears, held together only by the strength of my arms around her.

"Billie, wake up. You're going to miss it."

I picked our campsite for exactly this reason. At the high point on this barrier island, we have an unobstructed view of the horizon over the water. Billie may be freaked out by the concept of the sun setting over land, but no matter how bad things have turned, there is always a bright side. And today, that bright side is that she gets to witness sunrise over the ocean.

Billie peacefully wakes. "Miss what?"

"Sunrise over the water."

The sun slowly pushes itself over the horizon. First, the navy blues are chased away by cyan. Lines of rippled clouds light up in a hazy crimson, their tops still a deep purple. Tangerine washes over the horizon, then the first sliver of canary creeps above the ocean. Its reflection streaks across the tranquil water. We watch in awe as this spectacle fills our eyes.

"You know what they say about red sky at morning?" Billie asks, looking for something to go wrong.

"Maybe. If you're three miles out on the water."

She relaxes a little into my arms and we sit, content to be experiencing this everyday occurrence that somehow feels like it is becoming a fleeting memory even before it has fully happened.

Yesterday, we were playing pretend. Pretending Billie hasn't fled Maui without a word, leaving a staggeringly colossal hole in her wake. Pretending that we are back home and everything is normal. Pretending that I have any idea where we go from here.

"Billie, why am I here?"

"Because..." It looks like there's a disconnect between her brain and mouth. I can see her mind moving, but nothing will come out. It is finally broken by the one thing she still knows to be true. "I missed you, too."

Those four little words blanket me in a boundless peace. She misses me, too. Still wrapped up in my arms, she considers me, an almost hopeful glint in her eyes.

It is far too easy to get lost in the way she looks at me. I hesitate until my longing to know what her lips feel like melts my resolve. I lower my mouth to hers, and it takes everything I have not to lay her down on this deserted island and continue. I linger for a moment feeling her breath on my lips before touching my forehead to hers.

She lifts her head and beams up at me before contentedly wrapping herself back into my arms. The kiss leaves me weak, my heart overflowing with the joy I usually have to borrow from Billie and I want to lean down and do it again.

Searching for a distraction before I ruin the sweet simplicity of that first kiss, I move to the bag that I have been holding onto since I got here and pull out an old shirt with a T&C cartoon design of a surfing gorilla slamming into the pier pylon under a black-and-white magazine cutout of a group of onlookers atop the pier. In typical 80s neon, it reads, "Pier Pressure." Billie had been seeking out this one to complete her collection of all the original Steve Nazar designs for years. I hand it to her.

She unfurls it and hugs it to her chest. "No way! I love it. Where'd you find it?"

"A guy down the street from me was having a garage sale."

Billie strips down to her bikini top and slips the shirt over her head. "It's so soft, too. It's perfect."

She closes the distance between us. Standing on tiptoe, she wraps her arms around me and I don't miss the opportunity to kiss her again.

After a short paddle back into town, and returning our boards, we find a cute waterfront breakfast place that offers gluten-free pancakes but is suspiciously filled with pictures that make me believe we might still be on a fangirl tour of this town.

After filling up on more carbs than I have consumed all year, we stroll along the boardwalk. As we peer into the front window of an art supply store, Billie slides her hand into mine.

My heart is going a million miles an hour with each beat

reverberating through my chest like an echo across the Grand Canyon, the warmth of her hand only serving to speed it up until I swear, she can hear every thud of the damned organ.

"No way!" Billie sprints across the street, pulling me behind her until we are standing in front of a brick wall, her hand still in mine.

I begin to worry that maybe she is more broken than I had realized until she takes in a deep breath and lets it out in a giant smile. Her entire body relaxes like she has finally found the last missing piece of her journey.

I scan the wall. The small, dark-covered patio in front of it. The young tree in a sidewalk cutout. Looks like a whole lot of nothing to me. So, I check her face for any signs that this is an actual place of significance and not the ramblings of a crazy person.

She must pick up on my worried face. "Sorry. It's just that this is the wall."

"*The* wall?" I tease, still not knowing what the heck she is talking about.

"In *Dawson's Creek*, it's where Pacey paints his message to Joey, the girl he loved, the one that changed everything. It read, 'Ask me to...'" The thought seems to stop her in her tracks, like they opened some box of mysteries that, suddenly, she has to grapple with. Her gaze lifts to mine and I'm just as lost for words as she is.

"It was a significant moment for him and Joey," she explains just before the skies open up and unleash a tropical deluge. I pull her from her trance and we hustle to find a doorway to get out of the drenching showers.

Once under the overhang, she laughs infectiously as we swipe the water from our bodies. I run my hand over my short hair, flinging droplets of water her way. She lays a hand on my chest playfully pushing me away, the mere touch of her hand sending a warming shiver through me.

With nowhere to go but back out in the rain, I lounge confidently against the other side of the passageway, giving her whatever space she needs. But I send a coy smile her way, reminding her I'm ready for a replay of our kiss earlier this morning, eyes full of promises I fully intend to keep.

Her lean figure saunters towards me with a glint of wonder in her eyes. She smiles, thinking about her next move. Standing on tiptoe, she touches her lips to mine.

I return her kiss with reckless abandon. Hands on her hips, I spin her, press her against the wall, and cover her mouth with mine.

Raising my lips from hers, I whisper her name, before caging her in with my arms and leaning in to plant light kisses down her neck.

She, in turn, sets her hands on my chest.

And shoves me.

Then ducks around the corner.

I guess she isn't quite ready for romance. But I'll take playful, flirty Billie anytime. I round the corner to chase her, but by the time I do, she is a good twenty meters away.

And moving at a speed that is not at all playful. She has bolted.

I pursue her, but by the time I reach the corner, she is nowhere to be found. I don't know where she learned these counter-surveillance techniques, but she should be teaching them at Green Teams.

As I race in the direction she disappeared, I'm held up by a train waiting at the station and catch a glimpse of Billie ducking behind a uniformed man beside it. I sprint towards her.

"Stand clear of the closing doors," the announcement rings out.

As the train doors close, Billie slips onto the train before I even have a chance to move. She collapses into a window seat and we briefly make eye contact as the train begins pulling away. She must see the pain etched into my face because she hangs her head a split second later.

And once more, Billie is gone.

Gone without warning.

Without a word.

But this time I can follow her.

The attendant on the platform walks a young boy back to his frazzled mom busy with her four other unruly children.

I interrupt him as he passes. "Where does that train go?"

"Seventeen stops before it hits Key West."

Shit. "So, straight into oblivion?"

"I suppose," he says kindly.

"Fantastic."

Could I drive to the next stop and make it there before the train does? I pull up the train schedule and Google Maps and cross reference the times. Next stop is Myrtle Beach in fifty-eight minutes. Google says by car that would take ninety minutes, so feasibly I could make it in seventy. But that would still be eighteen minutes too late. The rest of the stops would be even worse. I'd need to call in a helicopter to get me there in time and I just don't have those resources anymore.

I lock my eyes on the train that is swiftly pulling Billie from my life once again and am immovable as it slowly dissolves into the coastal haze.

She left.

She up and left again.

And I have no clue what drove her to it.

After a perfect day, an unbelievable morning, I thought I finally had my Billie back. More than back. I could be entirely myself without having to put JJ's wants ahead of mine. Without having to hold back anything.

And I still couldn't keep her.

Chapter 26

BILLIE

What the hell did I just do? One second we are walking hand in hand along the boardwalk, peeking in store windows, making out in the rain, and the next my heart is slamming around inside my chest, I'm drenched in sweat, and the only thing I can think is, run.

Run.

RUN.

My head was screaming for me to run and I was helpless to do anything but listen. So, I ran.

But now that I'm held captive on this train, speeding away from the only comfort I have found in the last month, I have no idea why.

Why seeing Ryder lean in to kiss me sent me into a primal terror.

Why I couldn't do anything but obey that stupid voice.

The entire time I've been here, the only thing I have wanted is to be able to talk to Ryder, to have him hold me, and tell me everything was going to be okay. And, just when I have that, I bolt.

It doesn't make sense. That's not me. I don't run from things. I'm not scared.

Or, at least, the old me wouldn't have run.

This new me, this one is a mystery. I cry without warning. I shake and tremble. I'm afraid of everything. And I run from the one person who has been any solace to me. This new me, she is hopeless. And I'm not sure how much longer I can go on being her. Something has to change.

As the tracks near the Intracoastal Waterway, they bring homes on the opposite banks into view. Stately mansions with long docks out back, little white bungalows with bright blue roofs. Houses of all shapes and sizes keep watch over the waters as they drift by.

I know Ryder said I have post-traumatic stress, but I'm not a soldier. I haven't been to war. What happened to me is not the same. Nothing even actually happened to me. Kavika didn't *do* anything. All I know is I am broken and completely alone. I can't go on like this. Something has to change.

When the train finally stops, I hop off and pull my bike from the rack for the long ride home. The songs of crickets and cicadas fill the thick salt air as the monotonous hum of my tires against the pavement lulls me into a spiritless motion, legs spinning up and down, up and down, mindlessly.

Turning at the library onto my street, I let my legs ease up.

Library.

Ryder kept trying to show me proof that Kavika and his boys were locked up. That JJ wasn't involved. But, I refused to listen to him. *No phones. No internet. No trace of me.*

Though, I could use a computer in the library without having to sign in with my name.

I slow to a stop and let my gaze drift from the road ahead to the library sign over my shoulder. Even if it were all a lie, they still couldn't track me.

I swing my bike around and ride toward the library. Once inside, cool air engulfs me, sending chills down my back. I meander towards the computers lined up against the back window with a view of the marsh grass, not sure I can handle seeing JJ again, even if it is just a picture on a screen. But I have to know.

I slide into a chair, type in his full name Detective John

Gerdis, along with Maui PD and Kavika Kinske, and let my hand hover over the Enter button.

"Five minutes 'till closing," the librarian sings out.

That's all the warning I need. I scamper towards the door, grateful that I don't have to face him today. When I finally make it home, I collapse into bed in my clothes, too tired from the long weekend to even care, as scenes from our perfect day flash through my head.

The moment right before we jumped off the pier when Ryder knew exactly what I wanted to do without me having to say a word. And those kisses. Damn. Who knew just kissing could be so hot? Falling asleep wrapped in Ryder's arms. It was the first time in a long time that I slept without fear. I wish I had those arms around me tonight.

The look of confusion on Ryder's face when I stood awestruck in front of a blank brick wall. I know it sounds stupid to somehow find validation or direction from a TV show, but something just clicked for me in that place. Standing in front of that wall, I could still see the words, "Ask me to stay," hastily, yet adoringly written in red paint, as if the producer had left it up there after filming.

It was a plea from that boy to a girl who was always running from the things she wanted. He needed to know that she wasn't finished with him yet. And he knew, he had always known, exactly how to push this girl to be her best. From the very first moment they met. All it would have taken to get him to stick around forever was for her to ask.

For some reason, it felt like Ryder had written that for me. Like he was begging me just to reach out and ask him to stay with me. But I couldn't even do that right. There is nothing I wanted more than for Ryder to stay forever, but instead, I completely freaked out, ran away, and hopped a train speeding in the exact opposite direction.

Not very Joey of me.

But maybe it's time I try.

And it starts with finding out the truth about Kavika.

The next morning, when the librarian approaches the front door, I'm already sitting against the cold stone wall outside, waiting. I push to my feet as she pulls the keys from her cardigan pocket and unlocks the door.

"Important search, Dear?"

"Something like that," I reply.

"Well, come on in."

Hesitantly at first, then feverishly, I read everything I can find on Kavika. From the story about his arrest to a column in some obscure Surfing magazine from the late 90s to features about the wide-reaching arms of his crime.

So, Kavika is behind bars and probably won't ever be out again. One write-up even mentioned that his crimes were so serious and numerous that he might be tried for the death penalty. And several of his top men got picked up in the takedown, too.

The one that really catches my eye is the article with a picture of the U.S. Attorney General. Behind him stands an unnamed JJ alongside some other officers I don't recognize above a headline that reads, "Maui's Alleged Mob Boss Has A Well-Documented Life of Crime and Violence." It describes how he uncovered the site they used for the past decade to bury evidence of their numerous murders.

I get up and mill about in the cool air, trying to wrap my head around this new information. JJ wasn't dirty. He was just doing his job. And I somehow got wrapped up in it.

I stroll along the carpet filled with patterns of tropical fish and follow them to the back wall of the library.

Those guys are all gone now. They'll be in jail for years while awaiting trial and probably a lot longer once they are convicted. It might be safe to go home.

To see all the people I love.

To see Ryder again.

See him and then act like a complete idiot in front of him

when my brain melts down again? It's not just Kavika who is keeping me from home. It's my broken head.

Either way, I've wasted enough time in this library. I've got to get back to work to keep supporting my life in Hammerhead Key and stop daydreaming about everything going back to the way it was before all this happened because that is simply not going to happen. Not with my brain still completely screwed up.

I run my fingers along the seagrass encased in epoxy that makes up the end of each row of books as I read the topics. Food & Travel. Business. Psychology. History.

I take two steps back. Psychology. Ryder mentioned that he read about PTS. I wonder if they have anything on it here even if it's not what I actually have.

I walk down the aisle until the titles turn to trauma. *What Happened To You?* A little judgmental, don't you think?

Struggle Well? With a pic of a combat veteran on the front, I don't think that one's for me.

The Body Keeps Score? It sure feels like mine has.

Shoot. I'll just take them all. I pull any book with trauma in the title, practically clearing out the whole section, piling them up until I can't carry any more.

Loading the books into my bike rack, the smallest glimmer of hope shines from the horizon. Maybe there is some way I can put myself back together.

After four hours sanding down a twenty-eight-foot Danish cutter, my eyes slowly drift over to the blinking light on top of my bag. I made one more stop before heading into work this morning. After the success I found by breaking my *No internet* rule, I decided to break one more of my rules. I bought a phone and had the guy hook it up to my old number, complete with my old voicemails and texts. I didn't have the courage to read or listen to any of them, but it's been beaming at me ever since.

"Think it's time to call it a day, hon?" Rusty suggests. "Go out and enjoy the evening before it's over."

"I'll try." I clean up my area and head towards the door.

"You coming to the Pub with us?" Rooster asks.

"Not tonight. Maybe some other time," I reply and, for the first time, I think I may actually mean it.

"I'm gonna hold you to that."

I nod and put my hood back up as I head out the door.

At home, while lying in bed, my backpack stares at me from the foot of the bed. I've been putting it off all night, busying myself by cooking some mac and cheese, taking an extra long shower, and making the bed for the first time with actual sheets I pulled from the windows today. But everywhere I go, the blinking light screams at me. Even buried at the bottom of my pack, it calls out.

I stretch my leg to capture the strap and slowly drag the bag towards me. Digging my hand inside the middle pocket, a wrinkled paper grabs my attention. I retrieve the pic I forced to the furthest recesses of my bag earlier and unfold the half with JJ on it, trying to smooth the wrinkles. For the first time, I don't shudder when I look at his face.

I turn the phone on and pull up the voicemails. It lights up with a plethora of texts and voice messages. Some from friends back home, a few to remind me to vote in the next election, and tons from my parents, but those have been piling up unanswered for years now.

Scrolling back to that day, I see one from JJ. I tap the message, but let it play out before putting the speaker to my ear.

It was a practice run. That's all.

I try again, this time succeeding in listening. "Hey, Babe. I need you to do something for me. And it's really important. I need you to stay in Nalu Kai today. I know the only place breaking today is up in Fourmile's, but please, whatever you do, don't leave Nalu Kai. It's really important. Promise me you won't leave. I can explain later. Just promise me."

That morning, I was so sure I was going to break up with him that when I saw his face light up on my phone, I sent it to voicemail.

I screwed it all up. Every last bit of it. JJ tried to warn me and, I was so selfish, I refused to even take his call. Then I blamed him. I assumed he was some sort of evil monster who was trying to get me mixed up in his drug deals and would hunt me down afterwards to keep me quiet. How could I have possibly thought he'd do that?

And to pay him back for attempting to protect me, I bailed without a word. Radio silence for months.

But that's what I do. I bail. Push people away. I did the same thing after Brent. I went for years without talking to my folks or Piper. It was like I thought I could just walk away from it all and start a new life so I could just ignore all the pain. If I didn't see anyone who knew Brent, I wouldn't have to feel it.

And here I am, doing it once again. But this time, instead of moving to the other side of the island and not returning calls, I flew to the other side of the country and completely destroyed my phone.

The pot on the stove boils over and I jump to yank it off the flame. My mac is mushy and swollen, but I can't afford to waste it, so I mix up a squishy bowl of cheese sludge and flop on the sofa next to my stack of books. I pick *The Body Keeps Score* and skim the contents. Based in Neuroscience, stories from vets *and* kids, and a huge chunk on how to recover. Might be something in here to help.

The first sentence gives me even more hope. "One does not have to be a combat soldier, or visit a refugee camp in Syria or the Congo to encounter trauma."

I read that sentence over and over, through eyes blurred by tears.

Ryder could be right.

I say the words slowly.

Out loud.

Post. Traumatic. Stress.

It's a declaration.

Proclamation.

Acceptance.

I have post-traumatic stress.

And an insatiable desire to find out more.

Chapter 27

RYDER

On my flight home, the seat next to mine sits empty. It was the one Billie was supposed to be in when I brought her home with me. But I failed.

I should have known. Seen it. I could see the signs of her PTS. I knew the recommendations for a dating moratorium after trauma. But once again, I put my needs ahead of someone else's. I put my selfishness ahead of duty. Ahead of what I knew was right.

And I got the same shitty result.

Now, how exactly do I explain all of this to JJ?

I was hoping that by bringing Billie home, JJ would be so happy about it, he would overlook the fact that I lied to him about the trip.

Who knows if she'll ever reach out again? I took the one chance anyone had of bringing her home and, instead, ensured that no one will ever see her again. Now I have to go tell, not only JJ, but Charlie, Greyson, Finn, Piper, and Riley. I have to tell every one of them that I couldn't bring her home.

By the time Maui comes into view through my window, I move on from my wallowing and construct my plan of attack. I won't let this time destroy me like the first time she left. No dabbling in gluten. No flaking on the job. No punishing myself with fights. No drinking.

ERIN SPINETO

I have to employ the old strategies that helped me the first time. *Take action. Maintain order. Breathe. Your brain will heal.* I'll take extreme ownership of my part in all of this and tell everyone, all at once, at Game Night. And I'll take all their anger at my shortcomings.

Then I'll get my ass up and get my life back on track. Work hard. Book all the trips I can. Be a hospitable captain and stop taking it out on my guests. I'll make my workouts and eat the right things. Discipline in body and mind.

And it works. I'm up early the next morning for a swim, and Spooner seems to sense the change. He is ready to join the discipline train. He lines up in the sand, glances up at me, and sprints into the water before I do. I follow after him, totally surprised that he is able to keep up. He matches me stroke for stroke all the way to the quarter-mile buoy and back.

Later that evening, I make sure to arrive a little late to Game Night; I only want to have to say this once. I throw my pickup in park and try to settle myself for what I know is coming.

In the yard, Greyson lugs the cooler toward the fire pit where everyone has already gathered, ready for another night of fun. Little do they know that I'm showing up to destroy it.

I hold open the truck door for Spooner to hop out. I bend to pet him and, maybe, to stall a bit. Two painfully slow steps from my vehicle and JJ slaps a hand on my shoulder like nothing has happened. "Hey man, how was the charter?"

I can only shake my head.

"That bad? Cougars or know-it-all dumbasses?"

"Take a seat and I'll tell you."

He pulls a beer from the cooler and sits between Finn and Greyson. "Nice. It's story time."

I remain standing. Not going to be here too long. "I need to tell you all something. You think you could listen up for a minute?"

Charlie and Piper stop their conversation with Harley. Great, Harley's here, too. One more person who gets to witness my screwup.

"I have some info on Billie and then I'll take off." Everyone perks up, ready for any bit of information I can give them as I struggle to find the words I prepared while staring at the ceiling all last night.

"Read us in," Harley orders like she's being given an intelligence brief from her dad, Savage.

"She reached out last week. She's on the east coast." This brings a smile to Piper and Charlie, reassured they know where she is.

"Let's go get her," JJ demands.

"It's not going to be that easy. I went to go see her and she's in a bad way."

"You saw her?" JJ stands. "That weekend charter you said you had?"

"Let him talk, JJ," Piper tries to calm the situation.

But JJ is right to be pissed. I lied. I should have told him. And brought him.

"She's dealing with a lot from what happened with Kavika and it's taken a toll on her. I tried to bring her home. I tried."

"Which is exactly why you should have taken me," JJ barks. "I could have talked to her. Convinced her to come home. She would have listened to me."

Like she listened to you at Kavika's?

Wait. No excuses, Jax. Take ownership.

"You're right. I'm sorry."

"Where is she now?" JJ stalks towards me.

South of Wilmington? Somewhere in the Southeast? "I don't know, man. She took off before I could ask."

"You didn't ask? What did you do in this shitty recovery op? I thought you did this kind of thing for a living. It's no wonder you got fired."

That's one step too far. I get in his face.

He's smart enough to back down. "Whatever, man. I'm done." Long strides eat up the distance to his truck, followed by a dust cloud as he speeds off the gravel driveway.

I turn to the group waiting for the retreat of each of them. "I know I screwed up. I wish I could have brought her back to you guys. You all deserve to have her in your lives. I'm sorry."

Charlie stands and heads my way. I've seen her hitting the

heavy bag; I prepare myself for a solid right hook. But instead, she wraps me in a generous hug. "I know how much this must be killing you." And she stays there, holding me. "I know you did your best. Sometimes you have to wait for a person to be ready for your help. She'll come back when she's ready."

She pulls back and captures my gaze. "And she will come back, Ryder. Her home is here. We are, too. Especially you."

It's the first sliver of hope I've had. Maybe I'm important enough to her to convince her to come home.

Charlie releases me from her grasp. "Ryder, we all forgive you."

How could they? How could they look past all that I screwed up? Forget it? But her face convinces me. There's no hatred or derision there. Just welcoming love. I scan the other faces around the fire and find the same thing.

Greyson takes a long draw from his beer. "Are we gonna play some Mafia or what?"

I barely say a word during the game, my head far too wrapped up in sorting through the two things I never thought I'd get tonight; forgiveness and hope. As the night ends, Finn hands me another cider and drops into the seat next to mine, his silent signal for, "Hey, can we talk?"

I settle back in my chair, waiting for rare words from Finn.

"Let me know if you ever want to talk with someone who gets it."

"And who would that be?" In all the years I've known Finn, I haven't heard him talk about any girl, so I'm not sure how he could be any help.

"Me, man. I get it." He tugs at his beard while I wait to see if that's all he's got to say. "It's been five years since I've seen or talked to Em. Unless you count the one card I got from her on the one-year anniversary of the day I fucked it all up."

"She was your girlfriend?"

He runs a hand through his hair, pulling at the strands. "In the truest sense of the word. She was the best friend I ever had."

"And she left?" Sometimes you have to lead Finn to keep him talking.

He shakes his head. "I did. And I never figured out how to go back."

What if Billie never comes back? If I never see her again. I can muscle my way through life, disciplining myself so I get things done, but without her, I'm not sure I'll ever be happy again.

Maybe that's why Finn is eternally quiet. Without Em, he just can't find the joy in anything.

He taps my knee with the back of his hand. "But, Billie? She figured it out once, she'll figure it out again. You were the one she reached out to, Jax. That means something."

I take a long draw from my cider, hoping to gain the strength to ask the one question I've been afraid to ask.

What if I'm not enough for her?

But the strength doesn't come.

Chapter 28

RYDER

SAVAGE: Get your ass over here.

Not the way I wanted to wake up this morning. But in all reality, nothing short of Billie showing up on my front porch would fix this misery.

Ryder: Give me some time. Got some shit to do.

SAVAGE: By 1800. No excuses.

I have nothing to do today, but I won't be ready to be civil to anyone anytime soon.

After a long swim and staring out at the water for hours upon hours, her chair sitting empty beside me, reminding me of what I can never truly have in the way I really want, I make my way to Savage's. When I get there, he brings out a four-pack of Woodchuck Hard Cider, hands me one, and I know I'm in for it. He never goes out of his way to have cider on hand.

Harley pulls a grocery bag from the fridge and sets it on the counter. "You guys should go catch the sunset. Looks like it'll be a good one tonight. I'll start prepping the veggies in here, give you boys some privacy. Let me know when you're ready for dinner."

Savage leads me out the back door to low benches surrounding a fire pit. "So, how'd you screw it up with her?" he starts.

"With who?"

"Don't give me that shit. Billie. What'd you do?"

"I haven't screwed up anything. My *Others First* theory stops me from that."

His laughter had a sharp edge. "Where'd you come up with that stupid theory?"

I give him a look that says, *Shit man, why isn't this obvious?*

He waits for a real answer from me. "When putting myself first caused the shitshow with Emma."

"So tell me, what happened to Emma?"

"What the hell, Savage? You know what happened."

"I want to hear you tell me."

Knowing there is no fighting with Savage, or really, there is no winning a fight with Savage, I give in. "Fine." I toss my bottle into the can at the foot of the deck behind us. "I wussed out of that last mission. Decided I had to go home and baby myself. Get some R and R. And they throw Potter in my place because I couldn't get my shit together in time for them to give you a real teammate."

"I could handle Potter," Savage fires back.

"Potter was so busy fighting you on every decision that you were late getting back to TOC which gave the ADF enough time to find them, to find Emma, and..." I can't unearth the words.

"And what?" Savage demands.

I let my head fall into my hands. "And they shot her. They stuck a gun in her face and pulled the trigger. Do you know what that must have been like for her? She shouldn't have had to go through that. She was an analyst for God's sake. She shouldn't have had to deal with that."

"So, you killed Emma?" he prods.

I crack open another cider. "Fuck."

"Jax. Did you kill Emma?" Savage asks.

"Yeah. I killed her. You happy now?" I shout.

He lets my statement hang in the air.

I take a sip from the bottle, but it's as bitter as the words I let slip off my tongue.

Savage tosses another log on the fire before sitting back down. "So you think you should have gone into a mission so sick you could hardly stand and *that* would have had a better outcome?"

"Come on, Ollie North had dysentery when he raided the DMZ in Vietnam. He assaulted that place with shit running down his pants. And I can't get over a little GI distress from eating bread?"

"Look man, don't get me wrong, dysentery is bad, and Ollie was a rock star for doing that, but you didn't just have a bacterial infection. Your entire GI system was on fire and had been for way too long. You hadn't absorbed any nutrition for months. You had no strength to even lift your arms. I saw it. You were in awful shape." He sits forward in his chair, settling his gaze on me. "If you didn't pull yourself out before that mission, I would have done it for you. I thought it would be easier for you in the long run if you were the one to make that call. But from the looks of it, I probably should have been the one to do it. You've done a fine job of kicking the shit out of yourself for it all these years. I would have much rather you'd been pissed at me."

"It's still my fault. I was the one who couldn't go."

"I'm sorry to tell you, Brother, but you are not that powerful."

"What?"

"You heard me. I know we're all a proud lot, but, shit, Jax, you are not in control of everything. You cannot intercept every bad thing. And you're not called to." He turns to me and rests his hand on my shoulder. "God only calls you to love and protect your own and be as prepared as you can to help. He never asks you to prevent all the evil in this world. That's impossible. Not even I can do that. If He's gonna let it happen, you couldn't stop it if you tried."

"But I should have—"

Savage steps into my words. "Enough. The only thing you need to do is sit here in silence and think about what I just said. Don't try to come up with every reason in the book why I don't know what I'm talking about. Just absorb it."

"Sure," I grumble, but there's no way I actually agree. And he knows it.

"Fine. Then listen to Emma."

"What the hell does that mean?"

"You knew her, right? Pretty well, if I remember correctly," he says with a knowing grin. "She's up in Heaven, totally enlightened. She's been filled in on all the details. Does she think it's all your fault?"

Fuck. That's the last thing I want to think about. The only image I can pull up is the look on her face when those assholes burst into the room and shoved a muzzle in her face. It's the same scene that has kept me staring at the ceiling all these years. Every single night. All night long.

"You two are sitting in those chairs at the edge of your property. She's got some pink girly cocktail in her hand. You have a Stone Smoked Porter."

I give him a look.

"You don't drink quality beer in your imagination?"

"I guess so."

"So, you're sitting there, and the sun is about to set. The sky's all lit up. And she looks at you and says?"

It's the first time I can see her smile. In my mind, she *smiles* at me, and the tourniquet that has been wrapped around my chest since that day loosens, just a hair. I want to simply sit here and bask in that radiant grin.

Emma takes a sip of her drink and then mutters, "You know, where I'm at now, we have sunsets twenty-four hours a day."

"Of course you do."

"Well, if you think about it, the sun is always setting somewhere on Earth."

That draws a chuckle out of me.

"But I still think this is my favorite place to watch one."

"Even with me here?" I ask sincerely.

"That's the best part."

"Take your time, buddy," Savage interrupts my daydream.

I glance out at Hawea Point which is visible just beyond the fire pit. Following the coast east to the jetty in front of Nalu Kai, I count back four houses to the one I know Emma should be in right now.

"You ask her if she blames you..." Savage prods. "What does she tell you?"

"She says, 'War is brutal. Those assholes are to blame. You

got that, RJ? They are to blame. Not you. You did what I urged you to do; Go home and get better.'"

"She told you to go home?"

I hadn't remembered that until the words are slipping out of my mouth. "Yeah. We were sitting in this watering hole in the Congo and I couldn't finish my beer. And she says, "RJ, man, this isn't right. You're sick. You know that right? You can't tough your way through this. The only thing that's gonna get you better is doctors and medicine and rest. You need to go home and get healthy so I can have my old RJ back. The funny, happy, strong man I depend on out here."

"Emma told you to leave. Is she to blame, then?" he prods.

"Of course not."

"So, that means?"

I don't know why it's so hard to let it go. This guilt has been crushing me since the moment I found out about Emma. I should want to let it go—to get it the hell off my back—still, letting it go feels like I'm letting Emma go all over again. And that's a whole new kind of crushing.

But I force myself to say the words all the same. "I am not to blame."

"Look. I've told you, Emma has told you, and you've said it yourself. You are not to blame. Now you just have to repeat that to yourself as many times as it takes until you believe it down to your very core. And that might take a while to retrain your brain. It's been lying to you for a few years now. You have to blow it out of that old rut and run it over those new words so many times it falls into a new rut. Only this time, the rut will be the truth."

I mutter it under my breath. "I am not to blame." It's gonna take a while before I really believe that, but it is somehow calming to simply hear the words.

I am not to blame.

We settle into silence while my brain tries to process everything.

"You going to throw on those steaks anytime soon?" Harley shouts from the deck behind us.

"You want to stay for dinner?" Savage asks me.

"I could eat."

The kinetics of dinner preparations allows me a little space to make sense of that new revelation, but that is short-lived once we sit. Even though Savage's daughter, Harley, might have learned how to run CQB and break down an AR-15 before she was ten, being raised by a team of SEALs has left her lacking in tact.

"You stopped your crying yet since you spilled your guts at Game Night?"

I turn to Savage. "Is that why you staged this intervention? Harley ratted me out to you?" I look back to Harley. "Is that why you're on-island, to gather intel on me and report back to your dad?" I tease.

"She's my good little sailor," Savage praises.

"Actually, I wanted to check in with you and see how you were feeling about the whole situation, but I've found a lot of you team guys do much better if I don't mention the word feelings," she adds.

"And what do you know about talking to us about feelings?"

Savage leans back in his chair like a proud papa. "You know she's got a Master's in Neurobiology with a focus on PTS in top-tier operators, right? My little girl is the best there is. A perfect combo of knowledge of the inner workings of an operator's mind and all that super-smart sciency stuff."

"Yeah. I guess being raised by you, Hawk, and your team would do that to a girl."

"So, how are you feeling about Billie still being gone?" Harley persists.

"How am I feeling? Shit. I don't know. It's all a mess."

"See, I use that word and you freeze up." She stuffs a bite of garlic bread in her mouth and continues without chewing. "Let's try this, what do you hate the most about the situation?"

That's easy. "I hate that she won't talk to me. I hate that I can't protect her. I hate that I put myself first again and screwed everything up again. I hate that I let JJ down, that I betrayed him." That I went behind his back and kissed his girl. But I'm not opening that can of worms in front of a magic specialist in drilling down on a guy.

"Most. What do you hate the most?"

Really? All that's not enough to appease her? Fine. "I hate that my life is bleak without her in it."

I have no idea how she got that out of me. Harley should be conducting interrogations instead of whatever it is she does.

She leans back in her chair looking just as proud as her dad did, but she says nothing else. No commentary. No insight. No next question. Like the whole point of that operation was for me to just say something.

Not wanting to hear the echo of those words any longer, I try to fill the air. "I just miss the simplicity of being outside the wire. We had one goal. I knew what it was and whether or not I accomplished it. There's no way of knowing if you're doing it right back here."

"Sorry, Jax, but that's life. It's messy and complicated and the only way to know if you're doing it right is if you can surround yourself with great people that you love and who can actually tolerate you. And you don't hate yourself. I say, if you can do those two things, you're doing fine."

After a few more beers, and, thankfully, no more interrogations, Savage decides to put out the fire pit the old-fashioned way, driving Harley and I toward the door. Before I make it too far, he calls me back. "If you're serious about getting back in the game, I might have a job for you."

"What is it?"

"You remember Ambassador Witter. She's now in Nicaragua and her boy needs security there. He's fourteen and way too rebellious to be in that country. The Ambassador needs someone to make sure the boy's not going to make headlines by doing something stupid. Could be perfect for you."

We worked with Ambassador Witter on my first deployment. She was a straight shooter; one of the few politicians I've met who didn't reek of corruption. And she was doing good work with the Hema and Lendu tribes in the Congo to drive peace. She'd be that much more effective if she didn't have to worry about her son.

"Do I have time to think on it?" I ask.

"We'll keep talking, but I'm gonna need a decision by the fifth."

I'd love to be back in the game, but I'm not sure I could leave before knowing that Billie is okay and back home where she belongs.

Chapter 29

BILLIE

Over the next four days, I pour myself into research. I read all the library books I checked out within the first few days and go back for more. I print out all the articles that I can from scientific journals and psychology sites.

One of my favorite books is *Pacing the Cage*, by Scroobius Wilder. It's a small pocket-sized manual, each page with some quote or mantra over a beautiful picture of the ocean or an island. The backside has a little summary of what the phrase means and how to use it. I may have forgotten to return this one to the library. After I cut out all the pages to hang them around my place or keep them with me, I'm not sure they would have wanted it back anyways.

The page that has been in my back pocket since the day I saw it, says, "Action Beats Anxiety." The back explains that when you get stuck in that cycle of fear, doing something small can break you out of it. And that one small success leads you to take on something else a little bigger. And then, before you know it, you have broken out of the anxiety jail.

It also delineates how having a forward center of mass, just moving your body in the forward direction like walking or running, actually suppresses amygdala function which reduces threat detection, anxiety, and fear. I don't know if anything can suppress my amygdala right now, but, with all my research, I have determined to try everything and keep what works. So, I resolve to test it out the next time I feel the panic pressing in.

The more I learn, the more it feels like it's possible for me to recover from this and maybe go home.

Maybe.

It would take a lot to make that happen. Even coming up with the money to fly home is a huge hurdle. And then I'd need money to pay rent once I get there. Maui rents are nearly the highest in the nation, nothing like my current place.

That is if my landlord hasn't evicted me and thrown all my things on the curb for anyone to take. I would have nothing. But I have nothing here and I'm still surviving. I could survive there with nothing, too, I suppose.

After another long day in the soul-crushing heat, I arrive at my empty shack and ultimately decide it's time to go home—to my real home—back to Nalu Kai. But I need to leave my mark here before I set sail. If I don't arrange even a tiny installation, it was like this time never existed. And no matter how incredibly hard this time in my life was, it was mine. And it matters.

The conception is glacial in its formation. Usually, from the moment I have an idea for a piece, it only takes a matter of days before I have all the parts worked out and am ready to install it.

But this one? It is days before I even get to a starting point.

And even that is a repeat of an old theme. I know I will use little toy soldiers again. Instead of Hawaiian shirts, they will have little navy blue hoodies on. But that's all I got. I have no inkling where or what they will be doing or what any of it means. I just know it has to be an army guy in a hoodie.

With the first nebulous ideas of an installation brewing, I have the confidence to look at flights to Maui.

Until I see the prices. Maybe my army guy should rob a bank so I can afford to go home.

And then I remember. The Patreon account. There might be enough in there to offset the airfare. I log into the account and am floored when I see the balance. I have to check it several times. I even sign out of the account and sign back in to make sure it is the right account. But it is.

And although it is incredible to know that I have a little cushion to help me get back home—actually, a really huge cushion—I think it's even more encouraging to think that I have reached that many people with my portraits of joy. Most of the contributions are small, five or ten dollars, so this sum must represent tens of thousands of people, some of them even signing up to make their donations a monthly recurring donation.

I'm overcome with joy until I realize that means tens of thousands of people are expecting me to continue to create that same caliber of artistry. Right now, I can barely string together a cohesive theme. What are they going to think about anything I put out there now?

It's one thing to create art for myself with the misguided dream that it might bring joy to one person someday, but to have tens of thousands of people waiting on my next production when I have a brain that won't function? That's crushing.

What if I can't? What if the only creation I make from here on out is just one giant heap of steaming dung? How many people will I have disappointed?

My head starts spinning with all the *what-ifs*. I gnaw on my nails, cutting them all to the quick in seconds. I shove them in my back pockets to stop myself from gnawing off my fingers and find a small card. I pull it out and read it. *Action Beats Anxiety.*

Forward center of mass.

I swipe my keys from the table and head out the front door.

After a solid thirty minutes of walking along the water, I return home and book a ticket for two weeks from today. *Action Beats Anxiety.* I won't allow anxiety to keep me from this decision.

Two weeks should give me enough time to let Rusty know I'll be leaving and to figure out what the hell I'm going to leave here to mark my time.

But the art stalls. I cannot for the life of me come up with what to do with the army dude. I can't even convince my mind to focus on the problem for more than a minute without totally spacing out. Twenty minutes later, I awake from my stupor and have no memory of what I even set out to do. The PTS has mangled my brain and it may never come back.

Oh, God. What if it never comes back? I have no idea who I am if I can't create. Am I even Billie anymore? Have I become some wholly new person that only looks like the old me but has nothing else in common with her? How dismal life will be without producing my creations.

I remember the first piece of street art I saw. It was about a week after Brent's funeral. I found myself at Westies, staring out at the ocean for hours. It wasn't the first time I welcomed the growing darkness after another day squandered on those lava stones. I was trudging over the uneven lava towards the parking lot when I made it to the short wall that separates the cliffs from the road and caught my foot on the onyx rocks, splaying out like I was trying to slide into home plate. Having used up what little emotional energy I had left, I simply laid there, scuffed up and bleeding.

After a few brutal moments, I gathered the strength to roll to my side. On the backside of the street sign was this beautiful rainbow someone had painted. Next to it, they printed the words, "Someday we'll find it."

I found myself singing.

Singing.

When you hear any part of the lyrics to *The Rainbow Connection*, you can't help but to finish it.

Out loud.

And I discovered a miniature slice of solace in a time where I hadn't felt any for far too long.

A few weeks later, when the grief clouds began to burn off, I decided that I would drench the town with tiny pieces of joy so that everyone else could stumble on a sliver right when they needed it. Maybe I need to leave Key Largo with some happiness, too.

Immediately, I know exactly what that army dude will do. Finally finding direction, I sprint out to the store to pick up my supplies before I lose the inspiration.

Chapter 30

RYDER

I bob for a moment at the buoy, giving Spooner a chance to catch his breath. He has gotten faster during our last few swims, but he could still use a little recovery time, so I let him hang on me to rest as I hold onto the buoy.

From this distance, the coast is a spattering of green trees hiding the homes of my neighbors, brown mountains towering behind them. A dark figure sits on the empty pink chair at the edge of my yard.

Billie.

I take off at a dead sprint not caring if Spooner can keep up. He knows the way back in.

Every few meters, I spot the figure again to make sure she hasn't moved, the sun rising behind her, shielding her from full view. When the water is knee-deep, I stand, tear my goggles off, and find JJ sitting in Billie's seat.

No Billie.

I pitch my goggles onto the lawn.

And, to make things worse, JJ is here for another pound of my flesh.

As I near him, he tosses a towel my way. I let it fall to the ground and snatch another off the back of my chair, drying off as I make my way past him.

He bends to give Spooner a quick scratch. "Looks like you got a new swim buddy."

Like it makes up for the giant loss of swimming with Billie.

"Spooner, come," I command.

He runs to my side.

"You got a second?" JJ calls out.

I shrug but stop stalking away.

"Yeah, fine," he says, drifting my way. "I was a bit harsh last night."

"No, shit." That whole extreme ownership thing has passed. "You think I didn't try to get her home? You being a total dick didn't help either."

"I know you tried. I think it's just the whole situation. You're so much a part of it, it's easier to be angry with you than myself." He wanders over to where my goggles landed earlier and scoops them up. "How the hell did I let this happen?"

"There's plenty of blame to go around."

"But she called *you*. She doesn't blame you," he says.

"She thought you were dirty."

"What? Didn't she get my voicemails? I left about a hundred after it all went down."

"Nope. And she destroyed her phone before she heard them."

"Oh crap, she must hate me."

"That's an understatement. She even thought I was out there to bring her back for you to kill her. I told her you were on assignment. I think it helped."

"Either way, if anyone could have brought her home, it would have been you. You two have always had this unspoken understanding. I could never get past it."

I thought I could bring her home, too, until she fled from me.

He holds out his hand. "So, we good?"

"Yeah. We're good." I pull him into a back-slapping kind of manly hug.

───────────────◄

With concern for Billie being compounded with the dredged-up memories of Emma, and the pending deadline to make a decision on the Nicaragua job, my only option for dealing is a grueling run up Haleakala. Sometimes the only way I can think through a problem is on a run.

I drag JJ out before sunrise to drive to the head of the Halemau'u Trail halfway up the volcano. I'm sure he's still got some penance to pay, too.

"You want a/c or *au natural?*" I ask as we begin to gain elevation.

"Let's go car commando."

We roll down the windows, feeling the temperature drop and smelling the Eucalyptus trees. The sensation brings back memories of every trip up this mountain.

I flash my annual pass at the Ranger when we approach the station and he waves me on. Another mile up the road, we leave the truck in the lot, throw on our running vests, and take off at a sprint.

"Jax," JJ shouts from further behind me than I realized. "You have to slow down or I'm gonna have to lay down in the middle of this crater and let Pele take me."

He's right. This isn't an easy trail. Mostly downhill for the first half of the almost eight miles, I tend to push too hard on the way down and not leave much for the hike back out. It's 2300 feet of elevation to climb back out and no real way to bail out early. And with some super sharp cliffs, it isn't the place to misstep because you're tired.

I step to the side and wave him ahead of me. "Set the pace. I'll follow."

I must have run this path dozens of times over the years, starting when I first started training for BUDS. When I got back from the Congo, I used it to gauge my recovery. The first time I made it across the entire crater, I knew I was finally healthy again.

At over 8000 feet elevation, it's one of the only spots on the island where I can get out of the oppressive heat that settles on me some days. Today, with not a cloud in sight, I expect the chill will be short-lived, which is fine by me. I deserve the punishing heat.

The loose-rock trail beneath my feet crunches as I eat up the distance to the center of the depression that lies on the tallest peak on Earth if you measure from its base on the ocean floor. After the first mile, we start the real descent into the crater, apparently the quietest place on Earth, except when you go there with JJ Gerdis.

"All languages travel at the speed of sound, but sign language travels at the speed of light," he blurts out randomly.

"Hmm," I grumble.

"Ground Control to Major Thong," JJ sings out his version of David Bowie's Space Oddity. "Commencing countdown…" He can only get out a word or two without pausing for another breath. "…to pants down."

I try to let the views pull my mind away from JJ's nonsense. With red dirt as far as the eye can see and hardly a single plant, the inside of the crater always feels like being on a foreign planet.

Maybe if I push the pace a bit he won't be able to sing at all.

When we reach our turnaround point at the Hōlua Cabin, JJ plops down on the picnic table out front, crowding another family in the middle of eating their breakfast. Even though JJ set the pace, I'm sure he is feeling the descent as he rubs at his quads and knees.

I pull out a 3 Musketeers bar and practically inhale it. It's been my halfway reward for nearly every long trail run I've done. Then I wash it down with a few sips of water from my pack. "We're burning daylight," I say, and start back towards the car without waiting for JJ to join me. I know the moment he catches up to me because his antics return.

"Is it just me, or are circles pointless?"

I wish Spooner could have come with me today. He at least doesn't spoil the silence with his inane ramblings.

Three miles up the climb, the views change from the unearthly landscape inside the depression to panoramic vistas clear to the coast. The sun beats down on my back, but a cloudy midst is making its way up the mountain. When we pass Supply Trail, I know we are just over a half-mile from the car.

JJ stops without warning and I nearly fall off a sheer face

trying to avoid slamming into him. "So, I'm gonna do it," he boasts.

"Do what exactly?"

"I'm done being a beat cop. I took the job as an instructor at the academy."

"Wow. What spurred that decision?"

He looks at me like that was the dumbest question ever—which I suppose it was—I just never thought JJ would give up his position. It has been the only thing he has thought about for years.

"When did you decide?"

"I've been thinking about it for a while, I guess. I would think about it every time Billie would look at me when I put work before her, when I had to make huge sacrifices for that job, when those sacrifices started bleeding out to the people I loved." He starts walking back down the trail.

I suppose it's a fine time for a cool down, so I follow behind.

"It's been time for a while now, but I was too scared to do anything about it. I was comfortable in what I knew. Didn't know if I would hate teaching. But after what happened with Billie?"

We let the silence wash around us as the haze rolls in.

Billie has that way about her. She can immediately diagnose what's out of balance in your life, but she never bugs you about it. She silently leads you until you figure it out and then convinces you that you were the one to think of it in the first place. It's one of the many things that drew me to her.

The drive down the volcano takes forever when we get stuck behind some tourist who is so afraid of driving off the side, they take every single turn at five miles an hour. But the view from up here is spectacular and I don't mind having to take my time. Gives me time to think. And with a hard workout in my rear view, my mind has slowed enough to think rationally. Maybe it's time for me to make a change, too.

When Savage mentioned the Nicaragua job, I hesitated. But why? The simplicity of a mission I know I can accomplish sounds fantastic. Getting back into the fight could be the perfect remedy for the Billie situation. Especially since I have no idea how it will all shake out.

Hell, she may never even come home. Why should I wait around on a maybe, when I could be focusing on an absolutely?

When I return home later that night, I make my daily online search for Billie. I check her personal Instagram account—same old pics there—when the DM notification catches my eye. One message.

I pull it open to read, "@hibiovandal has tagged you in a post."

She tagged me. It was like a lifeline. A tiny, delicate thread between us.

I tap the alert to see her post and it's a new installation. A tiny toy soldier wearing a navy blue hoodie hangs off the top of a chain link fence surrounding an old abandoned lot of weeds. He holds a packet of wildflower seeds that are blowing out of the package, off on a breeze, to cover the entire empty plot.

I don't know how she got such a perfect shot of the whole scene, but the image itself is a work of art, in addition to the fact that she has taken an old worthless piece of land and in a few months will have transformed it into a field of wildflowers. Just beautiful.

I look at her tag. She wanted me to see this. She thought about me.

Is her tag a challenge? To go find the installation and take my usual pic in front of it?

That would be nearly impossible, to locate the exact empty forgotten lot. I scan the picture for any identifying clues. But there is nothing. No signs, no homes, nothing but marsh in the background. Even the seed type she chose can be used in any of the Southeastern States. I checked. No clue there.

Even if I found the place, and flew out there, there's no guarantee it would go any better than the last time. And that's not a hit I can take again. If she wants to see me, she can call. Or, hell, she can simply come home and knock on my door.

But she hasn't called. And she hasn't knocked. Which only leaves one conclusion.

She doesn't want me.

I pick up the phone and dial Savage.

Chapter 31

BILLIE

After leaving what felt like a Dear John letter for Rusty, confessing who I really was and how to contact me through my Instagram, not without a serious warning to keep that info private, I packed up what little I owned, left my bike for the next tenant, and hopped on a bus that would take me to the airport.

After nineteen hours spent on buses and taxis, in planes and airports, I arrive home exhausted. I shove through my front door, but the door shoves back.

It's locked.

Huh. That should be unlocked.

Hide-a-key. At the edge of the porch, I pick up Thor the Turtle and slide the door to retrieve my spare key before letting myself in and locking the door behind me. I check the lock a couple times before tossing the key beside the overflowing mail basket.

I pop open the fridge and find it empty except for dozens of Dr Pepper cans lined up neatly on the left-hand side. The freezer is stocked with vacuum-sealed fish filets. I pull open my cupboards to check the four cans I left in them, but there are new boxes of Lucky Charms next to them. Did the landlord re-rent the place? Shit, does that mean I'm breaking and entering?

Mail. I dash back to the front door and study the address on the envelopes. Billie Stiles. Thank God.

But that could just be because I never forwarded my mail.

I head to my bedroom and open the drawers, my dresser still filled with my clothes, painfully bright and such a lifetime away. But they are my clothes. I must still live here.

I glance around the room.

Ooh, bed. I missed you.

With nothing left in the tank, I pull the curtains closed, lock the bedroom door, and climb into bed.

Click. Click. Creak.

The front door? Someone's in here.

I'm on my feet in a second, my chest exploding with the feel of my heart hammering. Morning light fills the room making it easy to assess the situation.

They're locked up. It isn't them. It's not...

I slide my hand under the mattress and come up with a knife that I slip into my waistband and a bat I hang over my shoulder.

They could have sent someone. Or it's just a normal creep.

I position myself behind the door and wait for the perpetrator. A few moments later and the only thing I hear is the sound of keys on a table and rustling in the kitchen.

They don't know I'm here. I've got the advantage. I can surprise them.

I round the corner peering into the kitchen to find Ryder loading up the freezer with his latest catch. I tuck back in behind the corner.

You're not ready for this, Billie. For him. Not yet.

But I cannot pull my eyes from him. He picks up the mail scattered on the floor and throws it in the basket when he notices a bright red bill and opens it.

I can read the block letters across the top, even this far away. Overdue.

He slips it into his back pocket.

I retreat behind my bedroom door and peer out through the crack in the jamb before he strolls through the hallway. He stops at the pictures, runs his finger over a picture of me. "Forty-five days, Billie. Forty-five." He lingers for a moment longer before turning and opening the front door.

I hold my breath, waiting for the sound of the door closing behind him, and then collapse onto the floor.

What was he doing here? I have so much more progress to make before I can deal with him. I thought I had more time. I thought I could avoid him until I was ready.

But he was here.

In my home.

I try my tools to stop my head from spinning. *Action Beats Anxiety.* But I don't have it in me to move.

Whatever is true? I'm a mess, that's true. Yeah. That one's not working.

It's okay to ask for help. I pull out my phone, but I can't call the one person I want to help me. I can't face him yet. Instead, I do the next best thing.

"Oh my gosh, Billie? I'm so glad you called." Charlie's voice alone brings down my anxiety.

"I need help. Can you come over?" I eke out.

Chapter 32

RYDER

*E*very week I come here, needing a reminder of Billie. And, each time, I leave more empty than when I came. After forty-five days without her, you'd think, it would get easier. But every day becomes more and more of a struggle. Propelled by my need to escape the pain, I head for the door.

Creak.

The whoosh of a door moving.

Is she home? It could just be the wind.

Closing the door behind me, I wait for another sound. The last thing I want is to scare her again by searching her house, a house that I'm currently breaking and entering in.

Then, just like a songbird, her sweet voice drifts in from the other room.

Billie's home.

And safe.

Her voice meets me before she does. "Yeah, I hid. I did *not* want to see him."

She rounds the corner, phone in hand, completely oblivious to the fact that I'm standing in her house. I press myself against the door, wishing I could pass right through it.

She disappears again only to return with a blanket draped over her head like a hoodie. "I'm totally not ready to see him."

Her green eyes find me. She stops mid-stride, letting the phone drop to the table beside her. Crestfallen, her smile evaporates.

And that hits me dead in the chest.

"Shit. Sorry," I mumble.

Wrapped in a rainbow fleece blanket, only her face is visible. And everything written on it is screaming for me to leave. She draws the blanket tighter around herself.

I search for something to explain why I'm in her house. Or how happy I am to see that she is safe and home. But she looks like the perfect mix of frightened and pissed. One false move from me and she might attack. I've seen her moves and that won't be fun. Or, even worse, she could bolt again, like in Wilmington.

Either way, my heart would be demolished.

Her shoulders rise as she takes in a huge breath before blowing it out in a slow, controlled movement.

Do I split so she doesn't have to talk to me?

Or would that hurt her more than staying?

Do I pretend I didn't just hear her say how much she doesn't want to see me?

"I... dammit. I should go." I search her face for any indication she wants me to stay. "I'm gonna go."

I give her one more moment to stop me, before turning and twisting the doorknob. As I glance back to make sure I haven't wounded her by leaving, she drops the blanket and races toward me. She wraps her arms around my waist and buries her head in my chest as she breathes out my name, "RyGuy."

I wrap her up in a hug as her grip tightens on me as if she will never let me go.

I have my Billie back.

When she finally loosens her hold on me, she pulls back slightly as wispy strands of hair fall into her eyes. I push them out of her way, tucking them behind her ear.

She slides her hand from my back and pokes my chest with a soft touch. She peers up at me, her light green eyes meeting mine. "You're real. Like really real."

"Last time I checked," I laugh.

"Help is here," Charlie calls out from the front lanai.

"Looks like she already found her help," Harley amends.

Billie drops her arms from me and steps back, and I immediately feel the loss.

Charlie wraps her in an eternal hug. By the time she releases her, it feels like weeks have passed. "I'm so glad you're back, Billie. We all missed you so much."

"I know. I'm sorry. I didn't know how to..." she struggles to find the words.

"I have so many questions," Charlie says.

We make our way to the living room, the two girls surrounding Billie on the couch. I drop into the chair opposite her. Billie spends the next thirty minutes trying to explain what the last two months have been like. She tells us of her job and Rusty, Rooster, and the boys. Of her little shack and stories of the locals. She's spewing stories like pennies into a fountain.

I spent the entire day with Billie in Wilmington and didn't hear a single detail of her time on Hammerhead Key, but, then again, we spent the whole time pretending that world didn't exist. It was all an illusion.

"Be honest," Charlie says. "Rooster was a hottie, wasn't he? I bet I know where he got his name."

My gaze snaps to Billie, watching for any indication that she knows more about Rooster than she is letting on. Billie nervously laughs it off.

Charlie is good at asking questions to keep her going. Harley sits mostly quiet, taking it all in. Until she doesn't. "What have you been doing so far to combat the stress? What tools do you have in your tool belt?"

Harley's got on her clinical face, getting right to the point.

"Action Beats Anxiety," Billie starts hesitantly. "I'll go out for a walk when I feel it coming on. Or I'll make a plan to accomplish something easy and small."

"That's a good one. Then you can build on the momentum of that small win," Harley agrees.

Wow. Billie's been doing some work. Why didn't I take the time to talk with her about this stuff when I had the chance?

I was with her for a full twenty-four hours and I could barely get the words post-traumatic stress out of my mouth. Harley is with her for five minutes and is already discussing strategies to overcome PTS.

"Yeah. And then there's one that's from the Bible," Billie adds. "Whatever is true. Whatever is right. Whatever is pure. Whatever is lovely. I will fix my thoughts on these things."

I recognize that one from a song I've sung in church hundreds of times.

"How do you use it? Just say it to yourself?" Harley asks.

"No, I try to find at least one thing for each sentence. Like last week, when I went on my run and felt my heart spinning out of control, I stopped and went through it."

"Show me."

This is beginning to feel a little too much like a therapy session, one that I shouldn't be let in on, but Harley really seems to know what she's talking about, and Billie probably needs it.

"What is true? They are locked up. They are not here. It is only my brain trying to make sense of the situation and keep me safe. What is right? I'm running, so my heart is supposed to beat hard. What is pure? Exercising is good for me and being in nature will calm me down. What is lovely? Spooner. The feel of warm ocean water over my back as I swim. Sunset in..." Her eyes flick in my direction, then down to her hands as she flattens her palms over the blanket on her legs. "Like that."

Sunset in my backyard? Am I part of her 'whatever is lovely'? Was she thinking about me while she was gone?

"That's awesome. Sounds like you have some good tools. Have you worked on '*Feel. Process. Let go?*"

"No. What's that?"

Billie's eyes keep snapping to me. I wonder if she's having as hard of a time focusing on this conversation as I am. I only got her back moments ago, with no real time to figure out where we are before the girls descended upon us and took over. There is way too much that I need to know.

Will we pick up where we left off in Wilmington? I have not been able to stop thinking about the way she looked at me in the arcade, the feel of her in my arms that night, or the total ecstasy of kissing her in the rain. Or, when she bolted, was that a sign that she wants none of that?

"I find that tough people usually have a hard time with this one. They are really good at pushing through and occupying their mind with other activities so they don't have to confront their feelings about what happened. Instead, they focus on all the things they can do, distraction, exercise, cold exposure, meditation, but they forget to do the one thing that is critical if they are going to move on from the incident."

Sounds like Harley's been taking up residence in my head.

"Feel?" Billie asks.

"Exactly. You can't keep running from it or you will tire out. At some point, you have to turn around, face it, and punch it right in the throat, which for you will probably be you staying in your pajamas and crying all day. But it has to be done. That's the hard work of healing."

"You want me to cry all day? That doesn't sound very productive. I have finally gotten to a place where I'm not fighting the urge to cry all day."

"Not forever. But you have to do it. You have to feel your feelings if you want to be able to process them and let them go. Otherwise, they will stay lodged in the back of your mind, haunting you forever."

"Feel. Process. Let go. Got it," she confirms.

She looks back to me like she is weighing whether or not she needs, in addition to letting go of her trauma, to let go of me. Or maybe that's just me reading way too much into this situation. Maybe she had nothing to let go of and I'm the one who needs to feel, process, and let go of the hope of one day having her back.

Breaking the awkward silence, Charlie kindly changes the subject. "Tomorrow's Game Night. You gonna come?"

She turns to me. "You kept doing Game Night?"

I can't find the words to tell her how I dropped the ball on Game Night.

"It's at Finn's now," Charlie says, thankfully.

"What? Finn's hosting Game Night? How the hell did that happen?" Billie asks.

"The second Friday after you left, we all got this text from Finn. It just said. 'Game Night. My place. I need this.' I think we all needed it."

Total Finn text. If you could get that guy to utter more than a three-word sentence I'd be surprised.

"How'd it go?"

"Complete. Failure," Charlie laughs. "We get there and he has all these folding chairs set up around his big dining room table—the one he usually uses to paint on—and he tosses a bag of chips and a deck of cards on the table. Then throws eight spoons onto the table."

"For the chips?"

"You ever play spoons?" Charlie asks.

Billie shakes her head.

"It's a little like musical chairs with cards. You get four of a kind and you grab a spoon. There's one less spoon than people at the table. If you don't get a spoon, you get a letter. When you spell S-P-O-O-N, you lose."

"I give him points for trying," Billie says.

"So, we all sit down and he deals the cards and spreads the spoons out in the middle of the table. Then he counts the spoons and freezes."

"Had to go pour a beer?" Billie jokes. "Couldn't believe he would be at Game Night without drinking first?"

"He got up to drink alright. He pours himself a glass of whiskey, knocks back the whole thing in one gulp, and then solemnly approaches the table. He delicately slides one spoon off the table and walks it back to the kitchen."

"Dude, that guy is so weird sometimes," Billie says.

"There were only eight of us, so seven spoons," Charlie explains.

"Oh," is all Billie can muster.

Harley throws her thumb my way. "Jax, here, takes one look at JJ and slams his hand on the table so all the spoons jump—all of us too—and he points right at JJ and shouts, 'This is on you,' and stomps out the door."

"I didn't shout," I say, looking to see if Billie believes me. Her eyes darken with compassion. "And the next few game nights got better, anyway," I amend.

"I'm so sorry. God, I didn't even think what it would do to all of you. I was so damned selfish," Billie pleads.

"It's never selfish to take care of yourself first," Harley says.

"I know, but..."

Harley steps into her excuse. "Nope. It's 'I know.' Period. No buts need to follow."

I should have been doing the same thing. Taking care of Billie first. In Wilmington, I let what I wanted cloud what I knew was right.

And it drove Billie from me.

I won't make the same mistake again.

Others First.

Billie's in no place for romance, and who knows if she'd even want that with me. So, friends. That's it. Right now, that's what she needs, and I'm willing to do anything to keep her in my life.

Chapter 33

BILLIE

When I walk my friends out, a sunshower is busy watering my flowers.

When I fled Maui, I knew I would be hurting Ryder, but I never even considered that other people would be reacting, too. Everything, everyone, disappeared from my mind. The only thing left was survival. That's it. That was as far as my brain could go.

But now that I'm back, I have so much making up to do for it. I'm just not sure I have the energy to do it.

As Ryder disappears down the road and Charlie and Harley pull out of the driveway, I step out from under the porch and spin beneath the warm drops, letting them soak my skin, when I remember Harley's tool. *Feel. Process. Let go.* I give it a try and finally lower the barricade I have been holding in place since this started.

A torrential tsunami of tears overwhelms me as I let it all pour out. The feelings flood in without logic, without pattern or purpose, only images of all I have lost. Game nights without me. A total disconnect from everyone I loved. Waves and surf. My home. Ryder.

Then a whole different wave of torment hits, and it's chock full of Brent.

I allow the heartache to wash over me without labeling any of it. There are no words. It is only pain. It sits on me, pours out from my eyes, from my trembling limbs, from my soul. Too feeble to hold any of it back, I release it to fall among the gentle showers splashing down around me.

Then, just as quickly as it started, the downpour vanishes, leaving behind steamy puddles straining to evaporate again to join their brothers back in the clouds only to baptize the land further up-island. My tears evaporate along with the rain.

I rise to my feet and wring out my drenched shirt. Not wanting to drip through the house, I walk through the side yard to the board house. One of the reasons I rent this particular little shack is the outdoor shed that houses all my surfboards, towels, and other beach gear.

Looking for a towel, I swing open the door and my favorite shortboard screams at me, "Seriously Billie, how long am I going to have to sit here before you take me out? I'm dried up and crusted over. I need to feel the ocean again."

I run my hand along its rails. I remember the first day I got this board. My shaper had been trying out some new tail shapes and was convinced this would be the solution to the problems I had been having with my roundhouse cutback. I was losing speed through the bottom turn and he had pulled in the tail a bit to help with that. He was right. It fixed everything. My first cutback was a revelation.

I haven't touched it since Brent. I haven't touched any shortboards. But, right now, it sounds like the perfect way to avoid thinking about seeing Ryder again for the first time. I don't want to figure out what it means and what I want and if he will ever truly forgive me for bailing on him without a word.

Twice.

I pull the board from the rack and lay it on the grass in the backyard. Years of neglect have left the wax gray and melted in streaks across the top. While I let it heat up in the sun, I sprint inside to change into a bikini.

By the time I return, the wax is soft enough to come off without much effort. I strip it all with an old Costco card, then grab a new bar of wax and walk down to the water to cool off the board before laying down a fresh coat. Tucking the remaining bar into my bikini bottoms, I wade out until the water is about knee-deep.

The surf is on the bigger side and a bit blown out. I scan the lineup for a good place to sit. A set comes in, and I stare as some guy takes off on the six feet of crumbly foam. He can't get off a solid turn before the wave closes out. I study it all the way in until it slaps at my legs. Then I watch the next one do the same thing. But I cannot convince myself to hop on my board and paddle out.

The last wave of the set washes into me and the horizon goes flat. Should be a good four minutes before the next set comes in. Now would be a perfect time to make it beyond the inner reef.

But I might not make it out in time for the next set.

When the last wave of the next set rolls in, I'll start paddling. It'll be better timing, so I won't have to face the outside set waves on my way out.

Another guy takes off on an outside wave and manages to make something of it with a couple turns before it crumbles to a mushy line of whitewash. Without losing the wave, he lays down on his board and rides it the rest of the way in, giving a few strong paddles to make it through the channel before the wave reforms and brings him towards me. By the time the wave breaks again, I recognize him.

"Hey, Billie. You heading in or out?"

"Out. Just timing the sets."

He glides past me.

After the next wave, I'll go.

The next wave hits me, and I'm still paralyzed.

On the count of three. One... Two...

Four more sets wash ashore before I give up entirely and turn to leave.

First, it's art. Now, surfing. What more can my stupid broken brain take from me?

Back at home, I toss my board in the rack, not caring if it

gets dinged up. It's not like I'll be able to use it again, anyway. Pulling on a tank top over my bikini, I head toward my porch.

Sitting in the sun, Ryder is a picture of warmth and safety, leaning back against the railing, one leg pulled up on the bottom step. "Hey, I thought I should probably wait out here now that you're home. I'm really sorry if I scared you this morning. I had no idea you were back."

If I thought that Imaginary Ryder brought me a touch of comfort and security, the Real Ryder? He washes over me with solace and wraps me in love. Every ounce of frustration I felt walking back from that crappy surf session is wiped away the moment I see him, right where he belongs.

With me.

Chapter 34

RYDER

I wasn't scared, I just didn't know if you were..." Billie plays with the frayed hem of her tank top as she struggles to explain, "...real?"

She drops down beside me.

I lift my hands to inspect them. "Look pretty real to me." I turn them her way. "What do you think?"

She bumps my shoulder with hers. "Not like that."

She dips her head and says faintly, "You said this morning that I was gone for forty-five days, that I left you. But for me, that wasn't true. You were with me. That first night in my shack, when I finally collapsed after three solid days of running, when I was so scared that they would hunt me down, and when I feared that I would never sleep again, you sat at my kitchen table and told me you'd take first watch."

She spins towards me, a renewed strength lifting her gaze to mine. "And when I wasn't even capable of taking off my sweatshirt, your sweatshirt, working in the hundred-degree Florida heat because I felt too exposed, you were there to tease me about it, and, somehow, hearing you laugh about it, made it feel smaller like it was no longer crushing me."

Knowing she thought about me as much as I thought about

her while she was gone, I have to stop myself from reaching out to take her in my arms.

Others First, Jax. She needs a friend. Be that.

Her green eyes capture mine. "And after Wilmington, when you helped me figure out what the hell was going on, you were with me every single day as I tried so hard to get better so I could be with you. Every book I read, every meditation, every training run, you were the voice in my head, discussing the new tactics, encouraging me to keep going, and kicking my ass when I wanted to slack off. You've been with me every single day."

She looks off to the clouds now drifting lazily by. "Sometimes, it was the only thing keeping me anchored to reality. I mean how screwed up is it that a hallucination was the only thing keeping me tied to reality?"

"Well then, I think we're equally screwed up."

Her head swivels my way.

"It's possible I made a couple videos talking to you while you were gone," I admit.

"I knew it. That one with Spooner in your bed, huh?" Her smile, alive with affection and relief, brings a matching one to my face.

"And maybe a few others." I don't admit to talking almost incessantly to her like she was right next to me, on charters, in the water, around my house, and especially in her house.

She tips her head back, taking in the sun. "You know what would make this day perfect?"

I nod and we both answer in unison, "Fish tacos."

"Walk, ride, or drive?" I ask.

She considers for a moment. "Walk, I think."

I help her up from the stairs, holding her hand a bit too long once she's on her feet._

Others First, dumbass.

We make our way down the narrow road lined on one side with jungle-like trees and the other with short rock walls enclosing the front yards of small bungalows and huge manors.

"So, get this," I start. "This guy on my last charter starts going on and on about how he found the best fish tacos on the island. I told him there's no way it beats Paia Fish Market."

"Paia's? Five Ono's got the best fish tacos."

I push aside the leaves of an overgrown banana plant and let Billie walk under. "Yeah, like I'm gonna tell some tourist about Five Ono."

"Good point. Everyone knows about Paia's already. Not gonna spoil any secret spot there."

"Exactly. So, he tells me that it's better than Paia's. He goes on and on about it, the view, the service. And, get this, he's a food critic for some mainland magazine, so he might actually know."

"There's no way we wouldn't have heard about a place that good." She looks genuinely baffled.

We hop up on the sidewalk that starts alongside the Malua Kai Estates, one of the only new developments in Nalu Kai.

"That's the thing. They just opened. The owner is a good friend so he was out to review it for their soft opening. They open next week."

As soon as we pass the estates, we are back out on the road.

"We have to go prove him wrong," she demands.

"That's what I said. You want to go check it out?"

"Are they like a fancy, reservations-six-months-out kind of place?"

"Yeah, but he told me he can get me a table any time I want."

"No way. Let's do it."

Chapter 35

BILLIE

*Y*ou want me to what?" I ask the instructor in our Beginning Freerunning class.

"Do the whole loop again, but backwards this time," he tells me like it's the simplest thing in the world.

The crazy pick for our Sunday afternoon Girls Workout was a beginner freerunning class, but beginner is not at all accurate. He has us moving in ways I haven't moved since I was nine.

"Okay. So, the balance beams first, then the wedge blocks, then... wait, how am I supposed to climb that eight-foot wall?"

"No, backwards like this." He proceeds to hurdle over the three-foot block wall backwards. He's actually running and climbing backwards.

I look suspiciously at Harley before drifting past Charlie and Piper to hide in the back of the line. I am starting to think Harley chose freerunning to gauge how I'm doing with my fear response. And that eight-foot wall is bringing on a huge wave of fear.

On my first go-around, when I had to jump from the top forwards, I got stuck, one leg hanging over the edge, bracing myself with one hand and the opposite foot. I had to stare at the instructor's face to trick myself into believing the drop wasn't all that far, and then remind myself that they wouldn't have beginners doing something that was actually dangerous. The thick crash mat below helped a little, too.

But thinking about having to do that backwards now is overwhelming my coping strategies.

When class ends after a full sixty minutes of pushing my body to do things I wasn't entirely sure it could do, we get to play around on the trampolines. After exhausting myself with front flips and back flips, and teaching Charlie how to do them, I collapse onto the landing to watch as the non-beginners practice their skills.

That show alone is worth the cost of admission to this class. One guy is so talented he runs up the side of the wall next to the trampoline before pushing off into a double backflip and then does it again.

Charlie leans over to me to whisper. "He's giving you the eye, Billie."

"Nah. I'm just in his eye line. He's using me to spot so he doesn't get dizzy."

"Then, shove over so I can get a little male attention," Harley jokes.

"Yeah, Billie gets plenty of it from Ryder," Charlie adds.

"No, we... Well, maybe?"

"What? That's a totally new story. Do tell," Piper demands, barely holding in her excitement.

"Wait. What about JJ? Have you even talked to him?" Charlie had to go bring that up.

"No." I shake my head. What would I even say? "All I know is it's over. Has been since the moment I left."

That leaves an awkward silence hovering between us all.

Piper bumps my shoulder. "So. Spill. You and Ryder?"

"We have this dinner tonight, but I don't think it's a date."

We got reservations for Barometer Soup a few days ago and, ever since then, I have been so confused. When we're swimming or surfing together, it's like old times, completely platonic, like our makeout session in the rain in Wilmington never happened.

But then, Ryder's taking me on a pre-arranged dinner. And this place is fancy. I looked it up. Rooftop on the only hotel in

Nalu Kai, Barometer Soup has perfected relaxed luxury with views of the sunset over Lanai, live ukulele music from a local artist, and food that looks like it could actually beat out Five Ono. So, it has to be a date, right?

"Do you want it to be a date?" Charley asks.

"I think I do?" I say hesitantly.

"Hmm," Harley mumbles.

Piper stands and pulls me up. "We have to get you ready. You need to borrow an outfit?"

Charlie hops to her feet. "I have the cutest skirt you could wear."

It's like they have both been married so long, they need to live vicariously through my love life for any sense of excitement.

"You may want to wait until you feel like you're mostly out of the woods before pursuing anything serious with Ryder. Romance can complicate things in the early stages of PTS recovery," Harley says, bringing us back down to reality.

Yes. Right. That's the smart thing to do.

But it's not what my heart is begging me to do.

———————

Dinner is amazing. None of that first date awkwardness, though I'm still not sure if Ryder thinks this is a date. The sunset is one of the best I've seen. Plenty of clouds to catch the waning light, reflecting back the whole spectrum of colors.

And the songs that Bohdi K sang and played on ukulele? I swear he found my Mellow Maui playlist and played right through it. I knew every song he performed. And some of them were totally obscure songs. For a moment, I wonder if Ryder stole my playlist and sent it to him ahead of time to have him learn it.

After soaking up all of the beauty surrounding us, we hop on the elevator to ride back down to reality.

I wish there was some guide for figuring out if you're on a date beyond if he pays or not. If that was the standard, every time I've eaten a meal with Ryder, it's been a date.

Does he study you as you watch the musician playing, and

when you catch him, his eyes light up with mischief and desire? Date.

Then, does he angle his body away from you to keep an eye on the whole restaurant? Not a date.

Does he look amazing in a black button down with the sleeves rolled up, putting his forearms on display? Wear the most perfectly fitting jeans showing off his ass and strong legs? Date.

Does he finish the perfect outfit with a pair of flip-flops? Not date? Date? If he knew it was one of my favorite looks on a guy, maybe it'd be in the date category, but I don't think I've ever verbalized that in front of him, so, not a date?

Does he remind you, that you're just here to see if Five Ono still has the best fish tacos? Not a date.

Does he stand close enough in the elevator that you can feel the heat emanating from his body when no one else is in there? Date.

I want so badly for a repeat of our makeout session in that doorway in Wilmington. Minus my freak-out, of course. He turns slowly toward me, leaning a shoulder on the wall. His eyes are compelling, magnetic. I'm powerless to resist the pull. I mirror his movement letting my gaze drift over his broad shoulders before drawing it back up to his face.

The look in his eyes as I turned towards him? Date. For sure, date.

The elevator slows and dings. The doors open and six of the loudest, drunkest tourists climb aboard. Ryder rotates towards me as we get pushed to the back corner of the elevator.

"Did you see that chick with the huge rack? Holee sheeit," Yellow Shirt shouts.

Without taking his eyes off my face, Ryder slips his hand into mine and a smile slowly spreads across his face.

"Well, we did come here to get leid," says the guy with white socks under his sandals.

We grin at each other knowing what we're both thinking, "Neither one of them has been laid in years."

Yellow Shirt chest-bumps Socks-with-sandals Guy, sending both of them into Ryder, forcing him to brace himself with his hands against the wall behind my head to avoid slamming me into the corner.

Immediately, the temperature rises ten degrees.

And thickens.

It's nearly impossible to draw air into my lungs.

I have to get out of here.

I reach for the elevator buttons in hopes of escaping, but Ryder stands in my way.

My heart speeds up.

Sweat everywhere.

Blood pulses through my ears.

Have to get out.

Run.

"Hey. We'll be out in just a minute," Ryder says calmly.

There's no way I'll last that long. I shove him aside, but he won't budge.

"I have to get out," I growl at Ryder.

"When we get to the first floor you can."

Not gonna work. I jab at Ryder's stomach.

He flicks it away and spins me around, wrapping my arms to my side.

Blue shirt glares at me. To him, it must look like we're two lovers who can't keep our hands off each other. To me, it is a battle to survive.

I thrust my elbow backwards into Ryder's ribs.

He winces, but then tightens his grasp on my arms so I am completely immobile. He whispers in my ear, "Billie, babe, you're safe. Nothing is going to hurt you."

But there is no way of making my mind believe that. Everything is going to hurt me. I will never be safe again.

The elevator dings and the frat house pours itself out, but Ryder doesn't loosen his grip on me.

Footsteps shuffle on the floor.

"You're gonna need to take the next elevator," Ryder commands the intruders.

They laugh him off.

"Get off. Now," he growls.

Chapter 36

RYDER

There's no way I can allow Billie to face a lobby crammed with people like this. She is bound to do some real damage. And the way I have her wrapped up is bound to attract the attention of the security guards which will only escalate this situation.

I whisper in her ear, "We're going up a few floors so you can have some privacy when you get off. I'll let you go if you promise not to hurt me."

I pull one hand from her and hit the third-floor button. The doors close and the elevator begins to move. She starts to flail again. The only way to protect myself from another jab to the ribs is to hold her. I wrap my arms around her again but slowly lighten my grasp as we ascend.

When the door dings, I release my grip and let her escape. She stalks down the hallway. When she reaches the end, she spins on her heel and paces back towards me.

Readying for another attack I lift my hands up, palms toward her. "I'm not going to hurt you, Billie."

She slows as she approaches, but the aggression blazing from her hasn't lessened. She turns and tramps down the hallway again, stopping this time at the floor-to-ceiling glass window at the end of the hallway. She lowers her head to the glass, staring out at the waves of Pau Ole.

Knowing she is coming down from the panic, I take four full-lunged breaths to slow my heart so I can bring some peace to her when I try to talk with her. If I'm still in fight mode, there's no way I'll be able to help her calm down.

I slowly make my way toward her, keeping enough distance so that she won't feel trapped again.

BANG.

Her hands fly down on the wooden railing attached to the glass. I pray it stands up to her beating and doesn't shatter the entire window.

She faces me, eyes scanning the hallway like she's trying to decide if she can make it past me. I step to the wall so she has a clear path if that's what she needs to do.

She squeezes her eyes shut like she was just hit with a searing migraine. When they open, she balls her hands into fists and I prepare for her imminent advance. But instead, she raises them to her forehead and rubs the bridge of her nose. She drags her palms up and down her face a couple times then looks to the ceiling before walking to the side of the hall and sliding down the wall until she is a puddle of spent energy, her head resting limply on her knees.

A few moments later, I approach her, sitting against the opposite wall, two meters down.

She lifts her head slowly scanning the hallway. When our gazes tangle, she hides her eyes again on her knees. Her shoulders shudder in that uneven pace that can only mean she is crying.

Every cell in my being is demanding I go comfort her, wrap her in my arms, and hold her until she knows I won't let anything in the world ever hurt her again. But I worry my presence would only make things worse.

Her breathing settles and she peeks up again, grimacing when her gaze hits the elevator doors. She drops her head once more.

I should have known better. I should have known it was too soon to put this kind of pressure on her. Once again, putting my wants above hers blows up in my face.

She studies the elevator doors one more time and it looks like they are causing her physical pain.

"Stairs. End of the hall," I offer.

She nods before her shoulders rise and fall in three deliberate breaths. She tips her head again before placing her palms against the wall behind her and pushing up to a stand. Three more intentional inhales before she is able to disengage from the support the wall provided. I stand to match her.

She drifts towards me looking entirely spent. I lead the way to the maroon door enclosing the stairwell. I open it for her and let her wander past me, head drooping. When we get to the first landing, she lifts her eyes to me as she takes in a breath like she's ready to finally speak. But the impulse passes and she makes her way down the next flight of stairs.

We drive home in silence, her gaze tightly fixed on the green hills passing out the passenger-side window. I wish I could do something to protect her from the flood of thoughts I'm sure are assaulting her, but I don't think she has the headspace to hear them right now.

When we pull up to her place, I kill the engine and hop out. Rounding my truck, I glance her way through the back window. She hasn't moved. I'm not sure it has even registered that we have stopped driving.

When I open the door, she startles. She moves towards the door, getting caught by the seat belt, and just looks up at me like she has no idea how to solve this problem.

"You want me to?" I slowly reach across her to unlock the belt, checking constantly for any signs of panic.

When she's free, she slides out of my car and pulls at the hem of her tank. She whispers barely above the sound of the wind, "I'm sorry I'm a freak," before scurrying off to her front door. She is inside before I have a chance to tell her that couldn't be further from the truth.

Chapter 37

BILLIE

Sunday morning at first light, we are all gathered at the top of Nuipu'u Street in full pads and helmets. This early, there isn't a car to be seen on the road that gently winds down the side of the West Maui Mountains at just the right incline for a downhill skateboarding run of nearly three miles.

My legs are burning by the time we reach the bottom, but I manage to remain upright the whole way down, so I consider this a huge win. The last time we tried this over a year ago, I got the speed wobbles halfway down and spun out so hard, I swear, I slid down the rest of the hill on my belly. Had road rash so bad, I couldn't surf for a month. My neon yellow Maui and Sons t-shirt with a giant black shark atop the logo got ripped to shreds. At least it wasn't one of my T&C collection though.

I wonder if dubbing these crazy Sunday morning adventures Crunch and Brunch has become a self-fulfilling prophecy. Every week one of us seems to take a huge wipeout.

Piper has to check out right after skateboarding to go to a two-year-old's birthday party—one of the few times I don't envy her life with a loving hubby and cute as hell baby—but Harley is on-island for one more day, so the three of us decide to head into Lahaina for a proper brunch.

After ordering a plateful of breakfast carbs, I dial up a half-dose pre-bolus of insulin. Typically, I don't like to get insulin onboard before finishing a meal since I never know how much I'll end up eating or if something will happen to delay my food, but with this many carbs headed my way, I have to get a jump on my blood sugars.

I glance down at my pump and am so grateful to have a full cartridge of insulin. The ability to splurge and eat what I want without having to stretch my insulin is a luxury I will never take for granted again.

When Charlie dips into the bathroom, Harley asks "How's recovery going?" She tips her mimosa into her mouth while waiting for my answer.

Let's see. I ruined my date with the perfect guy because he got too close to me. I then nearly broke through a plate glass window trying to escape the flood of fear that followed. Yeah, it's going swimmingly. "Do we really have to call it that? It makes it sound like I'm an alcoholic."

"Okay. How about we call it rewiring?"

"Rewiring?" I laugh.

"Sure. It's what's actually happening. Or maybe retraining is better?"

"Let's go with rewiring, then. The rewiring's going fine." I scan the bar for Charlie, hoping she'll distract Harley from this topic.

"So, setbacks then?"

Am I that obvious or is 'crazy as shit' written all over my face?

I run my finger along the rim of my glass, picking up a couple grains of salt. I stare at them as I let it all spill out. "I freaked out last week. All that progress, gone. I spent the last few months working my ass off to 'rewire my brain.'" I lick the salt from my finger. "Nothing has changed. I'm still broken."

"Billie," she says gently.

I wipe my finger on my jean shorts waiting for her rebuke. When it doesn't come, I check to make sure she hasn't fled the scene. I wouldn't blame her. I look up to find her smiling sweetly.

"Healing is not a straight line." She swipes at the condensation around her glass with her thumb. "When your brain has healed enough, it's strong enough to start dealing with more and more of the trauma. It will come in waves like this for a while."

"Then, what do I do? The waves are holding me under. And, God, they're screwing up the only good thing I have."

She leans over to get the bartender's attention. "I have kind of a weird request. Can I get a glass of cold water, a glass of hot water, and three bowls?"

Sometimes I think Harley must have been raised on Mars. But I know better than to ask when she gets like this. If she wanted to explain herself she would. Instead, I prepare myself for a wild journey.

Her supplies arrive just as Charlie does and I breathe a sigh of relief knowing we'll move on in the conversation.

Harley fills one bowl with cold water, another with the hot water. Looks like I won't be that lucky.

"Mix up the bowls so I don't know which is which. One hand in each," she commands.

Charlie dunks both her hands immediately.

"I meant Billie." She gives Charlie a napkin. "Trust me, Billie."

I oblige, dipping a hand into a bowl. "Now what?"

Without answering, she fills the third bowl with the remainder of both glasses. I raise my brows waiting for direction. Keeping her eyes on the bowls, she asks, "Can you tell me what your socks feel like right now?"

"What? You have seriously lost it."

"Play nicely. What do your socks feel like?"

"Fine." I wiggle my toes trying to figure out what socks feel like. "They're a bit sweaty, I guess."

"And?"

"And I don't know. The little sticky part on the back that keeps them from sliding down my heel feels different," I shrug.

"And before I asked, before you sent your thoughts down to your toes and probably moved them around a little, did you consciously know what they felt like in this moment?" She pushes the third bowl in front of me, wiping up the splash of water that escapes like I wish I could escape this bizarre object lesson.

"No. I guess I didn't."

"Great. Now take both hands and put them in the middle bowl." She nods to pull me from my hesitation.

I dip both in the third bowl. "Wait. What?" The middle bowl felt like two different temperatures. To my left hand, it felt cold. To my right, hot.

"Exactly," she says, like this whole thing was supposed to somehow make sense.

"Exactly what? What kind of magic is this?"

"Your brain will send you the signals it thinks you need to be aware of. Under normal circumstances, you don't need to know what your socks feel like, so it stops sending that message." She takes a smug sip of her drink like she just illuminated the universe. I'm still in the dark.

She must sense my bewilderment. "Which hand is hot?"

"My right."

She points to the bowl on my right. "Cold water."

Charlie dips a finger in. "Yep."

"Great, so you're a magician. Nice trick."

"I'm not a magician. When your hand first felt the cold water, it sent that message to your brain loud and clear. After a while, it sensed it wasn't dangerous, so it dampened the message. When you changed to the warm water, it had adjusted your input scale so that the warm water feels hot. The hand that was in hot water, had its scale adjusted the other way, so the warm water now feels cold."

I'm starting to get this, but I have no idea what to do with it. "So, I need to adjust my hot scale?"

"With exposure therapy. You find something that triggers that freak-out response, as you call it, and let your hand sit in the water. You know, you just sit there with all those fear feelings until your brain gets the message that you don't need to register those feelings as loudly anymore."

"So, you want me to go find a gangster and make him attack me? No way in hell I'm doing that."

I shove the bowls of water away from me. No way in hell.

I wiggle my toes in my sweaty socks. No fucking way.

Harley lays her hand on my arm. "I would never want you to do that. Never."

She leaves her hand there as I fill my lungs to their full and let the air sit in there for five heartbeats before releasing it slowly.

She continues. "If you were in a situation with a gangster, you would want that fear reaction. I'm talking about something that you shouldn't be reacting to, but you are. What set you off last time?"

I bring myself back to the elevator. The drunk-ass shits. The crowding. Then Ryder boxing me in with his arms. I shake off the thought. Just recalling it makes me nauseous.

I can't tell them that's what is setting me off. That's completely crazy.

Shit. I'm going to be alone for the rest of my life. What every girl fantasizes about, a guy pushing her up against a wall right before kissing her, had me attacking him and fighting for my life.

Harley knows when to push. And when not to. "Whatever it is that makes you overreact, try to experience a tiny bit of it, maybe just imagining it. Then wait for your response. Use all your calming tools and wait until you can get yourself under control again. Then take a bigger dose. And a bigger dose. Until you can handle the full dose without a reaction. Or maybe just with a reaction that is small enough that you can handle it."

It makes logical sense—in a lab experiment sort of way--but how am I going to convince Ryder to give me a repeated dose of him like that? He already must think I'm a complete psycho. Asking him to do that would be nuts.

Chapter 38

BILLIE

I open a can of Dr Pepper and down the whole thing before lowering the can and swiping the syrupy goodness that dribbled down my cheek in my low-induced haste.

"I think I like you best like this. Just completely unguarded," Ryder sighs.

If he wants unguarded...

I toss the can in the recycling bin. "I kind of need a favor."

He holds out the box of Lucky Charms. "Anything."

I take a handful, putting them in my mouth one by one, striving to string this out as long as possible. When I finish off the last marshmallow, I dust my fingers on the back of my bikini bottoms. "I'm trying to get my brain not to overreact to things."

Ryder folds up the inner liner of the Lucky Charms and puts them back in the cupboard before washing his hands in the sink. I love that he is willing to risk a gluten exposure to make sure I have my Lucky Charms at the ready during a low, but I would hate to think what he'd endure if he wasn't really careful.

"I've figured out one of the things that triggers me and I need to slowly expose myself to it in increasing doses."

He wipes his hands on the dishtowel and then tosses it on the counter, waiting for me to continue.

How do I ask this guy to make a move on me so I can fix my

broken brain? Dammit. This is the stupidest thing. But it has to get done.

"When we were in the elevator?" I'm hoping he can fill in the blanks and I won't have to spell this out.

He nods. "Okay. You want me to go back there with you?"

If only it were that easy. "I don't think it was the elevator that did it."

I make my way to the living room and fall onto the couch, praying this will be easier if he's not looking right at me. "It happened before that, too."

Does he know? Does he remember me sprinting from him in Wilmington? Leaving him without an excuse? Without an explanation? Without even a way to contact me?

He sits next to me.

I can't look at him, so I let my gaze travel the room, stopping when I see the picture of my entire family jumping off our sailboat on the edge of the Great Barrier Reef. That was the day I climbed to the top of the mast before leaping headlong into the sea. That little girl didn't know the first thing about fear. I want so badly to get back to her.

I take his hand and lead him into the hallway right next to that picture. "Can I show you?"

"Sure," he replies, still thoroughly confused.

I lean my back against the wall and angle him so he is facing me but still a good foot away. I swallow hard as my breathing grows shallow. There's no way I can get him to trap me like this without needing to beat the shit out of him again, so I stay there in that position, trying not to let the fear drive me to run. I picture my feet trapped by blocks of cement too heavy to lift, so I don't flee. My fingers come alive, tapping on my thighs as the muscles in my neck tense up.

Ryder studies me as I turn into a lunatic in front of him.

"Shit," he mumbles. He retreats to the couch, grinding his palms into his face. "Shit," he repeats.

Damn. Why did I have to ask him to do this?

My feet are still locked to the ground, so I call to the other room, "I'm sorry I asked. This was so stupid."

"So, it's me? Being close to me does that to you?" He stops rubbing his face and looks up at me, crushed.

He doesn't think I'm crazy, he's hurt.

"No, RyGuy. It's not you." I cross the room and sit right next to him. "See, I can be next to you just fine. In fact, being close to you usually helps me calm down."

"I saw what happened, Billie. I just watched it happen."

I rub my thumb along my other palm and release a deep breath. "Kavika...he, uh, shit." I pull my thumb from my palm and study the indentation I dug there for a few moments. Wiping my palms on my legs, I try to continue. "He had me trapped." I begin to gnaw at my thumbnail.

After ripping it down to the nub, I go on. "I was up against the wall and he had his hands..." I lift my arms to place them against an imaginary wall in front of me. "So, when..." I cover my face with both hands and squeeze my eyes shut, praying it will hold back the tears.

"It reminds you," Ryder suggests.

"Yeah. It reminds me." I pull my hands from my face. "Harley thought I should try to recreate that in small doses so I can get over it."

"Whatever you need, Billie. For as long as you need." He hesitantly slides his hand on my shoulder. I fall into him and he folds me up in a revitalizing hug.

He pulls me back. "Want to try again? I promise I won't bail this time."

"Please." I return to the wall.

He returns to his mark. "Let me know where you want me."

"That's good for right now." I fight my rising heart rate by controlling my inhalations.

"You good?"

I nod. But I'm nowhere near good. It's full-blown panic setting in just picturing him trapping me with his arms. I grind my teeth together trying not to run. Or worse yet, slam my fist into his chest.

He steps back.

"What happened?" I ask.

"You looked like you were in physical pain." He leans against the opposite wall. "So, I stopped."

"It does hurt. But it's supposed to. I have to sit with the pain and let it subside."

"How am I going to know when it's too much? I really don't want to hurt you any more than you've already been hurt."

"I don't know. Maybe we could have a code word or something."

"A safe word?" he laughs.

"Sure. We have a safe word." Flashes of Ryder in a leather getup, whip in hand, asking for my safe word has me giggling. That's one way to bring down the fear. "How exactly do you pick a safe word?"

"Don't know. I've never needed one."

"That's good to know. Um, how about..."

"Sea slug," he declares.

I completely fail at stifling my laugh. "You seem confident in sea slug."

"Sea slug's perfect."

I'm afraid to ask why he thinks it's perfect. "Okay. So, unless you hear sea slug, you keep me there."

"You promise not to break another rib?"

"I am so, so, so sorry. Did I hurt you badly?" I lay my hand on his shirt checking for any damage. The only thing I feel is taut muscle under my palms. And my heart rate bumps back up.

He laughs. "You do know.."

I finish out his sentence with him. "...what I did for a living, right?"

"I'm fine. You want to try again?"

I resume the position and prepare myself. He stands in front of me, toe to toe, and the whole process starts again.

Heart thrashing.

Sweat pouring.

Breath racing.

The need to scratch at his flesh to get away.

I obsess over his nose, knowing I could head butt him and

knock him to his knees. I have to press my skull to the wall behind me to keep myself from doing it.

Breath first. Heart follows. I demand my lungs draw in a complete breath until they cannot expand anymore and hold it there until they are about to explode. I blow it out slowly and let my chest hang deflated at the end. Then I repeat the process.

Ryder glances at my face before returning his gaze to the ceiling.

A few breaths later, my heart is following.

Without letting his green eyes meet mine, Ryder breaks the silence. "How will we know when it's over?"

"When I can get— Oh! I know." I pull myself from the wall but am trapped by strong arms. "Let me... fine. Sea slug."

He lowers his arms and I race into my room to find my Garmin watch. Slipping it onto my wrist, I push the buttons to change the heart rate settings. Eighty is a normal walking-around heart rate. So above 120 would show I'm in fear mode. I set it to begin alarming above 120.

I return to the wall. "Resume the position."

My heart is already at 118 so as soon as he steps in front of me, the watch starts beeping. Ryder studies it.

"When I can get the alarm to stop, we'll be done."

He nods like any of this is normal.

After controlling my breath, I try some visualizations. I picture myself slowly strolling into Napili Bay. The warm water creeping up my body. I relax every muscle that the sea touches. By the time the water reaches my ears and I'm floating, the beeping has ceased. A smile creeps across my face as a sense of control and accomplishment spreads in my chest.

Ryder dips his head. "We done then?"

"Yeah. We're done."

He scuffles into the kitchen. I follow.

He pulls a Dr Pepper from the fridge, pops it open, and takes a long swig. It looks like he was the one who just confronted his biggest fears, not me. "Sorry. I know they're for your lows, but I really needed something."

"I agree. I feel like I deserve a treat."

"Like training a dog? You do a trick and you get a treat?"

"Well I am training my brain, so why not?" I search my cupboards for something sweet. Finding a pack of Caramel M&M's, I hold the package out to Ryder, looking for his gluten-free stamp of approval.

He nods.

I hand one over and take one for myself.

He gives me a hang-dog look. "One?"

"I don't want to start packing on the pounds."

"From one M&M?"

"One for each time."

He takes another sip while he considers. "We're doing more of these?"

"Well, yeah. Bigger doses every time. Until I don't even respond. Can you do that for me?"

He pops the M&M in his mouth. "Anything. Anytime. Anywhere. You just tell me where and when."

Chapter 39

RYDER

At the edge of my backyard, next to the chairs angled to catch the sunset, Billie has parked her bike and is waiting for me to show up for our morning swim. It has been far too long since I have done this with her and I cannot believe how much I have missed it.

I take my time crossing the yard, enjoying the delight radiating off her. Just watching her paints a broad smile on my face. Spooner and I meet her at the waterline without a word. This early, words will only serve to break the melody of the tropical birds high in the trees.

She bends to pat Spooner's head. "Hey, buddy. You come to see us off?"

That's right. She doesn't know that Spooner has been filling her shoes on my morning swims. "Not exactly."

She sends me a perplexed glare. No need to explain, she'll figure it out. "Slow is smooth," I say as we start our pre-swim ritual.

Billie finishes it off. "Smooth is fast."

I nod and all three of us dash into the ocean.

When Spooner beats her into the water, she laughs. "He's with you for a few weeks and you turn him into a seal?" she blurts.

"I needed a swim buddy. He was here."

Her face falls before she starts swimming again. *Way to hit her where it hurts, Jax.*

By the time we make it to the buoy, Billie has let my transgressions go and is once again beaming as Spooner paddles in circles. He hasn't learned how to tread water in place yet, so he keeps doggie paddling forward around the two of us.

She checks her watch as I wait for her update on time and her blood sugars. "We should get going, if we're gonna make it to Finn's on time."

And that widens my smile until it is nearly as big as hers. It was already such a coup to be able to swim with her again, I didn't think she'd want to show up to Game Night together. Not that we're together-together. But getting to spend any additional time with Billie is a huge bonus.

She missed the first two Game Nights since she got home. I think she's avoiding JJ, not ready to have that conversation yet, especially in front of all her friends. Billie's not the type to avoid a conversation if she has something to say, but I don't know if she's processed it all yet. At least not the part that JJ played in all of it.

I mentioned it to JJ last week. He decided he was going to be busy for the next few Fridays so she could enjoy Game Night until she's ready to be in the same place as him.

When we get back to shore, she shoulders her bag without even changing. "You mind if I rinse off in your shower?"

"It's all yours. You know where the soap and towels are?" I know she knows because I've caught her eyeing me in there a time or two, or at least that's how I like to think of it.

After a Game Night led by Charlie, who graciously took over as Gamemaster for Finn, we retreat to my place. Billie and I have been practicing her exposure therapy for almost a week now. And she is getting better. Each time she is able to bring her heart rate down faster. Which means, each time, I have to get closer and closer.

Her exposure therapy is turning into my exposure torture.

I know. Let's take the one thing I can't have and put it so close that I can nearly taste it over and over again. And let's make it so I cannot even let it look like I want it. Do you know what kind of excruciating torment that is? It should be outlawed right along with waterboarding.

The last time we tried, I almost broke. I'm toe to toe with her, but her heart rate never breaks one-twenty. So, with a steady heart rate, she asks for more. "Okay. I think I'm ready for your arms."

When we're only standing toe to toe, I can still study the ceiling to distract myself. I can fidget with my hands to get out the nervous energy. But locking my arms to the wall behind her takes away all my coping strategies.

"Whenever you're ready, RyGuy."

Damn, she has to go and call me that.

"Yeah. Right. Arms. Got it." I lift my hands and touch the wall with just my fingertips, leaving as much space between us as humanly possible. She inhales deeply and releases a sigh.

I match her next breath in. I think I could use some of her relaxation breathing, too.

I allow my gaze to dip down to her face. Her lips push out as she exhales. She rolls her bottom lip under her tongue, then takes in another breath. I lean my entire weight on my hands, bringing us even closer, and dip my head as I imagine following her tongue with mine.

She lifts her head from the wall behind her—the prolonged anticipation almost unbearable—before she pulls up her watch to check her heart rate.

And the cold realization smacks me in the face. We are not here in some sort of drawn-out foreplay. I'm only helping her get over something. And even though I know this going into it every time we do this, I get carried away in the moment, her nearness overpowering my resolve to keep my wits about me.

How am I going to continue doing this without screwing up?

Chapter 40

BILLIE

With my recent wins in exposure therapy, I decide it's time to tackle surfing again. By the time I reach the water's edge, I realize that is a lot easier said than done. I bend to refasten my leash around my ankle, pulling the Velcro strap back and sealing it again several times.

A repeat of my previous humiliating performance is looming. I can't get stuck in knee-deep water again.

Action beats Anxiety.

I need to go. Now.

Using one of my old tricks, I twist to look over my shoulder as Imaginary Ryder sprints down the sand, jumps on his board, and paddles past me. "You coming?"

I take off and paddle once I hit the water, following Imaginary Ryder into the lineup, sitting a little further out than the crowd. The last thing I want is to be caught inside when a bigger wave comes through.

Set after set barrels by and I cannot convince myself to spin around and paddle for a single one. A smaller ripple dawdles behind after the last set.

Perfect. I turn to paddle for it, but I half-ass it and miss entirely. I don't even know if I want to catch it.

It's only three feet out here today, held up by a fabulous offshore breeze. By the time I was ten, I surfed waves four times this big without a second thought. But now, I can't even convince myself to give it a real try.

For the last seventy-one days, I have been stuck under this busted brain, barely able to do the most basic of things. Running into walls. Losing everything. Tripping over my own feet. It has taken my art from me.

And now my surfing, too.

The next set rolls in and I'm determined to take one. I egg beater my feet, spinning my board around. Laying down, I paddle furiously. I can feel the energy of the wave pick me up and know it's time to pop up. I grasp the rails, push my chest up, look over the shoulder to find my line.

And then feel my feet dragging in the water behind me to pull out.

"If you're not going to take it, get the hell out of here, kook."

I turn to the local boy sitting to my right.

He splashes me in the face. Shaved head. Black trunks. More ink than skin.

I paddle away from him and I hear from over my shoulder, "Let's show her what we do with snitches."

There's no way. Kavika's locked up. It's not him.

But that doesn't stop my heart from battering my ribs.

Or my breath from growing shallow.

And is it possible to sweat in the ocean?

Slow it down. Come on, Billie. You got this.

I am safe. Warm ocean water on my back. Kisses from Spooner. Sunset in Ryder's backyard. You're paddling, your heart should beat this hard. You won't die. You won't die.

I make my way to the edge of the lineup to make sure I won't be in anyone's way again. Stretching my hands to the front of my board, I let my head drop until my forehead is resting on the nose.

It's been nearly three months since Kavika screwed up everything, I should be better by now. I may be healing, but it is happening so damned slow.

"Slow is smooth," Imaginary Ryder calls out from his board next to me.

I look up and picture his big, goofy grin smiling back at me.

I don't know how we got into the habit, but before every swim, when we line up at the shore, he says, "Slow is smooth," and I reply, "Smooth is fast." Then we jump in and take off. Every single time.

Halfway through the swim, when I'm getting tired and my form has broken down so that I'm spending more energy smacking the water than actually gliding through it, I say to myself, "Slow is smooth. Smooth is fast," and my form recovers.

It's okay to take my time in recovery. Slow is smooth. Smooth is fast.

My heart quiets. I force three long breaths in and out.

Lifting my head, I focus on the feel of floating up and down the swells before they crash into rideable waves. It's so similar to being on the front of Ryder's boat, feeling the spray from the bow dance up to hit my feet hanging over the edge.

The surface of the deep green water is like glass reflecting the scattered clouds lazily wandering above. I relax my hand to play with the water like a dolphin breaking the surface to jump and flip, only to dive again. A school of 'Oama begins to pool beneath me before darting off all at once.

I let the side-shore current push me west to the next peak while I pull myself out of my head and back into my body, allowing the ocean to bring me back to neutral.

When the next set hits, I spin and paddle for the first wave, this time finally making it to my feet. With the ocean flow still pushing me, all my experience comes back and I'm riding it like I was actually a pro at one point in my life, hitting the lip, powerful turns. I even throw in a little aerial at the end.

I ride until the wave evaporates and I'm left standing on my sinking board. I lay back down, aim my board out to sea, and paddle back out. I do this over and over until I run out of steam. One last wave brings me to the sand. I pull my leash from my ankle, wrap it around the tail, and look out at the waves.

I let a laugh slip from my lips. I still have it. It's been six years since I stepped foot on a short board, but it all came back to me. Maybe this PTS hasn't taken everything from me permanently.

It's all just temporary. I will get it all back. The art. My life. Friends. I can get it all back.

Now that I have my surfing back, and a full three weeks of exposure therapy under my belt, I'm almost normal. Like a routine, I assume my position against the wall and Ryder takes his. We have gone from him standing a distant foot away and taking a good ten minutes for my heart rate to return to baseline to him stalking up to me and ensnaring me without my heart rate ever rising above the threshold.

"So, that's it? You finally got one without going over one-twenty."

I reach into the caramel M&M bowl I stashed next to us on the hallway table to dole out our reward every time and toss it his way. He catches it midair.

I retrieve my training treat and slowly roll it over in my mouth, taking my time to bask in my growth. "I feel like I need some kind of last gigantic test."

"Like a final exam?" Ryder suggests.

"Exactly. Like a massive, scary, gnarly final exam."

We move to the living room couch. "I could come at you with a ski mask and—"

"No ski masks needed. But maybe if you looked more like... like Kavika did that day. Like a pair of black trunks and glasses on top of your head." I beam as I realize that picturing that night doesn't cause my body to react. "And you could come at me with a menacing look on your face. Like real mean."

He bares his teeth at me.

"No, for real. Like your actual fight-mode face."

"I have a fight-mode face?"

"I'm sure you had one when you needed it."

"Okay. Fine," he acquiesces. "And how about a surprise attack?"

I hop up on my legs and turn toward him. I feel like I'm playing a little war game. And it's kind of fun. "Yeah. We could have an attack window. Like any time between midnight on Saturday and midnight Monday. Anywhere in that forty-eight-hour window, without warning you trap me up against the wall."

He stands from the couch and glances out the front window, a nervous tick I've noticed lately. "Okay. Black trunks, sunglasses. Do you remember what color shirt?"

"No shirt."

He lets out a breath. "Copy that. Attack window is zero-hundred Saturday to twenty-four-hundred Sunday. I'll come with my game face on and not much else."

And now I'm really looking forward to this.

Ryder sinks into the sofa next to me and holds up the remote. "You want to watch something?"

"You did say you'd give *Dawson's Creek* a chance." I waggle my brows.

"Until I realized that would mean watching a twenty-year-old show about kids not old enough to drive. I couldn't even make it to the opening credits of the first episode. Watching fifteen-year-olds talk about transcending mounting sexual theoretics is too much for me."

I don't blame him. I'm floored he even tried to watch it.

He turns on another rerun of *Ridiculousness* and pulls me back to the couch, resting his arm on my shoulder. I settle into him as we let the mindlessness on TV try to distract me from the picture of Ryder in black trunks wrapped around me.

Chapter 41

BILLIE

Friday night, I prepare for my attack window. I slip my fully charged watch onto my wrist. Before I go to sleep, I do an extra-long meditation session, hopefully giving myself a little more heart rate wiggle room if he attacks tonight.

When I awake Saturday morning, Ryder still hasn't come. Not sure I expected him to try to rustle me up from a deep slumber to press me up against a wall. It just wouldn't make any sense, but it definitely would be hot.

Since he's going for a sneak attack, we couldn't very well work out together, so I swim a leisurely mile at the beach by my place. I forgot how enjoyable it was to take it slow. It gives me the time to really feel the water sliding across my back, the sun on my shoulders, and the sound of steady breaths in and out of my lungs. Of course, my watch was beeping at me continuously as I had my heart rate in the 130s the whole time.

After a quick lunch, a nap is calling, so I lay out a towel in the backyard and strip down to my bikini. Don't want any funny tan lines.

I set out to do a little meditation to lower my heart rate in case Ryder shows up soon, but my mind keeps pulling me back to my impending final. Maybe I should do some positive visualization to make sure I react the right way.

Before my NSSA surf comps as a kid, my coach used to have me do that before each heat. I'd sit on the shore and envision my heat, everything going perfectly. I'd get all the biggest waves, making every powerful turn flawlessly, hitting the lip with force, throwing in a few airs along the way.

I'd think about what it would feel like paddling in from my last wave, knowing I slaughtered my competition, the crowd hoisting me up on their shoulders to carry me to the stage where I get one of those huge checks and the most gigantic trophy anyone has ever seen.

I roll onto my back and let the sun warm up my skin as I try to envision a perfect score on this test. I will use my breathing skills and progressive relaxation as Ryder, in his black trunks, shirtless, tan, traps me up against a wall. But I can't seem to picture it in the right orientation. My mind can only conjure me lying on this towel in my bikini and Ryder, arms braced on either side of me, slowly lowering his weight onto me, as he dips his head to kiss me. His lips warm and moist--

Beep. Beep. Beep.

The alarm stops that thought from going places I shouldn't be if I my heart rate to stay low. There's no way I'm getting any sleep now. Maybe a grueling surf session is a better idea. Burn off some of this energy. And the cold water wouldn't hurt either.

After a good two hours of near-perfect waves at Westies, I wander up to Five Ono. Kaimana lives in a giant silver Airstream on the backside of the property and built a little shower right next to it. It's out of view of the restaurant and it affords me a little privacy. He's cool enough to let me slip in there to rinse off when I surf out front.

I settle my board outside in the racks of my parked bike and pull the bamboo door shut behind me. Although the ocean was warm today, the off-shore winds brought the temperatures down. I wish Kaimana had the foresight to build this shower with hot water as a chill passes over my skin.

I turn and close my eyes, letting the water run over my hair, when I feel two warm hands on my hips.

Ryder pushes me through the spray until I'm backed up against the Airstream. He lifts his arms to trap me just like we had planned.

But this feels nothing like what we planned.

There's a hunger in Ryder's jungle-green eyes as they rove lazily over my skin, leaving a trail of heat behind. His gaze stokes a raging fire in me that was gently growing since the day I first laid eyes on him.

I track a drop of water as it runs over his broad, tan pecs, before he shakes more water from his hair, pulling my attention back to his face. My body aches for his touch and I have to fight my overwhelming need to be closer to him.

He staggers closer and closer until he's left me no room at all. The metal shell of the Airstream is warm on my back, heated by the blazing afternoon sun. Ryder's skin is scorching as he presses his chest against mine, sealing me in a seductive cocoon of warmth. He dips his head as he drops his elbows to the wall bringing him only a breath away from kissing me.

I can feel my heart start to race, nearly setting off my alarm. Right when I know it is going to sound, Ryder says in a broken whisper, "I'll count that as a pass. Congrats." But he doesn't back away.

I try to come up with something to distract myself from his nearness. "No M&Ms for a reward. I was totally unprepared," I say with a shaky voice. "Imaginary M&M?" I mock retrieving an imaginary M&M from a bowl beside me and lift my finger and thumb like they are holding a training treat to offer it to Ryder.

He leans forward and wraps his lips around my fingers. The sensation sends my spirits soaring. The need to feel his lips on mine like that, unbearable.

A devilish grin spreads across his face. "Looks like we're going to have to find another reward for you." He leans his head and lays his soft lips on my neck.

My watch starts blaring. I flip it off my wrist and let it drop to the floor, silencing it.

Pride fills his eyes, knowing his kiss sent my heart racing. Encouraged, he drops his head to the other side and wraps his lips around my earlobe. The sensation is even more decadent than on my fingers. He slowly releases my flesh and that need to feel his lips on mine is even stronger.

He moves back in front of me and with a slow, secret smile that I fully understand, he pauses as he considers my mouth. A delightful shiver of wanting passes through me as I rise to—

"Who's in there?" The door swings open and Kaimana's face appears in the opening. "Woah. Li'l Bill! Why you making out in my shower?"

Ryder steps back, his face a clash of surprise and disappointment, then spins around to face our accuser.

"Sorry, Kaimana. We just got carried away," I explain.

"No worries. I'll get the kitchen firing up your usual, Billie."

"What about me, Kaimana?" Ryder asks.

"You wait in line like everyone else." He slams the shaky bamboo door behind him.

We look at each other and laugh.

"Maybe we should get out there before he decides to ban me completely," Ryder says.

After toweling off, I slip on my Goonies Never Say Die shirt and a flowy white skirt from the basket on my bike. As we make our way across the open lawn, Kaimana catches me and wraps his arms around me in a warm hug that nearly suffocates me. "So glad you're back, Billie." When he releases me, he lowers his voice, "I heard the Menehune kidnapped you and were waiting for their ransom to set you free."

"No Menehune, Kaimana."

"Then, did you make eye contact with the Huaka'i Po?" This guy will believe any Hawaiian legend if it can explain what he doesn't understand.

"No, I just had to take care of something on the mainland."

"Damn. I'm sorry. Mainland is way worse than the Huaka'i Po."

"Sorry to worry you, Kaimana, but I'm back."

He points to Ryder. "Too bad you didn't leave him on the Mainland."

"Kaimana. Ryder's good people."

"Ok, Li'l Bill. If you like him, I like him. How 'bout I bring you two of the usuals?"

"Thanks, Kaimana," Ryder says.

Once we find an open table, Ryder closes the umbrella in the middle, making sure I have enough sun to warm up, though after that near kiss, my body is still on fire.

Chapter 42

RYDER

All morning, the only thing I could think was, if Billie passed this "final exam," would that mean that she has a handle on her PTS and might be ready to date again? What would that mean for us? Could I finally see where things go without having to break my *Other's First* pact? Would both of our needs finally line up or would that Nicaragua job stand in the way?

I had to stop myself from showing up at her place at midnight so we could get this last test over with and figure out the next phase. I spent the morning with visions of what it might be like to be with her. To know her in that way. By the time I tracked her down, I was flooded with so many ideas of what that would be like, I could barely hold back in order to play my assigned role.

But she passed.

Sure, maybe I cut it short to guarantee she would pass, but from the hunger I saw in her eyes, she wasn't showing an ounce of fear. The only thing I read there was longing and desire. She wanted to kiss me as much as I wanted to. And from the way she moaned when I kissed her neck, she is more than ready to take this friendship to the next level.

Sitting, waiting for our food, Billie is captivating. She's playing it cool, watching the afternoon sunshine play off the surface of the water as surfers stream in and out of the lineup, but I can't keep my eyes off her. When she looks back at me, the sunlight dances off her freckles and the coy smile that graces her face is alive with affection and optimism.

She pulls her damp hair into a bun, spinning it around her fingers, revealing her neck, and it takes all my strength to not reach across this table and lay my lips on her neck again, to taste her skin.

The skies suddenly unzip and let down a fury of warm water, distracting me from my impending plans.

There is something so magical about being drenched by the rain while the sun is still beaming down. And the drop in temp is nothing short of delightful. The last couple eating nearby take the rainy delight as their cue to pack it in, leaving us alone in this wonderland.

I jump up to spread the umbrella so we can tuck under it. When I glance at Billie to make sure it is protecting her, her eyes rake over my body boldly as her mouth softens. She makes no attempt to hide the fact that she was watching me.

There is only one sensible response to a look like that. I round the table and straddle the bench to face her. She follows my every move, somehow sensing my intentions.

Taking her face in my hands, my heart hammers foolishly. I lower my lips to hers. The touch is tender before her calm is shattered by urgency. I give myself freely to the passion of her kiss.

"Damn, get a room kids," a voice that can only be Savage's steps into this phenomenal moment.

Billie jumps back, leaving my mouth burning with the desire to kiss her again immediately. Can't we ever get a second without someone poking their nose in where it doesn't belong?

I lift my head to Savage who has positioned himself under the umbrella in front of Billie. She spins away from me to chat with him.

"I'm Savage. You must be Billie." He reaches out a hand to shake.

She turns a proud smile my way. "Has Ryder been talking about me?"

"How could I not?" I say before stealing a quick kiss.

"So, Jax, you ready for Nicaragua?" Savage blurts.

I try to give him a look that says shut the hell up, but he is so busy charming Billie, he doesn't notice.

"Nicaragua?" Billie asks innocently.

It's not like I'm actively keeping this news from Billie, but I wanted to have at least a moment together before telling her I'm leaving before we have a chance to see where this goes.

"Yeah. Jax is giving up being a tourist guide for a real job. He'll be doing private security for an Ambassador and her son. "

I glance between Savage and Billie trying to scour her face for how she is taking this, but she won't face me, so I'm left to wonder.

"Oh," is all she can muster before her head drops.

A thousand-pound weight slams into me. I give Savage an angry, fiery look that says, "Thanks for that." He finally takes the hint and says his goodbyes. Billie barely acknowledges him.

The gentle sunshower turns to a seething rain, thrown from jet-black clouds. I scoot closer to Billie to avoid the deluge now pelting my back as it's blown at an angle. I dip my head to try to get Billie to look up, but she doesn't move. She sees me—how could she not, I'm sitting mere inches away—but she doesn't react. Nothing.

Kaimana sets down two steaming plates of chicken, rice, and fries in front of us. "You want me to make that to go? Looks like this rain is gonna stick around."

At that, Billie glances up. "That's okay. We'll eat fast." She offers him a smile as she picks up a fork. But she doesn't eat. She sits there, fork aloft, staring at her plate, frozen beneath the flood of thoughts that will bury her if she doesn't get them out.

"How long?" she demands.

"How long until I leave, or how long will I be gone?"

She sets down her fork and looks away. "Whichever answer is worse."

"I would leave on the fifth. Be gone for a year."

She lets out an exasperated breath as she nods. Rolling her lip under her teeth, she bites back tears. She shoves away from the table and stands. "How," she huffs out. "How could you do that?"

"When I made that decision, you were gone. There was nothing keeping me here. And knowing I would be of some use in protecting someone was something I couldn't pass up."

She pauses for a moment. "Then go save the world, Jax." The way she spits out my last name like she doesn't know me, doesn't even like me, my ribs constrict in ways they shouldn't be able to.

She strides toward her bike around the backside of the Airstream. I'm unable to move as she stalks off, rain drenching her white skirt until it clings to her legs with every stride. She digs a key out of her pocket to unlock her bike before tucking the lock into her basket.

And that's it. I can't watch this any longer. This time, I won't let her run from me.

Fully soaked, I race over to her and insert myself right in her sight line. My face is radiating rage, arms tight across my chest, as I growl, "You're not running from me this time. We have to talk about this."

"What's the point? You're going to one of the most dangerous places on earth to be a human shield. I can't do that again. I can't have someone else I love die. I won't." She pulls her bike from the rack.

I grab the front of the handlebars. She stares at my hands but won't look up at me.

"I'm not going to die," I assure her.

She looks up, her green eyes impaling me, as she shouts, "You can't promise that." She tries to shake her bike free from my grip. "No one can," she yells again.

Kaimana is finishing clearing a few tables nearby when our yelling catches his attention. He sets down the plates on the nearest table and paces towards us.

I lift my hand to settle him and lower my voice. "What do you expect me to do? This is all I know. Protecting people is the only thing I'm good at."

"I dunno. Maybe stay here? Do the things that make you

happy instead of running off to fulfill some sense of duty that has long since passed?"

"I don't know how to do that," I admit. How do you switch off something that has been running your whole life? Something that has kept you safe and functioning all these years?

I stand helplessly as she does a slow dissolve, pulling away more and more in front of my eyes.

She shrugs, completely emotionless. "Then go."

I let go of her bike and run my hands through my hair, tugging at the ends. "Billie." It's a plea for her to stop running, to come fight.

But she doesn't hear my plea. She merely wheels her bike towards the road, calling over her shoulder, "I'm not gonna watch it happen."

———————————

I'm still seething when I get home, so I leave the truck in the driveway and haul out my Scout Bobber Bike. This is going to take hours of speeding through the twists and turns of Kahekili Highway to rid myself of the flood of adrenaline coursing through my veins. The focus needed to take these narrow roads at this speed is exactly what I need. Everything shrinks to acceleration and the pull of my body on the bike as I take each curve.

I've driven these roads so many times, I know every turn before it even comes into view. Left, left, sharp right. The road goes from dark to light as the moon's brilliance sneaks through the valleys behind me, the only sound the hum of the motor beneath me as my attention narrows to the concrete.

Here and now.

It takes a solid hour of riding to force my mind into a place of rational thought. I pull over at the turnout next to the Nakalele Blowhole and stumble in the shadows toward the edge of the island.

I was going to tell her. In a calm planned way. So she would understand why I had to do it. Why the hell did Savage have to blow that whole plan to shreds?

I take a seat on the jagged rocks.

Billie has no clue what I need. This is me. This is all I have ever done. From the time I was eight, it was the only thing that has added any value to anyone. I spent half of my adult life preparing for this. Training for it. Focusing on it. How am I supposed to all of a sudden stop doing it?

I wipe my hand over my mouth.

Waves crash against the lava-encased edge of the island sending a light mist my way. Could we survive a long-distance relationship that long? It didn't work out so well last time we had a whole continent between us.

That thought drives me from the ground and soon I'm traipsing over craggy terrain back to the road. I point my bike home and rely on autopilot to get me there as weariness begins to show itself. I pull into the driveway that is now occupied by JJ's brown El Camino and hop off my bike. I texted him before leaving Five Ono with a brief on the shitshow that had unfolded.

"You finally kissed her?" he gushes.

I take off my helmet and stow it on the back of the bike. "Kissed her and lost her in under an hour. That's got to be a personal record."

"I'm sure you didn't lose her."

I shrug as I lead us into the house. "You need a beer as bad as I do?"

"You need a beer like I need a hysterectomy," JJ laughs.

"Beer. Cider. Same thing." I pluck two from the fridge and pop the tops. "Just for that, I'm making you drink cider, too."

JJ takes a slow drag, obviously processing the lackluster taste of cider and the new info. "What makes you think you lost her?"

"Savage opened his big mouth and told her about Nicaragua." I take a long pull from my cider as the look on Billie's face when she stormed off flashes in front of me.

"Damn. You explain to her why you're going?"

"Explain to her. Scream at her. Same thing."

He drops into the barstool. "It went that well?"

"It wasn't my finest moment. I chewed her out right in the

middle of Five Ono. I think Kaimana is going to ban me from that place for it."

"For sure. Kaimana loves that girl. If I were you, I wouldn't go back there any time soon."

Solid advice.

JJ goes on, "This is still salvageable. Go and talk to her, tell her why you have to do this. She'll understand."

"The way we left things, I don't think she wants to be in the same room with me let alone listen to me."

I lean my elbows onto the counter across from JJ.

"If she won't listen to you, how do we convince her?"

We both come to the same conclusion in unison. "The girls."

Now, I just have to convince them that long-distance for a year is worth the pain for Billie.

Spooner slaps his paw against my thigh, his sign for wanting whatever I'm eating at the time. Not sure he'd do good with cider, so I pull some treats from the cupboard and give him one. "Hey, love bug. Can *you* talk to Billie for me?" His ears perk up at the sound of her name.

I guess since I'm really leaving, it's time for Spooner to leave, too. Not that I'm looking forward to increasing my loneliness, but if Billie keeps pushing people away like she did me, she's gonna need someone to love her.

Chapter 43

BILLIE

Tourists scatter from the sand when a sudden rainstorm hits, the look on their faces like they've never seen rain before. They had no idea that water could come from the sky. The perfect Hawaiian vacation they had planned could never go off-book.

After our fight, I straggled out of Five Ono, hopped on my bike, and it brought me here. The tourists won't return to Westies for a couple of hours, finding new ways to entertain their broods. That's the best time to be at the beach. The cool drizzle cutting through the heat. Knowing that I'm the only one around. That I'm the only one who is crazy enough for this precise moment.

Sitting. Drenched. Thinking.

He's leaving. Nicaragua might as well be Peru. And he will be going out looking for the exact same type of people that took Brent from me. There is no way I can hold another person I love while watching the life seep out of him. And I wouldn't even be there with Ryder. I would have no idea it had happened. No one would tell me. I'm not his next-of-kin. I'm not family. I'm nothing to him.

All I have left now is Imaginary Ryder. And even he is wrecked. Every time I try to conjure him up to sustain myself, his voice grows angry as he growls, "I'm next, Billie. I'm next."

The wet sand feels coarse against my fingers as I draw circles, distracting myself while I attempt to find some way out of this agony, but I'm not sure if any of my tools can dig me out of this kind of unrelenting pain.

So, I don't even try. I let the rain encompass me, let the waves roll in and abandon me once more. Let the tears fall, to no avail.

He's leaving.

And he's leaving of his own accord.

No scary Peruvian locals are forcing him to. He wants this. Wants to go save the outside world instead of living with me in this one.

Soaked through, feeling like water has seeped through my skin and watered down all my insides until they float in a salty broth that threatens to leave with the next wave, I rise, unsteady, not sure if the shaking is coming from the cold or my own weakness.

Slow steps draw me towards my bike in the lot. I pause at the bottom of the rocks, overwhelmed by the energy it will take to climb the ten feet to the street above. A path I would usually bound up with enthusiasm is now too much. I'm too fucking weak to do anything.

No wonder Ryder is leaving. I would leave me, too, if I were him.

Collapsing back into the sand, I waste another fifteen minutes pouring out another batch of tears. When my eyes finally exhaust themselves, I try again to ascend to my bike, dragging heavy feet to the top. I draw my hand along the craggy lava rock wall as I make my way to the parking lot, enjoying the coarse sensation on my skin. When a street sign blocks my hand's path, I let my fingers tap the cool metal post, as a faint rainbow catches my eye.

I drop my eyes to where I know I'll see the words "Someday, we'll find it."

Today, I'm not convinced. I don't think I will ever find it. It's been almost six years and I still haven't found it.

I'm still in the same dark place.

Sitting on this beach crying my eyes out.

Still haven't fixed all the wreckage that Kavika caused.

That Brent caused.
That Ryder will soon add to.
Not sure I ever will.

––––––––––––––––––––

It feels like I finally wake up once I am in my driveway, not exactly sure how I rode home. Pushing open the front door, I'm greeted by Spooner nearly knocking me over. I kneel to hug him. "Spooner. I'm so glad you're here, buddy." He rolls over and I give him a big belly rub. "I missed you so much."

I toss my keys on the table next to the door. They land on paper. I slide it from beneath the keys. "Didn't want you to be alone."

Those words. Almost the exact words I remember Brent writing to me before my semifinals in Peru. I read it again and am overtaken by a need to see the words in Brent's handwriting.

"Come on Spooner." I tap my leg for him to follow, but he slumps down and stares out the open door. "Fine."

I head into my room and crawl under my bed, shoving aside boxes and dusty balled-up clothes to find the small white box where I buried my life as Izzy. I take it and a blanket from the foot of my bed and return to the couch. "Come here, Spooner." I pat the cushion next to me.

He won't budge and I'm gonna need him right next to me in order to unseal this box of misery, so I tow the rainbow blanket behind me as I settle in beside him on the tile floor.

Removing the lid slowly so I'm not engulfed in a cloud of dust, I'm accosted by a folded-up paper. No need to unfold it; I know exactly what it says. But I'm not ready for that.

I slip it under the box and pull out a pile of photos of two little towheads in trunks. We're maybe four years old. Copper skin beneath a bushel of white straw hair. Tiny surfboards under our arms. Smiles as big as the surf world we knew we would conquer.

The stack of pictures is like a time-lapse of my surfing career. My first wave on a longboard. The first time I got vertical. A huge spray of water from a cutback when I finally found my strength. My first aerial. And then pic after pic of me on the podium with trophies bigger than I was.

I thumb through my journals from those days with more doodles than words. Sketches of me on the podium at the World Championships. Brent right there beside me. Of the logos from every brand I knew one day would be begging to sponsor me. And folded up in the pages, newspaper and magazine articles predicting the same thing. The Styles Twins Will One Day Rule the Tour Together.

And then the item I was looking for. A Cosqueña Beer coaster. I flip it over and read the last thing Brent ever wrote to me. "You're gonna kill it in the semis. You'll never be alone out there. I'll be right beside you cheering you on."

I never made it to the semis. And I have been alone ever since.

Thoughts of that night come crashing down on me. Standing in that filthy alley. The thud of the door slamming open and the rustling. Then that muffled whelp.

And I knew.

But I was completely frozen. The only thing I could do is stand in that disgusting alley and hope they didn't come after me, too.

And then Brent, whispering my name.

If I had only kept my mouth shut, stayed chill back in that bar, Brent wouldn't have paid for my insanity. For my mistake. He never would have met with that knife. Or was it knives? It was so dark and there was so much damage it was impossible to know.

When he died in my arms in that filthy Peruvian alley, I made sure Insane Izzy died right alongside him.

Eventually, I gather the strength to pull the folded-up paper from under the box. I unfold his funeral program and cannot take my eyes off the pic of our family on the trip we took to the Maldives right before that year's tour began. Mom and Dad, Brent and I, after the greatest surf session any of us have ever had. Arms wrapped around each other and our boards. Smiles as big as the world we would soon lose.

That was the last time we really were together like that. As soon as we got back, Brent and I took off on tour. Only I came back. And then proceeded to shut myself off from everyone.

They called. They came over. They tried so hard to reach me. But I couldn't. Every time I saw them, talked to them, thought about them, it all came crashing back in on me and I couldn't move. The only way I saw to keep going, to continue to be alive, was to seal it all up in this tiny box and never look back.

As Ryder might say, Ignore and Override.

I've been doing that ever since and it cost me everything.

Ryder may be leaving me, but my parents never will. They still call and text and reach out. Maybe it's time to salvage the few relationships I still can.

I tap on my phone and pull up the last message from Mom from a couple days back.

MOM: Dad and I just did the Friday Art Night in Lahaina. We stopped to eat at this darling little place right on the water in your town. It's a place you would totally love. If ever you want to grab some lunch, we can drive over your way and eat there. Dad says it's named after some TV show. I don't know about that. Just know we love you and are always here for you, babe.

BILLIE: Lunch tomorrow? Your place? Noon?

She replies almost instantaneously.

MOM: We would love that!!! Cannot wait to see you again.

Chapter 44

BILLIE

I wake the next morning a little lighter. Sure, I'm nervous about seeing my parents again, but it feels like it is a move in the right direction.

To distract myself from the hours I have until I can head over to their side of the island, I take Spooner out for a walk.

I cannot believe how big and strong he has grown. And how stubborn. Looks like Spooner will be taking me for a walk, not the other way around. He heads along our street, stopping at every corner, looking up at me for permission to cross. It's the only time I feel like I'm still in charge of this stroll.

When we get to Ryder's block, I tug on his leash to turn up a side street but he is so big and strong and stubborn, there's no use. "Let's go back, boy." I give him the command that usually marks the halfway point of our walks and try to retreat down the road away from Ryder's, but Spooner pulls against his leash.

I approach him and bend to pick him up, but he growls. I don't think I've ever heard him growl before. So, I stand and decide to wait him out. If he wants to be stubborn, I can definitely out-stubborn a dog. He continues to pull until he somehow wriggles free and disappears behind the trees that arch over Ryder's driveway.

I gingerly step forward, dragging an empty collar behind

me, to peek through the opening in the trees that line the yard, making sure Ryder's truck isn't in the driveway. It's clear.

Spooner sits in the chair on the front porch looking out over the yard like he owns the place. Even my dog doesn't love me.

I hesitantly push through the gate. "Come here, Spooner."

He doesn't move.

Utterly unable to convince myself to approach the house, I sit against the fence post trying to persuade Spooner to come back to me. But it is useless. Everyone has left me.

I let my head fall as I try unsuccessfully to stop the tears from coming. The last thing I need is for Ryder to find me on his front lawn bawling, but I just can't bring myself to leave Spooner. I only just got him back yesterday and it has been so amazing to have another living being in my house to ward off the unyielding stillness.

Hot breath sweeps across my cheek as my arm is lifted by soft fur. I wrap my arms around Spooner's neck and give him a big scratch behind his ear. Maybe I won't have to leave him, after all.

I retrieve Spooner's collar from the wet grass beside me and unbuckle it. "Come on, bub. Let's go home."

As soon as Spooner sees it, he dashes off to stand watch over the yard from the foot of the porch as if he's spent every day of his short puppy life doing that very thing.

I let my head drop back as I close my eyes now gritty from too many tears. No matter how hard I work, what skills I master, the healing I endure, I'm still not well enough for even a dog to stay with me. A dog that I rescued from the street, fur matted with mud, body starved of all puppy fat, carpeted with fleas. Even he is smart enough to look for a better home. And I think he found one.

Snatching his leash from the grass, I push to a stand and take one last look at my puppy. "Take care of Ryder for me, boy."

"Unsweetened tea, especially for my Isabel." Mom, one of the few people in my life who still uses my full name, approaches with hands loaded with one pitcher of lemonade and one of iced tea. She sets them on the table that sits overlooking Nalu River at the edge of our yard.

The whole drive over, I was fearing that it would be tense and awkward to see my parents after avoiding them for so long, but it was like no time had passed. Mom and Dad were entirely welcoming and simply happy to see me.

I wish I could muster as much cheer. Not that I'm not thrilled to see them, but things with Ryder have poured so much sorrow into me that it is hard to simply be happy. Still, being back here is definitely lightening the load a bit.

"Looks like it's time for some salt," Dad offers.

"I just got here." I don't think I'm prepared to unload on him. "And lunch will be ready soon."

"Go paddle, honey. I'm pretty sure the sandwiches will hold."

I look to Dad.

"Let's go," he says.

We coast downriver to Nalu Kai Harbor, mostly letting the current drag us onward, Dad waiting patiently for me to be ready to open up. When we make it to the mouth of the river, we don't turn into the wind today. Dad must sense that I have no strength left, so, instead, we pull our boards onto the sand and simply sit. After a few minutes, he turns to me. "What's got you so low?"

Without knowing where to begin, I jump right into the mess. "I ran for so long. I ran from Brent's death. Ran from you afterwards. And then I ran to the other side of the country."

"What do you mean, 'other side of the country'?"

I realize then, that my parents had no idea I had left the island. I let my relationship with them grow so distant that they didn't even know I was gone.

I spend the next half hour filling him in on my adventures in Florida, how my brain changed, my journey towards healing. And Dad only listens. No sage advice. No stories with hidden messages I need to figure out about how to handle my situation. When I finish sharing, he simply says, "Looks like you have done an absolute bang-up job figuring this one out. Just keep doing what you're doing."

By the time we get back to the house, Mom has a complete spread waiting for us: sandwiches, fruit, chips, cookies, cupcakes. She even has a chocolate-raspberry cheesecake. She must have started prepping the moment she heard from me, making up for the years of family meals I have missed in my cowardice.

Over a lunch to end all lunches, I share what I have been up to for the last six years.

"What do you think you'll do now?" Mom asks. "Go back to Piper's? Something else?"

"I think I'm gonna give the art thing a real try?"

"Your Biovandal Art? Oh, that would be wonderful!"

Guess my secret wasn't as secret as I thought. "Yeah. Maybe sell prints of some of my favorite pieces or sell replicas of the mini soldiers. Maybe keep up with the Patreon account and find little ways to give my tribe little snippets of joy that come in a box every month like raindrops from heaven. I'm still trying to figure it all out."

"Whatever you decide, it will be great. Everything you do always is," Dad adds.

Chapter 45

RYDER

Hey, you want to go hike Waihee Ridge Trail while we figure this out? I got some energy to burn off," JJ, the Energizer Bunny, suggests.

My *Others First* principle dictates I agree, but he's in a super-caffeinated mood today and I have nothing left in me for that. And I'm not sure how much planning we'd get in with him bouncing all over the trail the whole way. "How about we hit the Coral Reefer? Shoot some pool. Maybe Finn and Grey want to join?" They'll also balance out all of JJ's enthusiasm with a little perspective.

Grey and Finn don't arrive at The Coral Reefer in time to prevent JJ from continuing to prattle on. "I got to know…"

The waitress lays down our drinks with a smile that says it's not the only thing she wants to lay down tonight.

"Thanks." I return her smile, but with one that says a polite no thanks.

JJ continues, "You love her, huh?"

"The waitress? Hadn't given it much thought."

"Billie, dumbass."

"I think it could head in that direction one day," I obscure.

He isn't convinced. And, frankly, neither am I.

Finn slips up to the bar and orders a pitcher with just a head nod. The cute waitress nods back, grabs a pitcher from behind the bar, and starts to fill it. That guy is some sort of covert mind-controlling ninja. I've got to convince him to give me his secret.

He turns to us. "Damn, JJ. Haven't seen you out on a weekend in decades."

"Yeah. I'm trying this new thing. It's called work-life balance. I think I like it," JJ laughs.

When Greyson arrives, we grab a table and order. JJ lays out the objective, then opens it up to suggestions.

"You've got to go big." Greyson stuffs a handful of fries in his mouth. "Make The Grand Gesture." I think Charlie's got Greyson watching a few too many chick flicks lately.

"Yeah. Pull out all the stops. The Fourth of July is coming up. You could get one of the shows to spell out your reasons to her in fireworks," JJ suggests with a straight face.

"Maybe something simpler. And actually doable," I try to bring JJ back down to reality.

"You've got to do something or she'll slip right through your fingers. Three weeks will turn into a year and then into ten, and you'll end up with nothing," Finn certainly lightens the mood with that one.

But maybe it's just what I need to hear. I certainly don't want to end up with Billie being someone I used to know. I spent the last few months doing everything in my power to ensure that wasn't the case. Why stop now?

"What about a Fourth of July party? She's not gonna miss that if everyone is going," I offer.

"Totally. You can propose under the fireworks," JJ says.

"No one said anything about proposing," I protest.

"I meant explain yourself. You know, propose your plan and all the reasons it will work."

"Yeah. It'll be all patriotic and shit," Greyson jumps on board this train. "So when you explain it, she'll have to understand why you want to protect and serve. She'll be so swept away by the romance of it all, she'll have to agree."

"But you have to wait until the fireworks. You can do that right?" JJ and his fireworks.

"So, let me get this straight. I have to throw a party, get her to come, even though she's pissed at me, then ignore her until the fireworks show, and then with all the noise of fireworks popping off, explain all the reasons she should give this long-distance thing a chance? That's the plan?"

"Fine. I see what you're saying. But I can fix it," JJ says. He's on a three-way call with Charlie and Piper before I know what's happening.

He puts his phone on speaker and slides it to the center of the table. "Hey ladies. I need you help with something."

"Sure. What's up JJ?"

"So, Jax is gonna throw this Fourth of July party. And we need you to get Billie to come so Jax can convince her to give him a chance."

Silence.

If this were on Facetime, I bet those two girls would be throwing each other some knowing looks right now. Looks that say, I'm crazy for thinking I can convince her of anything. Crazy for coming up with this huge plan to make some kind of Grand Gesture.

Several dings come through the line. Think the girls are having a text huddle about how to handle this.

Charlie sums up their stance. "We're not gonna convince her to risk her heart like that. Not this soon. Jax, we love you, but ..."

Piper finishes for her, "come up with a better plan."

"I totally understand. Thanks for listening. And would you be willing to not tell her about this crazy plan?" I plead.

"No worries, Jax."

JJ taps the call off. "Not a problem. We'll figure something else out. But now that it's in my head, we have to have a party anyways. You have a perfect view of the fireworks off Lahaina."

"Whatever."

It's probably better this way. I'm not a Grand Gesture guy and I didn't like the idea of trying to trick Billie into coming over. Not that we could even pull it off, I know how hard it is to pull anything over on her.

After we finish eating, we move back to the pool tables.

After a few games of pool, I escape to buy another round. In no rush to get back to the chatter, I take a seat at the end of the bar.

After finally making a shot, JJ hops around from one side of the table to the other, taking the opportunity to taunt Greyson, who, I'm sure, is really winning. Finn reclines at the tall table nearby.

The same table Billie and I sat in when she proceeded to deconstruct my entire personality at first glance. She always had that uncanny ability to see right through me.

Maybe if I simply let her see the real reasons I am leaving, she'd have to understand. She always understands.

But will she?

Shit. That doesn't sound like a reliable plan, either.

But it's more than just that.

Even if she sees all my reasons, if I convince her to give the long distance thing a try, is that really what's best for her? Or for me?

And that question she asked at Five Ono keeps playing in my head on a loop. *Why can't you just do the things that make you happy instead of running off to fulfill some sense of duty that has long since passed?*

Chapter 46

BILLIE

I was hesitant to come back to Five Ono this morning—I really didn't want to be reminded of everything going bad with Ryder—but I knew I had to face my demons as quickly as possible before they have time to fester and become just one more thing that I can't do, one more place that I can't go. So, I bribed myself with the promise of an Ulu waffle covered in whipped cream, bananas, and pineapple.

And it worked.

I may be back here, but I'm not ready to sit at the same table, so I choose one on the far side of the grass and whip out my phone. Since replacing my old phone, I've been burying my face in there when tension builds. It might be a habit I have to break in the future, but for now, it works to find a little escape.

As I wait for my morning dessert, I pull up my last Biovandal post. I've been putting it off because I know it wasn't my best work. My mind just wasn't in the right place—every detail was a struggle to figure out—and I really don't want to disappoint everyone who poured out so much love and support on my Patreon account. I just hope that one day, I'll be able to create art that is on the level with what everyone deserves and expects of me.

I hesitate to read the comments. For some reason, people

feel like they are justified in questioning everything about art. Usually, everyone is pretty positive, but there's always the one critic with a random complaint about how I should have used a different color or had a character posed a different way.

Basically, made *my* creation *their* way.

I vow to take the good and let the nasty remarks go. Whatever is lovely.

Except, every comment I read is lovely. Every single one of them is raving about it. It's remarkable to see the collective mind narrow down where the location must be. Someone even found it already and took a pic.

All the positive remarks fill my heart with the same joy I discovered when I saw that first rainbow on the back of a street sign. Maybe my brain doesn't have to be fully fixed to share comfort with other people. I begin to wonder if everything I went through will somehow make my art better.

Kaimana slides my feast in front of me. "That was pretty rough the other night. You okay? You want me to find that guy and knock the snot out of him for you?"

"No, Kaimana. I'm fine." I flash him a smile trying to convince him that I am fine. "And it wasn't him. I was the one who started screaming. If you should be knocking the snot out of anyone, it should be me."

I was the one who took a civil conversation and turned it into a screaming match. I hate that I told him he was going to die over there—I really don't want that to be the last thing he hears me say—but, I can't go through that again. I can't spend the whole next year in fear. I have been working so hard on getting my brain to get out of fear mode. I can't just make it go right back there. There's no way I'm strong enough for that.

"If you say so, lil' Bill. But I think I'll pass on that beatdown. Too beautiful of a day to throw hands anyways. Enjoy your sugar coma," he says, motioning to my food.

It will take an entire tank of insulin to combat the sugar I'm about to shove in my body, so I dial up a massive bolus and vow to eat slowly. As I take my first bite of waffle, the sun finally pops its head over the West Maui Mountains, shining its golden beams my way. I lean back to relish the warmth on my face in complete bliss.

It's amazing what I used to take for granted. The taste of fresh Ulu Waffles, or any food for that matter. Having an appetite. Owning enough insulin to eat when I'm hungry. The automatic relaxation when sunshine hits my skin. The smell of saltwater over the scent of sugarcane. The very feel of being home.

I lower my head to take another bite as the sweet flavor of the Ulu combines with the banana and pineapple.

The surf off the point looks small today, but that hasn't stopped dozens of people from flooding the lineup. Maybe later this afternoon, I'll pull out my longboard and go enjoy the clear skies and warm water with them.

As I suck in a deep breath, I take in the blend of locals and visitors as they begin filling the tables. Some will be tasting heaven for the first time. Others will be coming home to a taste they have known for years. But all of them will be starting off their day with a full belly and joy in their hearts. There is no other way to leave Five Ono.

At the table next to me, four perfectly mannered kids wait patiently for their breakfast while their mom peppers them with questions about their favorite activity so far and what they are looking forward to the most today.

Beside them, an eager toddler dressed in a tiny red pair of trunks chases one of the wild kittens under and through tables whether they are occupied or not. He dives beneath the legs of a guy who bends to capture the swift creature. He hands it over to the little boy who brings the baby feline to his mom on the other side of the grass. When the hero turns back my way, it's JJ. He smiles but doesn't make a move.

I have been doing a good job of avoiding JJ since I got back. But this is a conversation that has needed to happen for a while. And after the success of mending my relationship with my parents, I think I'm ready to give this a try.

I return his smile and nod as if to ask, "Join me?"

He slides into the table. "Hi."

How do you start a conversation with someone when the last conversation led to one of the worst moments of your life?

I guess you go simple. "Hey."

"Long time, huh?"

"Yup."

He laughs. I laugh. It's a bit awkward, but that's better than outright hostile.

"I cannot tell you how totally, profoundly sorry I am," he blurts. "I let you get into a situation you should have never been in. And I left you there. I will never, for as long as I live, forgive myself for that."

I look to the water as I gather my thoughts. "The only thing that is going to do is increase pain. You have to let it go, move on, and do better next time."

"But what I did..."

"You have to forgive yourself. I have."

I take a bite of my waffle to give him a moment to process. When I finish the mouthful, I ask, "Do you think you could forgive me for bailing the way I did and not letting you know the second I got back?"

"There's nothing to forgive. And from what I heard, if I actually was a dirty cop, you did an amazing job of protecting yourself," he says proudly like he somehow rubbed off on me.

And maybe he did.

We eat our breakfast in comfortable silence, as if we have, in some small way, found our way back toward how things used to be. Not the whole way back, but at least I could stop trying to avoid him.

"Hey, what are you doing tomorrow night?" he asks.

The awkwardness must show on my face because he follows up with, "No. I'm not asking you out. I know that ship has sailed."

He takes a sip of his lemonade suddenly struck by a long train of thought. When he has it all wrapped up, he shares. "I think that ship left port before we even started dating. I've always been so damned competitive. Had to be the best and prove myself at everything. When I met you, I just knew that, if Ryder wanted you, I had to prove that I was man enough for you. But we were never really that right for each other. You know?"

Why does this feel like a breakup speech? He continues with it, even though I assumed he knew we broke up the moment he stepped out of Kavika's house, dirty cop or not. "We tried really hard and I really do like you, but I think we both know you were meant to be with someone else."

Anyone else? Or someone else in particular?

He's right, though. I think I picked JJ because I knew I would never grow so attached that I would have to hurt if I lost him like I lost Brent. You go through one affliction like that and you do everything you can to avoid the next.

"But, tomorrow? You can't spend the Fourth by yourself," he says.

Is it the Fourth of July already? I have lost all sense of time lately. Or maybe I've been trying to block it out because I know what happens the day after the Fourth.

Ryder leaves.

"I guess not," I answer.

"Some friends are headed to this place with a great view of the fireworks off Lahaina. We're barbecuing. Kind of a pot-luck thing. You should come."

"Friends? Is..." I pick at the edge of the weathered picnic table. "Will Ryder be..."

"Ryder didn't get an invite."

A huge party with dozens of people sounds like torture, but I think back to the priorities list I wrote down last week. At the top of that list is Engage with People Again. Looks like I'm going to face a backyard packed with people tomorrow. "I have a freezer of fish I'd love to clear out?" I don't mention that they are the filets Ryder has been filling my freezer with.

"Pick you up around three?"

The next day, I get up and swim six loops of the quarter-mile buoy. I figured if I'm tired maybe my body wouldn't spaz out so much around the raucous crowd I'm sure to encounter tonight. I forgot how exhilarating it feels to finish a high-intensity swim. It flushes out my mind and I'm able to think more clearly. Not to mention the high that comes from a long workout.

When JJ arrives later that afternoon, he holds a huge cardboard box. "It was on your porch." The label says, "Post Office, Key Largo, New York. Hold for Izzy Styles," with my return address. Well, that explains that mystery.

I slide my keys from the table. Pulling the door closed behind me, I lock it and pick up the cooler I set out earlier.

"Never thought I'd see you do that," JJ teases.

"Well, I've changed a few things. You want to take my car or yours?"

"It's just around the corner. We can walk. You want to walk on the sand?"

I never really hung out with any of JJ's other friends—it was always him and Ryder—but I might be a little less anxious at a party filled with cops.

"Did I tell you I started my Academy job last week?" he asks.

I fling off my flip-flops once we hit the sand and carry them. "They sent you back to school?"

"I'm teaching now."

"Wow. Professor Gerdis. What spurred that change?"

We walk along the hard-packed sand near the water. I let it flow over my feet with each wave. JJ dodges each one, keeping his Converse nice and dry. "That last case took too much from me. I was ready to have a life that wouldn't ever be touched by my work."

That last case did take too much. Too much from me, and I guess too much from him, too.

A few yards later, lights and people fill Ryder's backyard. I stop dead. "What happened to 'Ryder didn't get an invite'?"

He laughs and shrugs. "Don't need an invite when you're throwing the party."

"He doesn't want me here, JJ."

"That's bullshit, Billie."

ANYTHING ANYTIME ANYWHERE

Maybe Ryder didn't tell him about our big blowup. "No, JJ. He really doesn't want me here," I try to convince him.

"I think you'd be surprised."

I doubt that.

Chapter 47

RYDER

hy the hell did I agree to this party when I'm leaving tomorrow? When tomorrow makes it final. A year without Billie. Maybe a life without Billie.

When JJ was planning this party, he convinced me it would be a good way to distract myself from zero hour. From the big dustup we had last week. From the next phase of my life which I have been dreading more and more each day it creeps nearer.

In reality, not much could distract me from that shitshow.

I've been replaying our last conversation over and over in my head. Half of the time I come out beating myself up for being so quick to defend my reasons without considering how it would affect her. The other half, I come out furious at her for not understanding why I have to go.

Knowing I won't be a sociable host tonight, I have delegated most of the work. That way, when I'm over the whole party atmosphere, I can disappear upstairs and no one will notice. With the backyard flooded with JJ's friends that I don't really know, I find myself near the edge of the yard with the only ones I do know, or at least the only ones I'm in the mood to endure right now.

A swath of high clouds that look more like a flat curtain of haze, lit from behind by the moon, gives the sky an eerie glow as dusk begins to settle in. Charlie is telling some story I cannot convince my ears to hear, the white noise in my head far too loud to let in any outside sounds. And all that white noise is about our dustup.

How can you do it? Leave me without warning? You're gonna go get yourself killed. And why are you too stupid to do the things that make you happy instead of running off to fulfill some sense of duty that has long since passed?

Long since passed.

During Charlie's storytelling, I smile and nod at all the right times, or at least I try to, but a time or two I awaken to her waiting for me to answer a question I didn't even hear. Greyson tries to help by jumping in, but I cannot convince myself to care.

Then go save the world, Jax. I don't care one bit.

When I unquestionably fail at appearing to be paying attention, I glance off towards the beach to find JJ walking up with...

Billie.

When she spots me standing there, she stops dead in the sand and says something to JJ. He shrugs and says something I'm sure he thinks is hilarious. But it is enough to convince her to keep heading in my direction.

He could have at least warned me she was coming. Give me time to plan. To practice my proposal. My reasons. Not that I haven't been playing that conversation out over and over.

He hops onto the grass. "Hey, guys. Look who I found."

She steps up next to him as he wraps his arm around her shoulders, pulling her tight to his side. She refuses to meet my eyes.

"Billie!" Piper and Charlie cheer.

"I thought you had other plans," Piper continues.

"Yep. Plans to go to a party with JJ. Didn't realize it was this party," she says with a smirk.

Billie finally glances at me, her eyes begging me to connect. The tension must be palpable because everyone is busy scrutinizing the length of the grass beneath their feet. But there's a forcefield keeping me from embracing her. This is not the place to get into it again.

While the grass evaluation drags on, I study her. Her mango tank top with a neon green lizard wedged between the words GECKO and Hawaii. Her little white jean shorts. The Neon pink strap of her flip flops. She is right back to the neon ray of sunshine she used to be, while I have returned to the grumpy asshole I was when I first got back from the Congo.

Trying to break the uncomfortable silence, Billie holds up a small cooler. "I brought fish."

Are those my fillets?

"And beer," JJ adds.

"Who could say no to fish and beer?" Riley says, always the peacemaker.

"I can take the fish over here." Grey and JJ take the fish to the barbecue. On JJ's way by me he whispers with a cocky smile, "Wait till the fireworks."

I'm not sure I even want to ask again. I shouldn't have to explain myself to the girl I thought could see right through me. The one who understood me fully.

Finn is on the beer like white on rice, taking it to the drink table. The awkwardness is so thick it drives everyone else in all directions with or without polite excuse, leaving Billie and me uncomfortably alone.

Billie flashes me one of her million-watt smiles. "Hi."

"Hey."

I rub my hand over my hair, look back to her. Where do I start? Do I beg her to give us a chance? Defend why I have to go? Or do I wait until the fireworks like the big Grand Gesture plan?

She wraps her hands into the hem of that mango tank top inspecting the lizard on the front.

I run my foot along the top of the grass, nudging a small seed out of my way.

She lifts her eyes to me, begging for me to say something.

But I can't find a way in. A way to open up a conversation that ended so badly last time.

All of it becomes too much for me. I spin on my heels and

leave. Following Finn to the cooler, I retrieve a beer right before he swipes it from me.

"I'll take that, Jax," he scolds. "No way I'm ready to witness that aftermath again."

I reach to the bottom of the cooler and grab a cider. After downing it, I open another and look for a place to get my head on straight, somewhere far away from Billie. But no matter where I go, I'm acutely aware of her. And the noise in my head has only grown louder and more disorienting with her presence.

This is stupid. I don't do grand gestures. And is having some new conversation going to change anything about the situation we're in?

Billie sits on the armrest of her pink Adirondack at the edge of the yard.

Is she sitting there, in that chair because she wants me to go talk to her?

While I'm debating making another approach, some total dork stalks up to her.

I drift closer. Close enough to listen in on their conversation. Just making sure she's safe.

"What's a pretty girl like you doing so far out here?" he blathers.

She doesn't bother looking at him. "Staying out of the way."

"That's no way to be. Where's the smile? It is a party after all."

She sighs. "Seriously?"

"Let's see if I can't bring a smile to that pretty face. You want to hear a joke?"

"Not really."

If he doesn't take a hint soon, I'm gonna have to drive it down his throat.

"What about if I juggle for you?" he persists.

On what planet would that impress a woman as phenomenal as Billie?

And clearly, it doesn't. Billie is not amused.

She finally peers up at him. "If I smile will you just go away?"

"If you smile, I may just have to kiss you." He leans in. Billie jumps to her feet to evade the unwanted attack.

My beer drops to the grass as my long strides eat up the short distance between me and her.

JJ meets my gaze for a second before following my path toward Billie and the douchebag suitor. He sprints over to the dead man, throws an arm around him, and escorts him away from his deserved beating.

Chapter 48

BILLIE

Some guys just don't know how to take a hint. Luckily, JJ steps in before I am forced to unleash Insane Izzy on his ass. JJ wraps his arm around the boy and drags him towards the side yard. I think he's being shown the door. Or at least the side gate.

As I watch the procession, my gaze catches on Ryder, fixed in the middle of the lawn, fists clenched at his sides, chest rising and falling in quick breaths.

And we're both locked there together, staring for an hour-long-minute, his face inscrutable.

Does he want me to apologize?

Does he want me to leave?

Does he want me to yell and scream at him for leaving?

Does he want me to break down and cry so he can come put me back together?

Does he want me to vaporize into nothingness like a summer-morning fog at Pipeline?

Like he will tomorrow morning.

His face is screaming at me, but I cannot for the life of me discern what it is saying. And so I stand, as still as he does, completely unable to choose a direction to move.

Heart thrumming.

Chest rising and falling in quick breaths.

And then, just as fast as it began, the moment ends.

We are unshackled.

He turns.

Swipes the beer bottle from the lawn where it dropped moments before.

Disappears into the darkness on the side of the house.

The conversations around me become discernible again. The drums of the music begin to beat. Piper is pulling me towards the picnic table with a view to Lahaina. "Come on. The show's about to start."

And that's when I first hear her voice. A whisper really. *You should go punch him right in the throat.* It's so quiet I barely make it out, but it's a voice I know all too well. Izzy.

I shake her foolhardy voice from my head and focus on the girls lined up on top of the wooden table, joining them to watch the fireworks. Piper bumps my shoulder. "You good?"

"I'm… whatever." But I am not whatever. I am the farthest thing from whatever. I'm a seething pot of emotions I have no name for.

Charlie leans my way and offers me a Truly. "You look like you could—"

Or maybe you should go shake him and yell at him until he tells you what he could possibly be thinking, leaving you like that, her voice more vigorous this time.

Insane Izzy. The girl who does whatever she wants. No matter the chaos it brings. No matter who might get hurt.

Looking down at the can in my hand, I wish I could just drink her away, but alcohol only emboldens her.

I scan the yard for Ryder. He's keeping his distance, leaning on the back porch railing surrounded by two doting girls who are committed to getting his attention.

Fireworks light up their faces in reds and blues. The sulfuric smell overpowers the salty air that just moments ago was calming me down, and although I know they're coming, the rhythmic booms send a flurry of little pulses of adrenaline

ANYTHING ANYTIME ANYWHERE

coursing through my body. With each one, I grow more and more tense, while everyone around me grows more euphoric.

Piper is fully immersed in the show. "No matter how many times I see them, I always—"

Izzy's roar steps into Piper's words. *Or maybe you should walk over there and kiss him.*

Insane Izzy, the part of me that would never change one thing about herself to make someone else happy. Never hide who she is for fear of the outcome.

But I am smarter than her now. I no longer have to listen to her every suggestion. To her every demand.

I shift forward to stand in hopes that moving will convince her to quiet down, but JJ slides in next to me. "You're not thinking about leaving are you?"

I nod. "I really do appreciate the invite though."

"Right in the middle of the fireworks?" He looks concerned.

"I don't think fireworks are going to fix any of this. He doesn't want me here."

This seems to amuse him. "You're serious? You honestly think he doesn't want you here?"

I glance back to Ryder who is reveling in the attention of three lovely ladies now. "Yes. Clearly. And honestly, I don't blame him after what happened."

JJ leans back on his hands, lifting his head for a better view of the pyrotechnics. "Do you know what Jax said to me when he came home from your little rendezvous?"

That pulls a laugh from my lips. "Rendezvous?"

"Yeah. I know about your little meet-up in Wilmington." He bumps my shoulder. "Anyways, he comes to me and sits me down all serious and gets me thinking that he's dying or something, and he tells me, listen to this, he tells me," JJ's voice drops to mimic Ryder's, "'JJ. Your friendship means so much to me.' Now, I'm sure he's dying. All that sun's finally caught up to him and he's got melanoma or something."

"What?" Was I so wrapped up in my own little drama that I missed something major in Ryder's life?

"Then he says, 'I've really screwed something up and you're

301

pretty much the only person who can help me fix it.' So, no cancer, but there's definitely a body he needs help burying."

"A body? Ryder? Yeah, like he'd ever do something like that."

Squeal. Bang. Crackle. More adrenaline.

"You saw how he looked at that kook who was hitting on you, right?"

I shrug, not entirely certain how far he'd go to protect me. "He wouldn't have actually done anything to him."

"Sure, Billie," he laughs. "Anyway, he tells me, 'I've fallen for your girl. And, usually, I'd step back and not pursue it, but, JJ, it's gone way past that point. And I'm not really sure I can stand down from this one.' Always the romantic, that one. Using tactical terms for love."

There's no way he said that. I leave without a trace, for the second time, and that's how he responds. He's fallen for me? There's no way he could look in the face of feeling that kind of pain again and not even flinch.

Izzy coos, *Billie and RyGuy sitting in a tree... Go get some.*

I scream back in my head, *Enough! JJ has no idea what he's talking about.*

I scan JJ's face for any indication that he is joking or making this up, but he looks totally sincere. "There's no way," I challenge. "And either way, that was before I messed everything up."

"You really think Ryder is that fickle?"

"I think he's really that pissed." About to detonate like the fireworks overhead, I have to flee. Somewhere quiet. Try to calm down. "I'm gonna go grab a drink."

"But, you'll stay? Promise?"

"I'll try." I pass by the cooler and snake my way through groups of people, necks craned upward, taking in the sky spectacle. Heading inside, I make a beeline for the bathroom, knowing it's the only place I can guarantee I'll be alone. Only if Insane Izzy will quit harassing me, that is.

Three people waiting outside the door destroy my escape plan. Seriously, though, who chooses the middle of the fireworks show on the Fourth of July to hit the bathroom?

You do know where the other bathroom is, Izzy tempts.

I do. Upstairs. Past the sign hanging on a chain, blocking the stairs to the master. NO ENTRY. ATTACK DOG ON DUTY. Definitely Ryder's style.

Sneaking under it, I make my way to Ryder's bedroom, the silence allowing me a moment to relax. Sitting on his bed, I pull in a few soothing breaths. Spooner rises up from his doggy bed and rambles my way.

I rub his head. "Hey, boy. You want to escape everyone downstairs, too?" If only I could escape Izzy as easily.

After using Ryder's pristine bathroom, I catch my reflection while I wash up. The bags under my eyes have lightened. My tan is coming back. I look halfway alive again.

My gaze drops to a card that says, "Take action. Maintain order. Breathe. Your brain will heal." Reminds me of my cards. Action beats anxiety. Whatever is lovely.

I pluck the card from the mirror to audition his mantra, speaking it aloud to my reflection. "Take action. Maintain order. Breathe. Your brain will heal." An easy smile flashes on my face.

When I try to replace the card, a photo stuck behind it slides upward. I slide it fully into view. It's the picture of Ryder, JJ, and me on the first day we met. Bent in exactly the same place mine is, leaving only Ryder and me visible.

See, he looooves you, Izzy practically sings.

He probably just hasn't had time to toss it yet, I counter. *Plus he's bailing tomorrow. He couldn't love me.*

But, then again, he kept this. Where he can look at it every day.

"Ahhhhhhhhhhhhhh," I scream, hoping the noise of the fireworks will cover my frustration.

Why is he so infuriating?

Chapter 49

RYDER

I get a brief respite from having to make pointless small talk with everyone here tonight. I make the most of the opportunity, lounging against the door frame overlooking the backyard, hoping no one will bother me back here. When the fireworks kickoff, I try to psych myself up to do this thing.

But it's not working. I rehearse all of the reasons I have to go and the reasons we should still try long-distance, but all I can see is her side. She is terrified of me dying while I'm over there. I can't really ask her to spend the next year scared when she pretty much spent the whole last year scared.

I can't do this to her.

But after the shock of having Billie back in my yard again and seeing her sit on her chair again precisely where she belongs, and being completely unable to utter a single word, I have to figure out a way to make things right. Get things back to where we used to be.

I have to find a way to have her in my life even if I will be on the other side of the world. We managed to get through her fleeing to the other side of the country before we even knew what we meant to each other. Why can't we be in each other's lives now that we do know?

The third riser of my stairs creaks, telling me someone has

failed to heed my warning. I spin to hunt down the enemy, only to find Billie hastily descending the steps, muttering to herself. Arguing, really.

I move towards her, to console her, but she stops dead when she sees me, her jaw tensing at the very sight. I hold.

A solitary tear runs down her cheek. I lift my hand to wipe it away, but she flinches and clobbers me with a look that just says, "I don't need your help."

I'm the only thing preventing her escape from this moment, so I step out of her path to let her pass by.

She drops her gaze to her hands as she makes her way past me, but pauses at the doorway, and looks over her shoulder, her eyes connecting with mine, begging me to say something to make everything better.

I have nothing.

And then she is gone, disappearing into the crowd.

***

The rhythmic murmur of ocean waves lapping at the shore draws me into my chair at the edge of the yard. How am I supposed to find a way to have her in my life when she's made it clear she doesn't care? That she's done.

I can't think of that. The mission comes first and, right now, that mission is in Nicaragua. I have to focus up.

But how can I leave my heart here with Billie and have the concentration to be there?

A few minutes later, a cold bottle hits my chest. "Rough night?"

I shrug.

JJ lowers himself into the chair next to me and sneers. "So, you chicken out on the Fireworks Confession?"

"I didn't chicken out. I just can't convince myself that it's the right thing to do."

"What do you mean?"

"I shouldn't be adding fear to her life. I should be the one to protect her from that," I admit. "She doesn't need me."

He takes a long drag from his beer. "You know that girl is perfect for you, right? You saw how she fought for herself, broke Kavika's nose, went off the grid. You're exactly right. She doesn't need the protection of Warrior Jax; she can take care of herself. But she sure as hell does need Ryder's love and support."

Could there be a difference? Between Warrior Jax and Ryder?

JJ rises from his chair, takes a few steps, and turns back around. "If you think there's any way you can get over your bruised ego and make something happen with her, you should fight like hell for it, just as hard as you would in any other battle."

I nod in hopes this conversation will end. "Copy that."

The low cloud layer lights up in blues and yellows and reds as the pace of incendiaries quickens, bringing on the much-awaited grand finale and giving me hope that this night, at last, might be ending.

Maybe JJ is right. Maybe it's time Warrior Jax finally retires.

When the sulfur in the air clears, people begin leaving, and I gather the strength to usher them out. The moment everyone leaves, I ignore the mess and head upstairs, but sleep is elusive as the sight of Billie in agonizing pain haunts me.

Do I go check on her? In the middle of the night? Or would that make things worse? She seemed pretty hesitant to allow me anywhere near her.

I can't just let her sit and suffer, but I'm not sure how much more rejection I can take. Besides, I'm supposed to spin up today for Nicaragua anyways, so what would be the point?

After tossing for hours, something Savage said last week hits me. "You can't warrior your way through matters of the heart. You have to open yourself up to attacks from the enemy if you want it to work. There is no minimizing risk when it comes to love."

That's easier said than done, though. I have been in warrior mode since I decided to be a SEAL, and probably well before that. I just don't know if it's serving me well anymore. I'm not in a war zone. I don't live in a house with an abusive dad. There are no real threats here that I need to defend against.

Maybe it's time to leave that coping mechanism behind and

finally move on to the next phase of my life. One where I might be able to find some peace. One where I could do the things that make me happy instead of running off to fulfill some sense of duty that has long since passed.

Once again, Billie has somehow managed to diagnose what's out of balance and convinced me of it with the grace she always shows.

By 0400, I give up my attempt at sleep and wander onto the lanai to call Savage. "Hey, man. I can't go to Nicaragua." A cool breeze washes over me.

"You sure?"

"Yeah. I have to see if I can find some value as a partner and not just a protector." I run my hand along the railing. "Sorry to leave you in the lurch."

"That's okay, I had Trapp on standby. I had a feeling it'd go this way. Now, go get her."

"Copy that." I hang up and fall back into bed, finally able to relax.

I'll catch up on a few hours of sleep before coming up with a new plan of attack.

Chapter 50

BILLIE

*B*efore the sun begins to pour through my bare window, I'm already pondering my next move. How could I sleep with Insane Izzy and Chilly Billie arguing in my head the whole night?

If I am ever going to be fully healthy, to get any sleep ever again, I'm going to have to forsake Insane Izzy and Chilly Billie once and for all. To simply be me, whoever that turns out to be.

Or maybe I don't have to leave them behind completely. I can take the best of both and shed their weaknesses.

I need Izzy's fearlessness, her willingness to go for what she wants, to say what's on her mind, and to take chances. But I have to take a minute and assess the repercussions of my decisions. I have to think about those around me when I make my choices. I can't run blindly into danger anymore in order to somehow prove myself.

Besides, I have nothing to prove now, anyway. I took on the scariest guy on this island and I survived completely on my own, with nothing, in a totally new place. I lived through Brent's death. I can do anything.

And I need Chilly Billie, to be someone who is overflowing with joy. Who brings happiness to those around her. Who shares that delight through her art. But, I also want to stop pushing people away when things get hard. I have to face those feelings and feel them, so I can process them and let go.

I think back to how far I've come, how I have rebuilt my brain, reclaimed my life here, and started to build something with Ryder. When he first told me he was leaving, the only thing I could see was the fear. But I am so much stronger than that. I won't let the fear make the decision for me.

Even if it means I lose him to some horrible people in the Congo, I won't let the fear stop me from pursuing what I want. I survived the death of someone I loved dearly, I will survive another one if I have to. Until then, I will love Ryder so hard that it will make it all worth while. I will focus on the good and happy and beautiful and lovely so that our life before that moment is amazing.

Maybe that is what being totally healed looks like. To be in a place where I have enough brain bandwidth to look beyond my own needs and consider what other people need, too.

"*So, what is it that you need?*" Chilly Billie asks.

"*Don't you mean* who *she needs? What incredibly sexy and studly man will bring back your joy?*" Insane Izzy chimes in.

"What if it's too late?" I ask an empty room.

I have to try. He kept that picture. That has to mean something.

I stand, pull a pair of trunks from the floor, and slip them on. The sleep tank I have on will have to suffice. I swipe the photo I stole from Ryder last night from my nightstand and toss it in my back pocket. Bypassing my bike, I sprint down the sand toward Ryder's house.

The sun is starting to peak over the top of the mountains to the west, sending thin rays of sunlight between the palm fronds that line the beach. I just hope that he hasn't left yet.

I leap up the back porch steps and peek inside the French doors leading to his living room. No sign of movement. I check the door and it's locked. Stepping back to catch my breath, Izzy chimes in. "*Throw a rock through the window. You need to tell him before he leaves.*"

"Or you could go sit on your chair and wait for him to wake up," Chilly suggests.

Not certain either is a viable option. I run my hands through my hair while spinning around trying to figure this out when I glance up to see the door leading to Ryder's bedroom wide open. I've seen Ryder scale the railing to the lanai plenty, I'm sure I could manage.

Although it takes me nearly four times as long as it would take Ryder, I make it to the door and peek inside. Ryder is asleep in bed, shirtless, sheet barely covering his ass. Laying on his stomach, his strong shoulders on full display.

I tiptoe closer. Like this, there is no sign that he hates me. If only he could stay like this forever.

I know he keeps his weapon within arms reach, and the last thing I want to do is sneak up on an armed sailor. I look around and spy a gun safe on his nightstand. I make my way towards it, lifting my hand to move it, but pause to take in his muscular biceps. Even asleep, he is a massive, self-confident presence.

The moment I make any noise, he'll wake up and this momentary peace will be lost forever. I waver, letting my hand drop and sliding my other hand to the edge of his sheet. There's enough room for me to slip in next to him.

Be smart about this, Billie.

I move the safe to his dresser and return, this time keeping my distance from his bed. No need to give in to that temptation.

I draw the photo from my pocket and look at the smile on my face that day. After bailing on the memorial paddle out for Brent, and avoiding every single one of those horrific emotions, I found my joy that day. And I found it with Ryder.

I need to know.

I hold the picture in the air and demand, "Why do you have this?"

Chapter 51

RYDER

I heard Billie sneak in the moment she swung her leg over the second story railing, huffing and puffing from the exertion, but there was no way I was going to spoil her fun. I try to hide the smile threatening to give me away.

She lingers for a minute before reaching for the Stop Box on my nightstand that protects my gun from unauthorized users and moving it to my dresser. Now, I really have to see what she has planned.

"Why do you have this?" she demands.

I roll over to face her.

She's holding my picture of the two of us on the day we met. "If you don't care enough to stay, why do you have this?" she repeats.

I had no idea this would turn out to be her own version of an interrogation. Good thing I'm trained to withstand one. "I care," I chuckle.

"You can't stand being within five feet of me," she objects.

There's nothing I want more than to be within five feet of you, Babe. I move my legs over the side of the bed, rubbing my head, making it look like I haven't been up all night thinking about her.

Billie stares, motionless in the middle of the room. I steady myself and leisurely close the distance, stopping a few feet from her. She marks off the floor visually, measuring the gap. Three feet. She looks up slowly, taking in every element of me in just my skivvies.

I take that time to appreciate her, hair a little darker than it used to be with streaks of auburn now, a white tank top stretched over her chest, and a strength that does not lessen her femininity.

And, then, I try one more time. I capture her gaze and repeat with a quiet emphasis, "I care, Billie."

Remembering the photo in her hand, she lifts it once more. "Why do you have this?" she repeats less angry, more pleading.

"You know that picture was taken two hundred seventy-two days ago?" That throws her. Billie is more confused now than when she started this interrogation. "Two hundred and seventy-two days, Billie. And for forty-five of them, you were gone," I continue.

I tap the pic that she still holds motionless in the air. "That was the day I knew. That I didn't want a single day to go by that I didn't talk to you, that I didn't see you, that I didn't have you in my life."

"Then why are you leaving?"

"I'm—"

"Wait, it doesn't matter. I can handle it." She steps forward. "I won't let the fear of losing you down the road make me lose you right now. I am strong enough to endure it."

I can't hold back my smile any longer. "Yeah?"

Her hands begin to gesture wildly. "Yeah. I'm done running. I can't let the fear of pain dictate my choices. I don't care if you are going to the moon on a no-return mission, Ryder, I want to be with you."

I slip one hand around her waist. "What if I told you you didn't have to risk it?"

"What do you mean?"

"I can't promise that I won't ever be taken from you. Right? You said so yourself. But, maybe I can cut down that risk by staying here with you."

She lays her hands on my chest. "But you need to go protect people, you said so yourself."

"Not as much as I need to be with you. I think it's about time I start doing the things that make me happy. And, Billie?"

"Yeah, RyGuy?"

"I think being with you is the perfect place to begin. Just promise me something."

With no answer, I have to search for the answer in her countenance. *What?*

"Promise you won't let another day go by without me?" I plead.

"Not another day."

As my lips slowly descend to meet hers, my hands slip up her arms, bringing her closer. She returns my kiss with reckless abandon. And I savor the feeling of satisfaction it leaves me with. Maybe there's something to this whole 'finding what makes me happy.'

Chapter 52

BILLIE

The navy blue sky blurs into the ocean, waiting for the first glimmer of light. It's one of my favorite times when you can't see the horizon. The hinge on which the sky hangs just disappears.

At the edge of his yard, Ryder stands, looking up to the fading remains of the Milky Way stretched across the sky. I take my time traversing the yard, absorbing the strength emanating from him. Just watching him fills my reservoir of boldness the day ahead is going to require.

I pull off my tank top, but leave on my black bikini, my favorite black and white striped Greg Noll trunks lending an extra layer of fortitude.

I bend to pat Spooner's head. "You're gonna have to stay here today, Boy."

His face is crestfallen as he lays down on the grass next to my chair, begging to come with us. I almost give in when Ryder lays his hand on my shoulder and nods to the waterline.

"Slow is smooth," he starts.

"Smooth is fast," I reply as we lay our boards on the water and begin to paddle out. Water slapping against our boards and our rhythmic breathing are the only sounds as we let the full impact of this morning wash over us. When we reach the quarter mile buoy and sit up on our boards, the sun finally peeks above the mountains, spreading its warmth on the verdant, green land below.

I glance towards Spooner, sitting in my pink chair at the edge of Ryder's yard waiting patiently for our return and the chance to splash in the warm ocean. The island behind him, full of friends and family who love me and want the best for me. And Ryder, out here beside me, encouraging me, supporting me, loving me. I have everything I have ever wanted. It's a perfect morning.

A perfect October 7.

Ryder looks at me to start, but I am not quite ready, so he takes the lead. "I really wish I got the chance to meet you, Brent. But you were such a huge part of who Billie has become, in a way I feel like I did know you. I wanted to thank you for the bravery and determination and drive you brought out in her. I even thank you for the part you played in making her Insane Izzy."

I gather my strength to say the things I have finally found the words for. "I miss you so much, Brent. I am so sorry. I couldn't have asked for a better brother. You taught me to push myself and to want a big, big life."

Finishing up our private paddle-out memorial, we lift the leis from our necks and toss them into the water before splashing and hooting and hollering.

As we turn to paddle back in, I whisper, "Love you, Brent Baby."

It was only last year that I was so ready to never again have an October 7. This year, it isn't the worst day of my life. It's one of the best.

Or, maybe not the best, but one that I have made peace with. Today I celebrate.

Celebrate the years I had with Brent. How much he shaped me into the person I am today. Gave me the things that I love today; surfing and shave ice and sharing my art.

I celebrate how far I've come. How I found my resolve to

face the hard things. To feel them and let them go. And how to capture those feelings to make my art deeper and more complex.

And today is a day I celebrate with the love of my life.

By the time we are a hundred yards from shore, Spooner cannot wait any longer. He sprints off my chair to meet us. I let him hop up on my board and ride an ankle slapper all the way in to the shore.

Ryder checks his watch. "We should get going. JJ's the type to turn a moving party into a packing party."

———————————

When we arrive at JJ's place, everything is already boxed up. I point out the labeling system on the side of each box to Ryder. "Looks like JJ is changing in more ways than one."

He is speechless.

The six of us make quick work of emptying out his place before making the long trek across the island to Finn's place.

When we get there, we let Spooner out to play with Baja, Finn's dog. They run off to the far reaches of the yard to chase geckos.

"It's funny that we still call it Finn's place when Charlie and Grey already live here and now, JJ, too. It's more like Finn is running a bed and breakfast. Maybe we should start calling it the Potter B and B."

Ryder groans at the reference. He has been a sport and is letting me torture him by watching *Dawson's Creek*. Never more than an episode at a time, and always with a few days in between for him to recover, but we are making our way past the dreaded second season and are heading into my favorite, the third season. I don't think he wants to think about it more than he already has to. "Either that, or Finn has just become Grams."

Hearing him throw out a *Creek* reference just warms my heart.

When the cars are unloaded and all the clearly labeled boxes get moved into their corresponding rooms, we settle in around the fire pit as dark settles in around us. But there is no fire tonight. I have a totally new activity planned for Game Night and everyone has agreed to help me out.

After letting everyone rest for an hour, I rub my hands together excitedly. "Is it time? Are we ready?"

Next week, I'll be launching the Biovandals Unite subscription box through the Kaulike Hanai app. Each month a box is shipped to subscribers that is filled with the supplies needed to create a piece of street art. It comes with a little history on the type of art with some pieces from amazing street artists who have elevated the style for inspiration. It also has directions about how to use the supplies and how to come up with creative and meaningful art.

I assigned one of the first four boxes to each person or pair here tonight and gave them two weeks to come up with a piece of art that will send a positive message. Those were the only parameters. And I can't wait to see what everyone came up with.

"Okay, in the anonymous spirit of Biovandal, I have your hoodies to hide your identity?" I pass out different colored hoodies with my Biovandal logo and handle on the back. "And you each have your design sketched out?"

They all hold up their sketches or plans, except for Finn. "Do you know what you're gonna draw, Finn?"

"It's emblazoned on my brain. Nothing I will forget anytime soon," he says with a sigh of despondency. Even though I set out to have everyone send a message of hope and joy, I'm not sure how much of those emotions Finn can muster up. I decided to let him lead the way and create whatever holds meaning for him. Who am I to judge or try to influence someone else's art?

As everyone works on their installations, I fly my drone overhead picking up the video I'll need for launch week.

JJ steps back to look at his piece just moments after everyone poured out of the back of the moving van we drove to this covert operation. With super-sized word magnets, he has crafted a haiku on the side of a utility box.

Waves wash upon shore
Life is continually
Transformed by the sea

I fly the drone further down the dark side street to where Greyson and Charlie have teamed up, but their work is so small I have to land the drone and grab my handheld camera. Their box was filled with AJ's Toy Boarders. I was so completely thrilled the first time I saw these. They're little figurines who surf and skate, but modeled in the style of little green army men.

Grey and Charlie have brought with them a small plastic wave form that they are affixing to the gutter. On top of it they have lined up six of the Toy Boarders. The next time it rains, the draining water will form a standing wave that the toys will be able to surf forever.

I get down close and take a few macro photos with the light from the street lamp streaming in from behind the characters.

"Hey, I brought a huge bucket of water to reveal Finn's creation. Want to use a little to test this out?" I ask.

Grey looks up from placing the last of his figures. "As soon as this one dries, that would be awesome."

"Perfect. I'll be back in a little." I toss the drone in the air again to capture Finn's progress. He is hard at work on what looks like nothing.

Finn's box contained a bottle of super-hydrophobic coatings. When it's dry out, the art will be invisible. But when it rains, as it does so often here, the art will magically appear. Some people use stencils to get their message perfect, but it looks like Finn is using a small squirt bottle and a paint brush.

The video from the drone shows Finn in his bright pink hoodie, a madman drawing invisible doodles. I think it may be one of my favorites.

As soon as he finishes, I'll grab a video of him dumping a five-gallon bucket of water across the art revealing what he is entirely engrossed in creating right now.

I gave Ryder the subscription box that was filled with chalk paint, but he made me promise not to peek at his creation until he was fully finished, so I make my way back to capture Greyson and Charlie's standing wave. Laying on the street to grab the perfect angle, I snap away as soon as Charlie sends a rush of water down the gutter. And it works perfectly. Now, every storm will send these figurines surfing a never ending wave.

I make my way to Finn with the remainder of the bucket of water and let him do the honors as soon as the drone is aloft. And the image it reveals is nothing short of spectacular. It's a stunning portrait of a young woman who looks somehow familiar. Scribbled beneath it are the words, "be good and you will be lonesome."

He stands stoic in front of his art, letting only the smallest glimpse of a smile of satisfaction turn up his lips. Even though it looks like this might have been a painful experience for him, Finn asks, "So how exactly do I sign up to get these each month?"

"You'd want to do this again?"

"Sure. It was kind of fun."

Having Finn admit he had fun might be the best review I have ever gotten for any of my creations.

With video and stills from everyone else's work captured, we make our way to where Ryder is wrapping up his work on the side of a building. He steps back, tossing his brush into the jar of chalk paint as the last brush strokes dry to a chalky finish.

On a background of white, he's drawn a giant red heart. Inside he's painted, *R.J. Loves I.S.*, just like an old school tree carving. Beneath the heart is the word forever.

It's perfect. Simple, sincere, and it stirs up a childlike joy that makes my heart swell.

Gathering me into his arms, Ryder holds me snugly. "You like it?"

My lips instinctively find their way to his, the kiss as tender and light as a summer breeze. "I love you, too, RyGuy."

I step back to admire his work, a beacon of our love. But I didn't give him any red chalk paint. And it's all too opaque to be chalk anyways.

I press my hand to the drawing and come away with white fingers. "This is paint Ryder! You painted this guy's wall. That's permanent."

He just laughs.

I shove my white fingers in his face. "This isn't funny. That's not what we do. JJ's gonna have to arrest you for vandalism." I look to JJ to gauge his reaction. He's laughing, too.

Behind me, Ryder wraps his arms around my waist. "Chill, Billie. I talked to the owner yesterday. We worked out an agreement."

"An agreement to permanently deface his building?"

"I thought it was time you did something a little more permanent. And big."

"Wait. You bought me a wall?"

"More like sold the owner an original Biovandal mural, but, same difference, I suppose."

"You bought me a wall."

I hand him the camera before I pull down my hood and lean up next to Ryder's painting like he had done so many times in front of my creations. He clicks off a few pics before I call him over to me.

He hands Charlie the camera, pulls up his own hood, and poses next to me. Then he turns to me and just before he kisses me, I pull down both our hoods.

Charlie drops the camera. I think they all know that my identity as Biovandal is a highly protected secret. But maybe it's time I stop running from that one, too. After facing my fears, and dealing with the fallout, I no longer have to hide from anyone.

I am lighter.

Carefree.

Peaceful.

The real me has appeared. And the real me is loved. There is no need to pretend anymore.

"Take a good one, Charlie. I'm going public."

The End

Want to find out if Finn will fix things with Em or end up with someone completely different? Preorder SOUVENIRS now at bit.ly/BuySouvenirs .

Stay up to date with new releases of The Warrior Women Series by joining The Salties Scoop at bit.ly/SPSscoop .

If you're the kind of amazing person who likes to leave reviews to help readers find the right books for them, here are the links to review California Promises on Amazon and Goodreads. Or spread the word and tell a friend about Anything Anytime Anywhere.

Diabetes Appendix

BILLIE

Thanks so much for reading my story and wanting to know more about diabetes.

I know diabetes or any chronic condition you don't personally have can sometimes be confusing. When you get diagnosed with diabetes or any chronic condition, you have to learn a whole new language and set and people try to simplify their explanations of the disease so inexperienced people can understand it without having to take a college course on the subject. But that sometimes can lead to confusion and incorrect conclusions.

The best way to really learn about what it is like to live with a chronic condition is to listen to those who have it. Be willing to learn with each new experience. Ask good questions. And realize that, although you will never fully know what it is to live with any condition you don't have yourself, you have a vast well of empathy that will allow you to be compassionate and informed about another human's experience.

To help you out, I have written out a little appendix to explain some of the situations you may have found me in while I was being a stubborn, boneheaded girl trying to find my way to love. They are all in chronological order with links to products mentioned in this appendix at the end of the chapter.

A DIABETES PRIMER

Here are the basics of Type 1 diabetes. It's a lot like the speech you would hear from a doctor in the fifteen minutes he spends explaining a disease that can take years to fully master.

Something in your body—a virus, an out-of-balance gut, excess stress—causes your body's immune system to go a bit haywire and start attacking the beta cells of your pancreas, thinking they are a foreign invader. The beta cells of the pancreas, along with a few other organs and hormones, help regulate the amount of sugar in your bloodstream by producing and releasing insulin.

The amount of sugar in your bloodstream needs to be tightly regulated. A lot like a thermostat in your house keeps the temp between 68 and 72, your body needs the blood sugar to be between 80 and 120 mg/dl (or 4.45 to 6.67 mmol for you metric folks). Too much and you begin to destroy the other parts of your body leading to long-term complications. Too low and your brain and muscles can't function.

Since the pancreas stops being able to keep up with the insulin demands, a person with type 1 diabetes needs to give themselves insulin via a shot or insulin pump. Adam Brown, author of Bright Spots and Landmines, has compiled a list of 42 different things that can affect the amount of insulin needed at any one time. Things like food composition, caffeine, alcohol, stress, sleep, illness, other medications, altitude, and sunburn. And each of these factors can have a different effect on the same person at different times.

With that number of factors, dosing insulin can be a very difficult and dangerous pursuit, which is why a person with diabetes will not always have blood sugars in range, no matter how diligent and wise they are with their diabetes care.

CHAPTER 1, PAGE 13
Checking blood sugars while swimming

Exercise can burn sugar, causing my blood sugar to drop. To prevent this, I take off my insulin pump which reduces the amount of insulin in my system. But every workout is hard to predict, so I have a Dexcom Continuous Glucose Monitor which measures my blood sugars and then sends the info to my Apple Watch. That way, I can see what my blood sugar is at any moment during my swim.

CHAPTER 9, PAGE 67
Preparing to leave and grabbing diabetes supplies from her diabetes pantry.

The supplies needed to manage a chronic condition like diabetes can take up a lot of space. They are often ordered and received for three or six months at a time. So, to make a lame part of diabetes a little better, I like to make my storage pretty. I took an entire "coat" closet (totally unnecessary in Maui) and turned it into my diabetes pantry.

When I was about to run, I knew I'd need supplies for a while. So I grabbed what I could carry and hoped I would figure it out before those ran out.

CHAPTER 9, PAGE 68
Preparing to leave and correcting for a high blood sugar.

Since blood sugars can be unpredictable, it is always a safe practice to bring along some quickly absorbed source of sugar with me everywhere I go. That can be candy, energy gels, or even little packs of sugar. I usually call them sugars for short. But like every other thing you have to do every day, sometimes I forget.

The Dexcom Continuous Glucose Monitor only measures glucose to 400. Anything above that just registers as HIGH, which could mean I am 401 or 1200. HIGH's happen, but they are usually short-lived. A long-term HIGH can mean some serious consequences.

To correct for a high blood sugar, insulin is given. But every person's body responds differently to insulin. Over time, you figure out what your correction ratios are. That's the amount your blood sugar will drop for every unit of insulin you give yourself. Mine will drop 60 points for every unit. So I count units needed by reciting numbers that are 60 points above 120. (180, 240, 300, 360, 420, etc.) For each number, it is one unit of insulin. I've done it enough that it becomes second nature to calculate my dose.

CHAPTER 9, PAGE 70
Pump infusion site pulled out.

A few hours after correcting for a high blood sugar, I expect my levels to be back in range again. But if it hasn't, that usually means something went wrong and I have to try to find the source of error. In this case, the infusion set that allows the insulin pump to get insulin under my skin had been pulled out. So all of the insulin I thought I was giving myself was really just pouring out into the air.

CHAPTER 13, PAGE 93
Rationing insulin

Each time I eat, I have to give a bolus of insulin to take the sugar from the food I eat and tuck it safely away in my muscles. With a limited amount of insulin left, I knew I could reduce the amount I needed if I went without eating. Not a good idea to maintain my health, but unfortunately is a decision many people face.

Sometimes individuals without a steady supply of insulin will take this further and reduce the basal amount of insulin they use to stretch their insulin. This will drive blood sugars higher and higher and can be harmful and potentially fatal. This is called insulin rationing.

An estimated 1.3 million adults with diabetes in the United States had to ration their insulin in order to save money.[1] Another study of 982 insulin users found that 16.5 % skipped insulin doses, took less insulin than they needed, or delayed buying insulin, all due to cost.[2]

CHAPTER 13, PAGE 94
Insulin and heat don't mix.

Insulin can be ruined by exposure to heat. If it is left out in the Florida heat, it would be nearly unusable. So, it is typically refrigerated. Even the insulin in a pump is vulnerable to this, so

1   Briskin, Andrew. "Insulin: No More Rationing." diaTribe, 14 Nov. 2022, diatribe.org/insulin-no-more-rationing#:~:text=Rationing%20insulin%20can%20be%20harmful,coma%20and%20death%20without%20it.
2   S;, Gaffney A;Himmelstein DU;Woolhandler. "Prevalence and Correlates of Patient Rationing of Insulin in the United States: A National Survey." Annals of Internal Medicine, pubmed.ncbi.nlm.nih.gov/36252243/. Accessed 9 July 2023.

it is important to keep an insulin pump out of the heat as much as possible.

CHAPTER 16, PAGE 108
Diabetes supplies dwindling and the ramifications of running out.
When the ten-day period of a Dexcom sensor is finished, it will beep five times and display a message on a linked pump or phone. Typically, that means I will insert my next sensor and move on with life. Since this was my last sensor, it meant I couldn't use my Dexcom any longer.

Having a Dexcom measure and report my blood sugars is such a vital part of my diabetes regimen. It means that anytime my sugars go out of range, even when I'm not thinking about them, I will be notified. So, I no longer have to constantly think about diabetes. In a time of upheaval to my food, exercise, and stress regimen, my Dexcom is that much more important because blood sugars get even more unpredictable. It was the first of many major hits to my diabetes care that would follow.

With a reduced insulin and pump site supply, I would run out of insulin in five days. At that point, it wouldn't take long before my body starts to shut down. It may take 48 to 72 hours before a trip to the ER would become necessary, maybe less. If insulin can't be obtained, the body continues to get sicker leading to coma and death from Diabetic Keto Acidosis.

To prevent this situation, many states have passed new laws that allow pharmacies to give out emergency vials of insulin without a prescription, like Kevin's Law in Ohio and Florida in 2016; Arkansas, Arizona, Illinois, and Wisconsin in 2017; Idaho, Oregon, Pennsylvania, South Carolina, and Tennessee in 2018; and Colorado, Indiana, Kentucky, Oklahoma, Utah, and West Virginia in 2019[3] and the Alec Smith Insulin Affordability Act in Minnesota in 2021[4].

---

3   T1international - Kevin's Law Fact Sheet, www.t1international.com/media/assets/file/Kevins_Law_Fact_Sheet.pdf. Accessed 9 July 2023.
4   "'No One Should Have to Choose between Affording Their Lives and Affording to Live': Ag Ellison." March 15, 2021 Press Release, www.ag.state.mn.us/Office/Communications/2021/03/15_InsulinAffordabilityAct.asp. Accessed 9 July 2023.

CHAPTER 19, PAGE 125
Finding black-market diabetes supplies.

Because insulin is in fact life-saving, and because so many people struggle with finding insurance or cash to cover the high prices of diabetes supplies, those with extras for one reason or another will often share their unneeded supplies.

It is illegal, which on one hand makes sense because it is important that you know exactly where your supplies have come from and that they have been handled safely. On the other hand, it is hard to stomach the fact that it is illegal to share something that could save a life. Groups have popped up on social media that facilitate the sharing of extra supplies.

CHAPTER 19, PAGE 126
Walmart insulin, a less-than-ideal solution.

Walmart does produce a generic version of insulin called ReliOn. In emergencies, it is better than not having any insulin. It still comes at a cost, at the time of writing, $72.88 for a 10mL vial which can last anywhere from 5-30 days depending on a person's sensitivity to insulin, and two types are needed every day pushing the price up even further.

It is a synthetic human insulin, a different kind of insulin, than the insulin analogs currently prescribed to most people. They work very differently than contemporary insulins and changing to them is a process that can cause severe blood sugar fluctuations and be potentially fatal. They cannot be used in an insulin pump. So, although they are better than no insulin, they are not an easy or completely safe solution, especially in a time of general upheaval.

CHAPTER 21, PAGE 133
Overpacking for trips. The overabundance
of love in the diabetes community.

When packing for a trip, it is common for people with diabetes to pack more than enough supplies for the duration of the trip. If you only pack one backup, you can pretty much guarantee that you'll need two. If you pack four, you might just get away with it.

Whenever I travel, nearly half of my bag is full of supplies, oftentimes divided amongst my bags, just in case I lose one or leave one on a taxi or whatever other harebrained thing I might do while in a new place.

One of the most amazing things I have noticed is the outpouring of love in the diabetes community. If you need something, people will often jump at the opportunity to help. Most times, they will give and give until they know you will be taken care of. Often this is from complete strangers, too. Though in the diabetes community, you hardly ever stay strangers for long.

CHAPTER 24, PAGE 153
Commandeering free sugars.

Since my blood sugar can potentially drop at any minute, I always have to pack a quick-acting source of sugar to bring it back up. My favorite is a Gu Energy Gel. They work really fast and come in a small discreet package. They taste even better after I've been in the salt water. But they can be costly. So sometimes, I've had to find cheaper sources. And the free, small sugar packets at a restarant fit the bill.

CHAPTER 24, PAGE 154
Paddling fixes blood sugars.

Even in times of high stress which normally would cause blood sugars to skyrocket, a long, steady workout like walking or cleaning the house or even slow paddling, can bring down blood sugars to a more-stable range. It is one of the reasons, I always bring extra sugars when I go to a mall. For some reason, I always go low at the mall.

CHAPTER 37, PAGE 236
Pre-bolus insulin.

Even contemporary, fast-acting insulins take a little bit of time to get from the injection site to where they begin working in the bloodstream. This can be from fifteen to thirty minutes. So if you wait until after you have finished eating, you are already fifteen minutes behind the sugar being dumped into your blood from your stomach. Many people will give themselves an insulin bolus fifteen minutes before they eat to counterattack this time difference.

I have tried this, but in a restaurant, I have been caught off-guard by a slow kitchen and then have my blood sugars drop before my food even comes and that can be terrifying.

Or I expect to eat more than I actually do. So, in that case, if I gave myself the full dose of insulin before I ate, I would have to keep eating until I ate the correct amount of carbs for the dose I gave myself earlier.

I typically won't pre-bolus unless I am eating a super high-carb meal. And even then, I will only give myself half of the dose before and then follow it up with the other half after I eat. This allows me to adjust for the amount I did eat and only puts half as much insulin on board for a minor low if the kitchen is slow.

CHAPTER 38, PAGE 241
Dr Pepper and a lack-of-filter for lows.
One of my loves that I had to give up when I got diabetes is full-sugar Dr Pepper. And for some reason, it tastes so much better when I am low. And I have some weird cravings for shredded sharp cheddar cheese or Lucky Charms cereal. Who knows why?

Everybody feels lows differently. And every low can feel different. For me, when I get low, the filter that usually prevents me from saying exactly what's on my mind shuts down so I often say things I normally wouldn't.

CHAPTER 46, PAGE 286
Diabetes jokes and the appreciation for good medical coverage.
I am not one who gets offended easily. So, when the people in my life who know all about my diabetes make a small joke about it, I know they are doing it out of love. I've spent enough time educating the people around me, and I know they mean no harm. That, coupled with the gallows humor I got from my dad, makes it easy to enjoy the absurdity of this disease and to laugh at the craziness.

Eating a sugary meal slowly is one way to minimize the sugar peak. The slower the food gets into your stomach the more drawn out that peak is.

"This book is just the most fun, swoony, flirty, slaps you in the face with happiness RomCom and you need it!" – Rubie Clark

Find out how Charlie and Greyson first got together in California Promises, Book 1 of the Warrior Women Sweet Romance Series full of female surfers who happen to have diabetes and other autoimmune issues and the men who are strong enough to be with a warrior woman.

In an angsty, friends-to-lovers romance about a brilliant, surfing tomboy and her anxious, fireman best-friend, Erin Spineto spins another "Inspiring tale of being just the right balance of strong and vulnerable."

You'll love the hilarious, double-dating summer goal, breezy escape to the beaches of San Diego and Maui, and fantastic group of friends.

California
PROMISES
Erin Spineto

Pick up or download your copy today!
ErinSpineto.com

Sea Peptide Publishing

"...honest, funny, touching, incredibly relatable, and wonderfully sarcastic in all the right places."
--Kelly Kunik, Creator of Diabetesaliciousness

In "the most entertaining diabetes book I've read to date...," Erin navigates her twenty-two-foot sailboat down the Florida Keys as she fights winds, currents, and swells that threaten to capsize her. (Amy Tenderich, Founder and Editor of Diabetes Mine)

In a time when doctors advised people with diabetes "avoid any extreme exertion," will Erin push the boundaries of what is possible or find out the hard way she should have listened to the warnings?

Pick up or download your copy today!
ErinSpineto.com

SEA PEPTIDE PUBLISHING

About The Author

*E*rin Spineto started her writing journey in 2011 with Islands and Insulin, her memoir of sailing solo 100 miles down the Florida Keys with type 1 diabetes back in a time when doctors were foolish enough to recommend against this kind of wild adventure with diabetes.

She followed it up a few years later with Adventure On, a nonfiction book on using adventure to increase motivation to take care of chronic conditions like diabetes. Since then she has moved on to fiction and is currently working on Warrior Women, a four-book angsty RomCom series full of female surfers who happen to have diabetes and other autoimmune issues.

Erin's journey with autoimmune conditions started in 1996 with type 1 diabetes. She added hyperthyroidism to the mix in 2007, and has rounded out her collection with a little Anti-Synthetase Syndrome, which she thinks is so appropriately abbreviated ASS. Not letting anything slow her down, Erin is also a long-distance endurance adventurer and autoimmune advocate who uses stories to encourage others with chronic illness to go big.

Erin started surfing at age five when she stood up on her boogie board and realized waves were so much more fun to ride standing up. Since then she has had a love affair with empty beaches, warm water, and a post-surf lunch of fish tacos and Diet Dr Pepper (though she's had to give that up to fight the ASS) eaten on a patio in the sun with her own real life hero, Tony, and their two surfing teenagers.

You can learn more at SeaPeptide.com

www.ingramcontent.com/pod-product-compliance
Lightning Source LLC
Chambersburg PA
CBHW030520120726
47904CB00005B/1547

9780988206588